Fate's Prison

Tara Fox Hall

Published by
Melange Books, LLC
White Bear Lake, MN 55110
www.melange-books.com

Fate's Prison ~ Copyright @ 2016 by Tara Fox Hall

ISBN: 978-1-68046-224-1

Cover Art by Caroline Andrus

To my best friend Brandon

Chapter One

That next morning, I woke first. Glancing at the clock, I saw that I'd woken a good hour early. Lash and Devlin were still asleep, but entangled with me to the point I knew I'd wake them up if I moved. So instead of moving, I lay there thinking, my head resting in the crook of Devlin's outstretched shoulder, absently stroking Lash's arm that lay across my chest.

The last months had been peaceful to the point I sometimes felt as if I were dreaming. Apart from an attack by a group of vampire hunters who hadn't gotten even to our front yard, and the traumatic loss of my faithful black German Shepherd, Darkness, to cancer, my life was close to Heaven. Devlin's dual Ruling duties for both the Canadian and United States Territories kept him busy, and Lash was also busy with his own "work," both on Dev's behalf and as a private contractor. That uncomfortable fact, in addition to Lash's predilection for live food, his endless nightmares and resulting violent awakenings, and hot temper, had taken some time to adjust to. But our Oath was working well, by and large. Devlin's insistence on me meeting his two dearest friends, Cain and Kyle, for some private time—read: orgy—hadn't gone over so well with either Lash or I, but we'd negotiated that landmine, too. I was no longer a creature controlled by my desires; I was the woman I used to be, if a little more laid back, a few years older, and with more than a little maturity to show for the last years of greater than my fair share of supernatural stress.

My daughter Elle was in college, my son Theoron—better known as T—was running Solutions, Inc. with my ex-husband Theo and Terian, and my other daughter V was already onto texting as a recreational activity, being best friends with Europe's vampire lord's daughter, Sharon. Terian had married his longtime lover Sundown last January and

1

they were expecting a baby girl very soon. Theo had married my replacement, Jenny, the newly-turned werecougar, and they were living at Danial's old house with T, and also trying for a baby. I had Oathed to both Danial and Devlin close to Christmas, with Lash as part of my pact. He and I were officially mated. And I was NOT trying for a baby with either of my lovers, and very glad of that fact.

I was still grieving the loss of my werecougar son Devon, but that was healing little by little, too. After all the bloodshed and death and struggle, these last months had been just what I needed: a chance to recover and rebuild my life. With my newfound peace, I was hopeful again about the future the way I hadn't been for a long time.

* * * *

Lash and I took Kyle to the airport later that same day. He'd only stayed a short time, but I'd enjoyed the half-faerie's company. Not only did we enjoy the same taste in movies and books, but I'd finally discovered why Devlin and he were such good friends: Kyle could sing. Better yet, he had an innate talent for coming up with "alternate" lyrics for popular songs that had me in tears laughing. He'd been singing his latest creation to Dev just last night, a variation on Uncle Cracker's "Follow Me":

"Won't give you money, I'm kind of a bum. Don't seem to matter when I tell you to come. You're feeling guilty 'cause you've gone astray, so on your knees is fine if you need to pray."

Devlin and I had laughed uproariously. Kyle had paused a moment, then gone on.

"You don't know how you met me, you don't know why your blood starts to boil when I touch your thigh. All you know is when you're with me I let you try all that kinky shit you can't do with your other guy."

I grabbed blindly for the tissue box, tears leaking out of my eyes as I laughed hysterically. Devlin grasped it as I almost knocked it off the bedside table, and handed it to me. I mopped at my eyes. "You've got talent, Kyle."

Kyle shrugged. "Some of my usual crowd on karaoke night appreciate my wit, others get angry I don't sing the song word for word like I'm supposed to."

"Then the latter have no ear for talent, as Sar says," Devlin decreed with a wave of his hand. "Your voice improves yearly, Kyle, not that it was ever lacking. But you have range now that you hadn't when we met over a decade ago. And your song-writing talent continues to delight me, especially your inventive phrases such as these."

And this is why they are friends; shared love of music. "I agree," I chimed in. "I can't speak to your growth as a singer, but I love your choice of words. Having dabbled in poetry years ago, I know how hard it is to come up with not only good wording, but the perfectly right number of syllables."

"Thank you, ma'am," Kyle had said, nodding to me.

We got him to his gate with barely a few moments to spare. He shook hands with Lash, and then I gave him a hug. He embraced me tight, then released me.

"Take care of yourself," I instructed, handing him a package. "Here are some cookies for the road."

"Thanks," he said with a boyish grin. "They won't last till the plane."

"My mate's a good cook," Lash said proudly.

"That she is," Kyle said, giving me a smile. "You and Dev have found a good woman, Lash. I wish you the best."

"Be careful," Lash hissed, his eyes shifting form to snake suddenly. "Call me, if you need help."

"Thanks, but no," Kyle said carefully. "I couldn't take your help again."

"Sure you could," Lash hissed easily. "You get into a bind, you call me."

"You and I aren't friends," Kyle said, looking at Lash a little sadly. "And it's better that way. I don't want to bring more shit to Hayden's door. You have enough with Devlin's enemies, and your own."

I looked from one of them to the other. *What's going on?*

"Kyle, stop being such a stickler for etiquette, and be practical," Lash hissed angrily. "If that person who's looking for you finds you, he'll steal more than your money this time, he'll steal your life!"

"Lash, with respect, we both steal, too. But we steal lives, not cash."

"That demon will steal your soul, besides your life," Lash hissed,

3

baring his snake fangs. A few scales formed on the backs of his hands. "And you won't be able to stop him. You'll be screaming in Hell for eternity!"

Kyle let out a resigned sigh. "He comes for me, and I'll call. Happy?"

"Yes," Lash hissed in relief, changing back fully to human. "Dev will be, too."

Kyle rolled his eyes, shot me a last smile, and hurried onto the plane.

"What was that about?" I asked, as we walked away.

"Don't ask," Lash hissed, rubbing his eyes. "Just consider him protected to the extent he can be, and leave it at that."

The old Sar would have demanded to know what was going on, but the new Sar was glad to leave alone some danger that had nothing to do with her now. Kyle was a man who could take care of himself. And even if he couldn't, it wasn't up to me to save him.

* * * *

That next morning, Devlin and I were teleported by Titus to the first of our vampire "engagements."

Looking back, I shouldn't have been nervous for that meeting. Devlin's presence was required to settle some sort of dispute between the head vampires of the States of Missouri and Arkansas. Apparently, a younger vampire had been made by the Arkansas Ruler, and killed some of the human populace in Missouri. Missouri's Ruler said by rights the rogue killer was to be executed, and it was his place to carry out the sentence. The Arkansas Ruler said it was his duty to execute the killer, as he was that vampire's sire. Neither of them were giving an inch.

Devlin handled it well. He killed the murderous vampire himself with a sword, decapitating him. Then he ordered the vampire's maker to grant the "wronged immortal" blood equal to that illegally taken by the rogue. An amount measured in blood donors was agreed on and sworn to. Within a total of two hours, we were home.

"That was easy," I remarked in relief. "Will they all be like that?"

"I wish," Devlin remarked darkly. "The others are much more complicated, Love. Get some rest. We will need to leave soon for the next one."

"Why do these happen all at once? I thought we'd do one a week, like you spoke of back—"

"Kyle's no-shows made us push these back repeatedly," Devlin interrupted. "We can't wait any longer now." He expelled a breath. "As it is, I think we've waited too long already."

I sighed, and went into shower, resigned to my impending fate.

* * * *

Devlin was right. The next visit was horrible. We arrived to find a crazed vampire savaging a woman, amidst the remains of other dead humans, and dead, half-changed wereanimals of some bird type. Blood painted the tapestried walls, and was standing like water on the ornate inlaid stone floor.

Titus killed the vampire quickly with blue fire, before he even noticed us. But I threw up repeatedly, finding the nearest bathroom by my second time, as Devlin and Titus began cleaning up the bodies with magical fire. I stayed in the bathroom, sitting on the toilet seat with the door locked, unsure of what else to do. When Devlin did not come looking for me for the next hour, I knew whatever else he had discovered had to be even worse that what I had witnessed.

When he finally knocked on the door, I reluctantly opened it. He was covered in blood, his fine suit ruined. My dress was ruined as well, the hem bloody, and my shoes sodden. I'd tried to clean the blood off in the bathroom, and made an even bigger mess of both my gown and my shoes. "So much for my brand-new outfit," I said, reaching for his hand.

"Come," Dev said tiredly, taking my hand. "We'll go home, Love. There is nothing left we can do here."

Titus appeared, looking grim and also bloody, and teleported us to Hayden's kitchen. He left us abruptly. Devlin and I undressed right there, and cleaned off our feet enough to walk upstairs to his bedroom. We showered thoroughly, after which Devlin removed all of our clothes from the kitchen to the garbage and asked Serena to clean up the bloody floor. Wanting to help, I went downstairs and grabbed the Oreck from the hall closet, spraying about a bunch of lilac-scented air freshener as I vacuumed our path from where we had arrived to Dev's bedroom door, and the entire bedroom. The stink of carnage gone, I replaced the vacuum and went to thank Serena, but she was already done and gone, the kitchen floor sparkling like new.

Resolving to leave her a note of thanks, I rejoined Devlin in his room, where we lay in throws before a fire he'd made.

"I knew there would be some dead," he said in an ancient voice. "But I had no idea he would've turned on not only his guards, but his mistress..." he trailed off. "I should've acted sooner."

"Why did he do it?" I asked.

"He was insane," Devlin replied, adding a new log to the fire. "Clearly his subjects waited too long to report him, from all the evil we found. His journal was rambling. Half of what he wrote of were hallucinations. From the little I could comprehend, he'd begun to think of himself as some kind of dark god, one whose destiny was to drink the world dry."

I was silent. Part of me wanted to know what he'd found, and part of me thought I was better off not knowing.

"He has been dealt with, and several would-be successors have already emailed me," Devlin said, taking my hand. "The dead have been buried. There is no more to be done. Don't let it haunt you."

Uh huh. "Does this happen often?"

"No," Devlin answered. "But when it does, it is always like you saw. Bloody. Wasteful." He sighed. "Tragic."

"I don't want to accompany you anymore," I stated as nicely as I could. "I'll stay here, if you have future meetings where bloodshed of that level is expected."

"I'm sorry you saw that," Devlin said, squeezing my hand. "But I need you with me, Sar. The wedding is a month away. And I must attend the other visits with you along, our relationship requires it."

"Can you guarantee they will be carnage-free?"

"No," he said honestly. "But you will be safe, I promise."

You don't know that, not for certain. "Dev, I'm going to have nightmares, just from the one glance I got of that room."

"Sar, you must come with me to the rest of these appointments. There is no danger."

"You don't know that!" I countered. "You said yourself that you didn't know how bad this last situation had gotten!"

"Those dead men knew the risks, they were his guards," Devlin said coldly. "And the woman was his mistress, she had to know of his state of mind, and she chose to stay anyway, instead of either fleeing or contacting me. I am content that no innocents were killed, Sarelle. You should be, too."

Dev, you're bluffing. For all he knew that woman had died screaming for someone to save her, and had tried to get away, only to be imprisoned in the home she'd probably loved as much as I was growing to love Hayden. Seething, I took my hand out of his, and got up. I slipped on some clothes, and before he could stop me, I teleported to Anna's grave.

I sat on the stone bench, as I had before. It was a cool night, but spring was finally here, and the varied scents of newly blooming flowers were fragrant in the surrounding misty air. In a short time, I felt that same presence attend me, though I saw no one.

"I don't want to go," I said vehemently. "It was awful, Anna. There was blood everywhere! I'm so sick of blood and death."

I felt Anna's ghost come closer. Though it seemed sad to me as always, its familiarity was a comfort. I needed something familiar and soothing with the mood I was in.

"I'm sick of vampires, sick of the killing, and the carnage…"

I looked off into the distance, my words trailing off. The sky looked lighter over there. *Is that dawn already?* God, maybe we'd been gone all night and I hadn't noticed. *No, it's the highway.* The faint sound of the interstate miles away was just noticeable. *It's different out here at night.*

Shit. I cast a look around me, standing. *What other things roamed Hayden after dark?*

Screw it, I'm tired of being afraid. I sat back down. *I'm not going back yet. I have to think some more.*

A rustling came from the trees to my right. Big rustling.

Screw this, I'm going. I tried to teleport, and couldn't. *Fuck!*

I ran instead, tripping over branches, and cursing under my breath. I made it to the first part of the graveyard, and ran smack into Devlin. He grabbed hold of me. "What is it? Your heart's pounding!"

I turned fearfully, looking behind me. "I heard a noise in those trees!"

He scented the air. "A weasel, with her family. And an owl, hunting them."

I hugged him, glad of his company and decided staying mad at him wasn't worth it. "I was frightened, I couldn't teleport."

"I asked Titus to block you from leaving Hayden's grounds. I didn't want you going somewhere I couldn't find you."

I suppressed a shiver. "I'd already told you before I wouldn't leave the grounds without telling you. I kept my promise."

"Why did you come out here?" he asked gently. "I was sure you'd go to Lash's room, or—"

"Anna's presence comforts me."

Devlin gave me a shocked look. "What presence?"

"I feel her at her grave. When I come here, I sometimes talk to her."

Devlin was already moving. "Come with me there. Now, Oathed One."

We walked there, hand in hand. Devlin eased down on the bench, and I sat beside him.

A few moments later, I felt Anna's presence arrive, stronger than I'd felt it before. I watched in awe as a silvery shape drifted close from the tomb, and settled before Devlin.

"It is I, Love," Devlin whispered tenderly. "I am sorry it has been so long."

I felt a wave of intense longing and empathy emanate from the being. Devlin held out his hand, and the being touched him, or appeared to.

"I am glad to see you, too," he said. "I am sad, yes, but it is not because of you. Sar and I had a difficult day. Be at peace, my love."

Anna sent forth another burst of love and longing to us. Then she hovered near the flowers. Suddenly, a fading flower revitalized, and burst into fresh bloom.

Devlin touched it appreciatively. "Thank you, Love. But rest, and do not trouble yourself. I will be fine. Know you are loved and remembered."

Anna gave a sort of sigh, then she faded away back into the tomb.
Wow.

8

"Come," Devlin said quietly. "It is time to head back."

We walked only a few steps in silence, just long enough to get out of sight of the grave, before I spoke. "Dev, I have been to Anna's grave twice before. But I have never before seen anything manifest itself. I've just felt a presence."

Devlin looked over at me. "Nor have I," he murmured in a hushed tone. "She usually always fades away, before I even have a chance to tell it was her, and not a cool breeze. She has never manifested to me before this."

A lot of conflicting emotions churned within me. Some were jealousy, some were sadness for both Anna and Devlin, and some were for how unbelievable the experience had been. I had never encountered a true ghost before. "Why has she not moved on?"

"I thought she had. I don't know, Sar. I want to believe it's love," Devlin whispered. "Her love for me. Because if that's not the reason, she must be haunting her grave because of how tragically she died."

"Can't Titus send her to Heaven, or help her get there?"

"He is demon, Love. He is banned from Heaven. He'll be no help. Nor would Terian. Leri, though skilled, is also a dark witch—"

Good point. "Is there someone else we could ask?"

"Tatiana would not know," Devlin murmured. "She is the only white witch I know, and she dislikes me anyway. And I want no other magicians here near Anna."

I gathered my courage. "Devlin, who is buried by the pond, beneath the black diamond marker?" I swallowed. "Is it…at some point did Lash have a child?"

Devlin stopped, but didn't turn to look at me. "There is no one buried there," he said finally. "But you are right to think it is there for Lash, in remembrance of a young life lost."

"When was this?"

"Many years ago. Don't mention that you saw it, Sar, or ask him of it. He'll tell you of it someday, when he's ready to."

"All right."

Devlin was muttering to himself. "I need to know why she's still here, damn it! There has to be someone I could ask, someone I could trust to tell me the truth—"

He suddenly stopped walking, then turned to face me in a smooth motion. "I need your help. Will you help me?"

"What kind of help?" I asked cautiously.

"Come with me. There may be a way to find out what we need to know."

We walked for a while in the darkness in the direction as if we were walking back to Hayden. Then we took a sharp turn, and all of a sudden we came out of the trees into a small meadow. What had been a meadow once, anyway. There were younger ash trees here now among thick grass, and the remains of last year's scraggly late white wood asters. In the middle of the meadow was a thick tangle of brambles.

"Come."

I followed Devlin to the brambles. When I got close enough, I saw that underneath the thriving branches were the remains of a foundation.

"Whose house was this?"

Devlin didn't answer, he just parted the thorny tangle, stamping the prickers down with his foot to create an opening, and held out his hand. I took it.

We walked closer to the old stone and up onto it, until finally we sat before the remains of a large fireplace. It was crumbling badly, but the workmanship was good, and only a few stones had fallen out. Devlin built a fire, slipping some matches from a hidden metal box beside the hearth, and before long, the flames were warming us, even if my bottom was a little cold.

Devlin lifted a stone, and unwrapped something zippered in heavy plastic. I was amazed to see it was a thick fleece blanket, which he laid before the fire, and sat on. "Come into my arms," he whispered.

I let him hold me, and before long, as he liked to, he leaned into me and put his head over my heart. I stroked his hair.

"Do you trust me?" he whispered gently. "I'll need you to trust me, Sar."

Years ago, I would've had a smart reply for him, and maybe a stake. A year ago, I'd have just told him no. But something had changed in me, in the last few months. This was my life, the life I'd chosen. I'd picked him and Lash, because they were what I wanted. They'd picked me for the same reason. Love was about trust. Devlin had been there for me

10

more times than I could count. If he needed me to do something for him, especially for Anna, I was going to do it. "Yes," I said gently. "What do you need me to do?"

"I am going to say a few things, as I love you. You may feel something take hold of you—"

I bit my lip so I didn't laugh. If we were going to make love, I certainly wanted something to take hold of me.

"—and I need you to let it. Can you do that for me?"

I nodded.

Devlin looked at me for a split second, then began kissing me passionately. I was nervous for a few moments before succumbing to his embrace. As our loveplay intensified, we stripped off our clothes and I lay down, so he could love me. But after entering me, Devlin paused a moment. "Come back to me," he whispered longingly. "Come back to me, Rene."

I froze up, and stared at him in shock. "I thought this was about contacting Anna? Who the hell is Rene?"

"Shh," he said, putting his fingers to my lips. "Trust me."

Reluctant, I let him kiss me again. He began gently moving, stroking me with his shaft. I responded, kissing him fiercely as his hands roamed my body.

"Come back to me, Rene. Let me love you, as I did so long ago. Come back to me!"

Something slid across my shoulders like an icy tendril. Then it was sliding into me. I gasped, but Devlin clutched me to him tightly, still loving me.

"Come back to me!"

Abruptly, I lost control of my own body. It was bloodcurdling, and I grabbed desperately with my mind, but I couldn't make my body obey my commands.

Instead, my fingers ran up to touch Devlin's lips almost hesitantly.

Devlin froze above me. "Rene?" he whispered.

"Are you going to talk, or love me?" I heard my voice say with a French inflection.

Devlin kissed me so hard he hurt me, and then he was thrusting into me with abandon, even as someone else screamed with my voice in a language I barely knew for him to have me, to kiss me, to take me!

We came together, my pleasure barely noticeable in my rising fear. He eased off my body, and rolled me onto him, hugging me tightly.

"Again please, mon Coeur," Rene said through my mouth in that lilting voice. "I did not wait so long to be so quickly finished with you."

Devlin was already slipping into me, and kissing me frantically again. Resigned, I gave myself up to the pleasure I was feeling, telling myself if I was going to be possessed, I might as well get something out of it.

* * * *

At least two hours later, we lay before the fire, covered in sweat. Devlin was still clutching me tightly, and kissing me over and over.

"Shh," Rene said finally with my voice. "You will bruise her, if you aren't careful."

Devlin paused. "Can you feel me?" he said hesitantly. "Can you feel what her body is feeling, everything?"

"Yes and so can she," Rene answered. "She is a little wary of me, but otherwise, Sar is with us. We both enjoyed your lovemaking."

Rene used my hand to reach up again to caress Devlin's face. "But I know you did not call me back just to make love to me. What do you want to know, Lover? What future can I see for you?"

"Is Anna tormented?" Devlin said, agonized. "Does she haunt her grave? And what can we do, to make her let go, so she can cross over?"

Rene grabbed Devlin's face and kissed him passionately. "It was not her that you saw and felt all these years," Rene whispered. "It was me. It was always me, Devlin."

What? I never was talking to Anna at all? Why hadn't Dev told me of this Rene? And why the hell was she in Anna's grave?

Devlin didn't ask what I wanted to know, of course. "Why did you not go on?" he managed. "I got you your choker, as Ravel said you'd like that. I fastened it around your neck."

Now I couldn't get past the choker. Devlin had been Oathed to a woman I hadn't known of? What the hell was all this? No one had ever spoken to me of a woman named Rene!

"I couldn't, for fear Shaker might try for my soul," Rene said sadly.

12

"Just because he told you he would not take it does not negate my agreement with him. So it was safer to stay here, hidden. I wanted to be close to you, anyway."

"Why did you never show yourself to me before today?"

"It was time," she sighed. "I told you when last we touched that I saw to the bitter end, Dev. This is the end for me, this night."

"Must I stand by and let you leave? Can I do nothing to stop you?" he pleaded hopefully, tears in his eyes.

"Sar is the one who must do it. She must ask Shaker to relinquish my soul. As his kin, according to demon custom, he will agree. As soon as he does, I can move on."

"Will she agree to ask?"

"Yes," Rene answered. "But she's going to want an explanation from you about me. She is upset she didn't know of me. Very upset."

"I have never told anyone of you," Devlin said lovingly. "I wanted to keep you all to myself, Love." His voice turned black with hate. "There have been enough attempts through the years on Anna's remains by my enemies, looking to use my love for her against me. I finally had to have Titus put a magical barrier on your resting place that would admit only me and—"

"I know," Rene broke in. "But you must tell her, Dev."

Yes and he can start by answering why he buried two women in the same grave. I continued to stew, forced into silence.

Devlin nodded. "Is there anything else you can tell us?"

"You are building a good life together," she whispered. "Do not let jealousy rule your actions. Hope is not lost, Devlin. There is much joy to be had for you and Sarelle, together. But you're going to be tested sorely, too."

You're not much of a sorceress, I remarked mentally. *That's close to every single prediction that I ever heard from a soothsayer, that bad and good times were coming.*

"You were wrong, all those years ago," Dev whispered lovingly. "You said I would only love one woman, save Anna. But I have loved three, Rene."

Her tone was chiding. "You did not know me long enough to love me, not as more than a friend—"

"I love you. I've loved you since the moment you gave me your Oath. I came back so many times to remember you here by this fireplace! I wanted us to have so much more than what we did!"

"You did not love me then, you were grateful to me, for all I did for you," Rene corrected in that same chiding tone. "Be truthful, Dev. That you didn't love me then does not make what you feel for me now any less."

Devlin opened his mouth to protest, and she put my finger to it. "Hush. Call Titus, Devlin. Have him summon Shaker here. It's time."

Would Shaker know where to come? Had he been here before?

Rene heard my question, and told me 'yes' with her mind. I had other questions, but waited silently, now worried. Devlin was already speaking to Titus on his cell.

Two minutes later, Shaker appeared. "Titus said it was an emergency?" he rumbled, looking with interest at me in my nudity, even as Rene hastily grabbed some of my clothes to cover our body. "Do you need a third? I could easily be persuaded to join."

"Sar?" Devlin said, glancing at me.

I took a breath, and felt my body obey me. I let out a gasp.

Shaker raised his eyebrows. "I take it this isn't an invitation to bed her. So what is it?"

"Relinquish Rene's soul," I said flatly.

Shaker gave me a "get real" look. "No."

"Please? I'm asking as your kin."

"No," he rumbled. "It was promised to me. Lucifer knows this. I let it go without another soul in trade, my ass is charcoal."

"Sar is your kin, as she said," Devlin said amicably. "You are allowed a loophole."

"My deal with Rene predates Sar's kinship with me by centuries," Shaker said with a laugh. "That rule does not apply, Vampire." He turned to me with a gleam in his red eyes. "I thought I smelled faerie! You can't hide yourself in a human, witch. You might fool others, but I own your soul. You sold it to me to save your vampire lover, and I put a marker on it that day you promised it to me. That marker is long overdue."

Shit!

14

"I've been looking for you for a long, long while, Rene," Shaker rumbled in an evil tone. "I thought your soul had been destroyed along with your body, after Titus told me you'd been hit by a blast of his Hellfire. I never thought to check Anna's grave." He paused, and smiled. "But you're outed now, sorceress. It is you who must come along to Hell with me, by law, as you no longer have a body to inhabit."

"She does," I stated harshly. "Rene can stay with me."

Chapter Two

Shaker gave me another incredulous look. "You want her sharing your body, sharing your mind, making love with your lovers? How's Lash going to come to terms with that?"

"That isn't your concern," Devlin hissed at him, before I could reply. "Get out, Shaker. You are banned from my employ, forever. You come here to see Titus, you stay out of the main house." His golden eyes bled to glowing red in his fury. "You ever come near Sar or Rene, ever, and I'll send you back to Hell myself. And Rip and Titus will be following you!"

Shaker laughed, bearing his rows of dagger teeth. "Who'll guard you then, Vampire? Who'll make Lash his potion every month?" He took a menacing step closer. "Get out of the way, so I can draw Rene's soul out of her."

Devlin didn't move an inch. "Leave, you fuck! To think it was you all this time that was making her hide, keeping her from revealing herself to me!" His hands were inch-long claws, taloned in his rage. "I'd send you back to hell tonight, if I had the means!"

"But you don't!" Shaker sneered. "You have no faith, vampire!" He reached out for Devlin. "You get in my way and I'll tear you apart. You have nothing to threaten me with!"

Pure rage filled me, along with relentless determination. I grabbed up the fireplace poker, and a burning stick, and crossed them in front of me, brandishing them at Shaker. He looked at me, went to laugh, and instead let out a yelp.

"The Lord is my Shepherd, I shall not want. He maketh me lie down in green pastures, He leadeth me beside the still waters—"

Smoke began to curl up off of Shaker. He snarled at me.

"—He leadeth me in the paths of righteousness for His name's sake!"

"Stop, human!" he hissed at me. "You don't want me for an enemy!"

"He prepareth a table in the presence of mine enemies, my cup runneth over—"

Shaker was steaming now, and snarling, but he did not reach for me, or make any move.

"Yea, though I walk through the valley of the shadow of death, I will fear no evil! Thy rod and thy staff, they comfort me."

"Stop, or I'll take your soul to hell with hers!"

"Surely goodness and mercy will follow me all the days of my life! In the name of Jesus Christ, begone!"

Shaker screamed as he burst into dark flames, and abruptly disappeared.

"Shit, I messed up the lines..." I whispered, dropping the poker and stick.

Devlin caught me as I sagged in relief, easing me down beside him. "Shh," he said tenderly. "You were very brave, Sar. Your faith was what mattered, not the words. What you did worked. He's gone."

"Rene, are you there?" I asked aloud.

Yes, I'm here, she said tentatively in my mind. *But are you sure you want this, Sarelle? If you want, you can teleport me somewhere else.*

"What is she saying?" Devlin said impatiently. "Is she still within you?"

"Shh," I said to him. "I'm trying to hear her. This is not as easy as it probably seems."

As long as Shaker can't find me, I'll be safe, Rene continued. *But we must hurry. What you did weakened him to the point he had to leave or face physical wounds from your faith. He'll return here as soon as he regains his strength, no matter what Devlin told him. He'll search everywhere here, until he finds me, or he determines I've left.*

"Stay in me, for now," I said aloud, hesitantly. "I don't want you to go to Hell. Maybe there's some way we can find to break your agreement with him."

Maybe, Rene echoed in a disbelieving tone. *But I'll gladly stay, if you don't mind. I have spent too many lonely years here, with only the beasts and trees for company. It will be good to be among people again.*

"Then let's go," I said, getting to my feet, and reaching down for my clothes. "I'm getting cold."

* * * *

Devlin and I walked hand in hand back to Hayden. Rene let out a gasp in my mind, when she saw it.

So much has changed, she said in awe. *It is more beautiful that I could've imagined.*

"What is it?" Devlin said insistently, squeezing my hand. "Sar? Rene?"

"Use my voice, if you like," I said aloud to Rene, imbuing my words with a note of warning. "But don't fight me, if I want it back. The same with my body."

Understood, she said in my mind. *Just tell me 'Go" from now on, and I will close myself off from you, so you can be alone.*

I gave my assent, and Rene assumed control. "It is beautiful," she said in her lilting voice. "Much larger than I thought it would be, Dev."

"Come and see it, Love," Devlin said tenderly. "I want to show you everything."

We walked in the back door, and Ghost trotted up to me, tail wagging. Then he began to growl at me and shake, his eyes anxious.

Rene relinquished control to me. I called to my faithful dog. Ghost let out a whine, and then he was bounding to me, wagging his tail.

"You don't have to be afraid," I said, hugging him. "It's just me and, um...a new friend, Ghost."

Ghost whined, when he felt Rene hesitantly take control of me, but he didn't growl. And when she petted him tentatively with my hand, he licked her. "He is beautiful," Rene said in my voice. "Ghost? How appropriate."

Ghost whined again, looking at me quizzically.

"He is Sar's dog," Devlin said eagerly. "We have cats too, four of them, including Danial's cat Briar—"

"Danial lives here?" Rene said coldly. "With you? You have forgiven him?"

"Much has happened in two hundred years," Devlin said in a

18

mollifying tone. "Much I'd not want to admit to you. Yes, we are brothers again. A large part of that is Sar. She healed our rift, Rene. Sarelle is Oathed to us both, though Danial thinks her dead—"

"I got that, from their conversation awhile ago at Anna's grave," Rene said, rubbing our eyes. "This is very confusing."

To me, too, I said to her mentally. *I'm not even sure how to refer to us. I can't say myself anymore.*

"Come and sleep," Devlin said, leading us to our bedroom. "I'll tell you the rest over breakfast—"

"Is there a child?" Rene interrupted haltingly. "I saw one for you and Sar, Devlin. A girl, with your eyes."

Devlin hugged us tightly. "Yes, Love. Her name is Venus. We call her V. Would you like to see her?"

"Not tonight," Rene said in a wobbly, unsure tone. "I am overcome that so much has changed. There are objects all over I don't recognize, materials that are not wood or metal, and noises, there is so much noise—"

I spoke to Rene in our mind. *That is the TV downstairs, and we are getting a fax, and one of the phone lines is ringing.*

"I want just to sleep in your arms, and not think," Rene said aloud. "Please, Dev."

"Then come in," Devlin said, opening his bedroom door. "Come in, and we'll rest."

"About time!" Lash hissed in irritation from the bed, tossing down his book. "I've been waiting two hours! If Titus hadn't said he knew where you two were and that you were making up from a fight, I'd have come looking for you."

Devlin looked at me, bugged out his eyes, and exhaled deeply. Rene made to leave me, but I told her not to.

I went to Lash, and sat beside him. "I have to tell you something." I said haltingly. "Tonight, I let someone else inside me."

"Fuck, I knew it!" Lash shouted, instantly angry. "Who were you off with? Devlin, I'm gonna kill him, whoever it was."

"Please do not be upset," Rene said in my voice. "I am a woman, not a male. You are Lash, no?"

Lash went utterly still. He changed to snake partway, and put out his tongue, scenting the air. "Sar?" he hissed softly. "What have you done to her, Dev? That's Sar's voice, but that's not her, even if it smells like her."

"It is Rene, a woman I knew long ago. Her soul is inside Sar," Devlin said calmly. "Shaker wanted her soul, and Sar did this: let her inhabit her body, to save her."

"Ravel's sister," Lash hissed finally. "The sorceress you came here with, when you and Anna first arrived in America. I've heard you speak of her before. Why is she here now?"

"She was always here, since she died. I just didn't know."

"Fuck, I don't care about that! Why is she in my mate?"

"I told you! Sar let her in, so she wouldn't go to hell."

"I want her gone," Lash hissed menacingly, advancing on me. "Get out of my mate now, you witch! Get out of her before I make you get out."

"Stop!" I shouted, holding up my hands. "Lash, I agreed to let her in! We can find a way to break the agreement she made with Shaker, but we need time! Just relax!"

"How can I relax?" he shouted back at me. "I wanted to make love with you, and now I can't, because there's some other woman in there with you!"

"I can wall myself off in her mind, while you're with her," Rene said in my voice. "Please, Lash. Please don't make me leave!"

Lash hissed at me, baring his fangs. "I don't trust witches! More than twenty have tried to kill me over the years. The only good witch is a dead one!"

"I am walling myself off now," Rene whispered aloud. "Sar can call to me, when she and you are finished." I felt her presence flicker, and then disappear, as if she had completely left me.

"She's gone," I said, relieved. "I can't feel her."

"Good!" Lash hissed happily, taking my arm. "Let's go to Leri right now. She can draw her out of you, and stick her in a jar or something—"

Devlin belted him in the mouth hard. Lash hit the floor like a ton of bricks. "You fuck," Devlin hissed. "You are not doing anything to Rene, or I'll skin you in reptile form, and make a pair of shoes out of you."

Lash shook himself, and looked hatefully up at Devlin, his eyes flat.

20

"You wanted this, you fucking deviant vampire! You couldn't have Sar with another man, so you found a way to invite another woman to our bed."

I knelt beside him. "Please, Sweetness, stop it. I offered this. Devlin had nothing to do with it. It was my decision."

"Why?" Lash hissed, changing back slowly. "Why help her? What's she to you?"

"She means a lot to Devlin, and I can feel her love for him. It almost consumes her, it's so strong." I offered him my hand. "You know me, Tryst. You know how I feel about not helping, when it's in my power to do something. Was what I did for you less than a year ago so different?"

Lash looked at me for a moment, and then he let me help him up. "No," he hissed softly. "But I thought you helped me because you loved me. Because you cared about me."

"I did," I said, hugging him. "But I'd have helped you even if I didn't. You'd done too much for me, and for Devlin, not to help you."

He hugged me back tightly. "Are you sure?" he hissed. "I've never been possessed, but it's got to be odd, having someone in there with you, seeing all your thoughts and feelings."

"I told you, she's not here. We agreed already that sometimes I'd need her to go—"

"Get out," Lash hissed, looking over at Devlin. "Get out and leave us alone for an hour. When you see me leave, come back in."

Devlin didn't insist that this was his bedroom, or say anything, which I found odd. Instead, he just nodded, and left.

"You're sure she's gone?" Lash hissed sternly. "She's not there just hovering quietly?"

"I don't feel her—"

Lash cut off my words with a rough kiss, and then he was pressing me to the bed with his body, frantically removing my clothes. I kissed him back and let him, breathing an inward sigh of relief.

* * * *

Two hours later, Lash reluctantly got up. "I need to go, Sweetness," he hissed ardently, giving me a last kiss. "I've got to get some sleep. You get some sleep, too, okay? Tomorrow we'll go see Leri, or Terian or

21

even Tatiana, if we have to. And we'll find a way to break her agreement with Shaker, so she can get to Heaven, and out of you."

I nodded. He kissed me once more, and left.

A moment later, Devlin came in. He shut the door behind him, locked it, and came to my side, gathering me in his arms. "Is she still there?" he said frenetically. "Rene?"

I called out to Rene in my mind, and she answered, *I'm here.*

"She is here," I said.

Devlin squeezed me against him with something like a sob. "I'm sorry for Lash's behavior," he began. "He doesn't know you, and he's right, a lot of witches have tried to hurt him—"

"I'm not angry," Rene said tiredly, assuming control. "He had every right to be upset, finding me where he did. I'm just glad he agreed to let me stay."

"Rest with me, and know you're loved and safe," Devlin said emotionally. "I'll be right here, if you need me."

"It's good to be back in your arms," Rene said, sighing. "I wanted to be, for so many years."

"Shh," Devlin said, kissing her gently. "Rest. There is tomorrow for talking. Just be with me, Love."

Rene snuggled against him, and fell asleep. I felt asleep soon after, too, from sheer exhaustion.

* * * *

The next morning, I woke up. As I was thinking about whether or not to get up, in my mind Rene told me chidingly that I should.

I let out an involuntary cry of surprise.

Sorry, she said apologetically. *But don't you need to see to your daughter?*

"No," I said aloud, relieved. "Serena usually makes her breakfast on weekdays. Devlin's schedule is a night one, but V's tutor comes days. Caitlyn's a relative of Leri's—"

I should've known that sorceress was here, Rene said in a put-out manner. *Wherever she is, Titus is, and vice versa.*

My natural curiosity perked up. "How long have they been together?"

22

Three hundred years, or so. But it's true it is an off-on relationship, though Titus always calls her his wife even when she is with another, not speaking to him.

I was taken aback at her harsh words. "Do you not like her?"

She's a faerie witch, like me, Rene said, as if that explained it all. *We've had a few run ins. We aren't enemies, but she tends to dabble in the darker stuff. I often wonder if Titus has the rights to her soul, and that's why she stays with him—*

"Lash said it was his size," I commented, then flushed.

Rene was dead quiet a second, and then she laughed for a long time. *Could be!* she said, still chuckling. *Demons are known for their size.*

Is it true? I thought to her. *Do you know for a fact?*

Yes, she whispered back in my mind. *But don't think you're missing out. Devlin's no twig.*

It took me a minute to get what she was saying and then I was laughing uproariously.

I smiled. "I think we're going to get along fine," I said aloud, as I got up from bed.

* * * *

All that week, I spent with Rene showing her how daily life had changed since her time. She was astounded at so much I took for granted, like the TV, warm running water on demand, and electricity. I stayed away from the computer for the moment, figuring the Internet should wait. Rene did have some knowledge of cell phones, having seen Devlin use one on many occasions near Anna's grave. But even given how much I enjoyed myself with Rene, that isn't to say we didn't begin immediately to try to solve "my ghost problem" as Lash referred to my situation.

I went to Terian's lab the very next morning after acquiring Rene. But he wasn't there.

I was very pleased to see Asher, but she freaked out, either from not seeing me for so long, or sensing Rene in me. I left her hiding under the table, and went to Sundown's room. Before I got there, I ran into Theo.

God, just my luck today to run into the one person I'd had the good chance to avoid for months. "Hi."

"Hi," Theo said in a tone that was mostly growl. "What are you doing here?"

"Looking for Terian."

"Why?"

"Titus said he'd asked to see me."

"He's at a meeting," Theo growled. "I'll tell him you were here."

No, you won't. Sigh. "I'll wait, if you'll know when he'll be back."

"I don't. Sun doesn't want you hanging around anyway, bothering her husband. Go back to your forked-tongue lover."

Nice. "Thanks, Theo." I turned and walked away.

"How could you do it?" he hissed under his breath, as I made to go out the door. "How could you, Sar?"

"We fell in love. I didn't mean for it to happen—"

"I remember you in my arms that night three years ago! You were bleeding badly, because he nearly drained you! How could you go back to him, and want to live with him?"

I belatedly realized he meant Devlin, and not Lash. "I love him, Theo. He was there for me when you weren't. When no one else was."

"You aren't the woman I fell in love with," Theo said in repugnance. "You've become someone else."

"I have," I said, feeling to my surprise a little sadness, but mostly pride. "I couldn't be the woman I used to be, not and live in this world of danger, killings, and archaic vampire laws. I have children I care enough about to put what is best for them before what's best for me."

"Cut the crap," Theo growled. "This was about you wanting him, it was never about what was best for Theoron, or Elle."

"I have another child, or did you forget?" I said scathingly. "Venus needs me, and she needs her father. Hunters have been trying for us both!"

"Then maybe you should've stuck to your husband," Theo said just as scathingly. "But then one man has never have been enough for you, has it?"

This was pointless. I turned and walked away. " 'Bye, Theo."

This time, he let me walk away.

I'd gotten outside and into the woods before I realized I'd forgotten to leave a note for Terian. I cursed mentally.

That was an ex-lover of yours? Rene said in my mind. *He's handsome.*

"Ex-husband."

I'm sorry for what happened to you, Rene murmured quietly. *I gather from what was said that Devlin hurt you, before he realized you were the woman I foretold for him?*

"Yes," I sighed. "It was a long time ago. I forgave him."

Good, she said soothingly. *I'm glad you had V with him, Sar, that you helped him regain some of his lost humanity. He loves you very much—*

I walked to Danial's cemetery, not really listening to her. It was a nice day, and I wanted to forget Theo's angry words, and the pain of the past. But I ran smack into it, when I came upon the grave of my son. Theo had indeed carved the headstone. It was the spitting image of Devon as he'd been, life-size, made of stone, dates carved into the base near the words "Beloved Son."

I walked up to it and touched the likeness. "I wish I had Aslan here from Narnia," I said, wiping away a tear. "I'd make you real, Devon. I'd bring you back to me."

I'm sorry, Rene whispered gently. *He was as noble looking as his father.*

I wondered how she could tell that, Devon being in lion form, and Theo in human form. Maybe she was just being nice. "Thanks."

"Lady, what are you doing here?" a gentle voice called from behind me. "And who are you talking to?"

I know that voice, Rene said bitterly.

I turned to see Danial walking toward me, dressed in jeans and a denim shirt. From the gun at his hip, it looked as though he'd been doing target practice at the outdoor range.

I forced a smile. "Hi, Danial. What brings you here?"

"Meeting T for some gun practice. I haven't for a long time, and it was a way to try to mend fences with him. I think we may have made up. At least, we didn't fight this time."

"Good. I came here to see Terian, but he isn't here."

"He's at a meeting in Dallas. But call his cell, he'll be checking messages."

Now why didn't I think of that? *Duh*. I used my phone, and left a message quickly, just asking him to call me ASAP.

As I hung up, I felt Danial's cool arms encircle me. "Must you run off?" he murmured, beginning to kiss me. "I would love to steal a kiss or two."

He's after your blood, Rene hissed, sounding pissed off. *Tell him to get lost!*

Go, I said in my mind. *I want to give it to him, Rene. He's my Oathed One.*

She cursed in French, and then her presence left me.

"Lady?" Danial said hesitantly. "Do you not want to be with me?"

"Tell me," I said gently, turning to face him. "Do you feel anything for me at all, beyond friendship?"

"I have told you I do," Danial said carefully. "I would not be here with you now, if I didn't. As soon as I scented you on the breeze, I came to look for you."

Can he come to love me again? And do I want him to? "Then take it," I said, putting my arms around his neck.

Danial gave me a seductive smile, and leaned in, giving me a sensuous kiss. But he broke it abruptly. "Quick, behind the tree!"

Chapter Three

Danial pushed me behind the tree.

"This looks familiar," Theo's sarcastic voice called out.

It does, Rene growled.

Dev knows, I growled back at her. *He wants me to do this. Knock it off.*

Sorry, she said, cowed.

"What I do is not your concern, Theopolis," Danial said loftily. "Do not interfere in my business."

"I don't give a fuck," Theo growled. "Not anymore."

"Did you come to see Devon?" Danial said back to him, in a much more respectful tone.

"Yes," Theo growled. "He's my son."

"Then visit," Danial said. "I will leave you."

Danial headed back the way he'd come through the trees, and I followed him, not looking at Theo. Soon, we were at the shooting range. It looked exactly the same, the human form targets set up a good fifty yards away in various positions. Sure enough, there was the fresh smell of burnt gunpowder on the wind.

"Good grouping," I said half-heartedly, looking at the nearest target. "You hit the heart ten for ten."

Danial wasn't fooled. "Excuse him," Danial said gently, hugging me. "He's been angry since losing Sar to my brother and me, no matter that he has his own mate now. That together with the death of his son has made him bitter."

"Do you remember Devon?" I asked quietly.

"He was a noisy cub," Danial said, smiling. "And when he was human, he was the very image of Theo, from his blond hair to his blue eyes—"

Theo had helped him change to human form…and kept it from me. I staggered, and leaned against a nearby tree.

Danial's arms were around me in an instant. "Lady?"

Get out the words before you miss the chance! "You saw Devon as human?"

"Theo helped him shift once or twice, and I was on hand to see him. It was for a few moments only."

I choked back a sob, and cursed Theo again, for not sharing that with me.

"Lady?"

I turned to Danial and kissed him hard. He recoiled a little, then his arms tightened on me, and he kissed me back passionately. His mouth devoured mine, pricking me gently with his fangs.

He eased me down onto a fallen log, still kissing me. He pulled me onto him so I sat astride him, straddling him. I could feel his organ stiff through his pants, and resisted the urge to stroke him. Instead, I rubbed my hips against his gently yet provocatively, still kissing him.

Danial let out a groan. I expected him to shove me away, but instead he cupped my buttocks in his hands, bringing my hips tight to his. He thrust up gently with his hips, kissing me with abandon. I threw my head back, grinding my pelvis into his, as he bit into my throat.

I let out a cry, and ground harder. Danial withdrew his fangs, just as I felt a small orgasm wash through me, enough to dull the pain a little.

Danial kissed my wound, healing it, and then hugged me tightly. He drew back from me some minutes later, looked at me with his dark eyes, and gave me a final long kiss.

"I care for you, Lady," he said gently. "But this is all I can offer you. Are you sure this meets your needs, as it meets mine?"

I wanted to say bluntly that I still felt his rigid penis throbbing against me through his pants, so it was bullshit that all his needs were being met. But there was no point trying to make him acknowledge something he was so vehement to deny. "Danial, if there comes a time I need more, you'll be the first to know."

Danial nodded. "Then let me escort you back."

* * * *

As we walked back, we talked a little. Rene was still silent, though if she was back and listening or still gone, I wasn't sure.

"I have spoken to Elle," Danial told me in a worried tone. "She said she may settle for an associate's degree, instead of a bachelor's."

"Why? She said things were going well, not to mention she'll regret that—"

"I think some classmates were mean to her. That, or she had a brief affair with a fellow student, and it ended not to her liking."

"She's not mentioned any boyfriends to me, or even any dates." I frowned. "I'm worried about her, actually, that she's avoiding all males."

"Nor to me has she mentioned any boyfriends, though I would be quite content to have her focus all her energies on her studies. But something is different, Lady. There is something in her voice that wasn't there before. It's happiness, but it's wrapped tight with fear."

For all that Danial sometimes annoyed me, his astuteness was something I was and would be eternally grateful for. *If he says there's something off with Elle, then there is something wrong.* "She's doing the therapy," I said in a low tone. "But it's going to take a while. She may need some time to work beyond her fear, before she can have a normal relationship."

"I should have been there," Danial said in a rough tone. "I failed Elle. I wasn't there for her when she was hurt."

"You were there for her many times. You've always been a good father...um, from what Devlin has told me."

"It's true Sar was not a good mother, not at first," Danial said sadly. "Though she tried hard to be. I had the benefit of having been a father before when I was mortal. I was not half so good, the first time." His voice turned emotional. "She used to do so many small things for me, things I don't think I ever thanked her for. She was so kind, and loving. And it's those small things I remember most—"

I didn't want to hear anymore, even if he was going to tell me good things about myself unknowingly. "I need to get back, I'll be missed."

"Then till our next time, Lady." He blew me a kiss as I walked away.

* * * *

29

Terian returned my call that night. He said he was sorry, but he wasn't going to be able to help. "Nothing I know can break a demon's soul deal, unless another soul is offered in exchange."

I thanked him, and consulted with Rene. "We could go to Leri?"

No, she said. *She'll say the same. Try the other woman Lash mentioned.*

"Tatiana. I don't know much about her. I only have met her a few times, at Danial's parties, and at her nightclub—"

We'll go there. Do you know the way?

"Sure, but we can't go alone. We need at least one guard, probably Lash."

Rene grumbled, but allowed that him accompanying us was probably best.

"Should I call her, ask her to meet with us?" I mused aloud. "It may give her the chance to say no."

Let's just go there, Rene replied. *If she can't help, we'll know that much faster. If she can, perhaps she can do something immediately.*

Three hours later, Rene and I arrived at The Haunt with Lash. I looked around, and saw Tatiana talking to an important looking couple who were sitting at what had to be the best table.

Lash saw her, and made a beeline for her. I followed him.

Tatiana looked at him with distaste when she saw him coming toward her, though she had a fleeting smile for me. "Hello, Sarelle, Lash. What can I do for you?"

"There's a faerie witch in Sar, some old friend of Dev's," Lash said bluntly. "We need to buy her soul back from a demon and get her out of Sar. Can you help?"

Tatiana gaped at him. "Run that by me again?"

"You heard me the first time," Lash hissed in his deadly low voice. "Can you help or not?"

"Come with me to my office," Tatiana said, rising. "Excuse me," she said to the couple. "I'll be back very soon."

"Getting her out of Sar isn't a problem," Tatiana said to Lash, once we were out of earshot. "But getting her soul back from a demon...that's not going to be so easy."

"Technically, she still has her soul," I put it, "But it has some kind

30

of marker on it. Shaker owns it."

"Nice," Tatiana remarked sarcastically. "But better, actually. Possession is most of the law, at least as far as souls go. What did she trade it for?"

Help for Devlin, Rene whispered in my mind. *I had to.*

"She did it for Devlin, because she loved him."

Tatiana nodded. "I've heard the stories of the great lengths some women have gone to for that vampire. Again, this is good. If it had been for evil purposes, like money, revenge, or power, that's harder to ask forgiveness for."

"So what do we do?" Lash hissed impatiently.

"Rene needs to either offer Shaker something he values more than a soul, or she needs to get a higher power for good to intercede for her, to negate the deal."

"What higher power?"

"A saint, an angel, or God, Himself."

Lash gave me a dubious look. I was pretty dubious myself. "How do we do that?"

"Pray for it," Tatiana said. "We will pray now. I'll use some of your faith to try to make contact."

"You've got a conduit for God in your office?" Lash hissed sarcastically. "Going to yell up to an angel? You've got a screw loose, Tat. Give us a potion, and we'll give you some money, and we'll be out of your hair."

"This is not dark magic, this is white magic. It doesn't work like that," Tatiana said nicely. "There are no potions for this. Be quiet, Lash."

"I say how this works," Lash hissed in his killing tone. He unsheathed his knife. "Give us what we need, sorceress. Or I'll take you back to Devlin, and he can convince you instead."

Tatiana murmured a few words, then looked at Lash as if she expected something to happen. But nothing occurred as he advanced toward her. Her eyes widened and she hurriedly pressed a button. Two men appeared in her office via teleportation. They grabbed hold of Lash, and then all three of them disappeared, Lash struggling hard.

"Where are you taking him?" I accused sharply.

"Back to the gates of Hayden," Tatiana said just as sharply.

"Threatening me in my own club! That snake and his master are banned from now on, Sarelle. If you come back, don't come back with them."

Great. "Can you help? Please, we have no one else to go to, Tatiana."

"Pray with me."

We prayed for about ten minutes, with no visible results. Tatiana rubbed her eyes, and then sighed. "It's not working," she said tiredly. "That means the saint I'm praying to won't help, or it would already be done. I'm sorry."

"Can we try someone else? Another saint?"

"I don't have any pull with any other saint except the one who has guardianship over me. He's the only one who has ever answered my prayers. I've never even seen an angel, Sar. Sorry."

"What else can I do?" Rene said stridently through me. "I need help! Please!"

"There is one more thing," Tatiana said, studying me. "But it's involved."

"Yes?" Rene asked quickly.

"Rene, you'll have to become flesh again. Your soul will naturally go into your body. Then go to a convent for at least a month. Pray, and let the sisters pray over you. They may be able to intercede on your behalf."

"What's the catch?" Rene's tone was suspicious.

"You'd need someone to run a complicated spell of epic proportions, to create you a new body."

"Can't I just get a body that's not being used, like a person ready to die?"

"No," Tatiana said in disdain. "Your soul needs its own body. As it is, you'd need a lot of magic to form it for you. Plus, you need raw material: flesh, blood, hair, and bones—"

"Can I give her some of that?" I asked, breaking in and wresting control of my mouth back from Rene.

"I have my own bones," Rene said stiffly, taking control back from me. "I can use them."

"Are they dust?" Tatiana said with raised brows. "That's harder."

Shit.

"Maybe," Rene whispered, obviously terrified and horrified. "I don't know."

"Sar, yes, you can give her what she'd need, without too much trouble. But it'll take time to make. There'll be pain, too, most likely. I can't do it. The spell is a dark one, and I don't do that kind of thing."

"Who can?" I asked, irritated.

"No one I know," Tatiana said. "You'd need a really knowledgeable sorcerer."

I can try, Rene said to me confidently. *I was very skilled, when I was alive.* "What else?" she asked aloud.

"You'll need faith. Faith of your own. Once you are flesh again, you have to ask the demon for your soul back, and believe enough in God's power that He'll do it, to actually make the demon back down. That's it."

"I know someone who has a good deal of faith," Rene said emotionally. "I can try to emulate her, in that."

We both thanked Tatiana and teleported home to Hayden. After checking in with Lash, who was unharmed but still very pissed off, I walked downstairs to put in some overdue time on the treadmill.

"We'll work together," I said as I walked, trying to reassure Rene. "We'll figure it out. Terian will help, and so will Titus."

They're Shaker's brothers. They won't want to help me.

"I'll ask for you. Titus thinks of me as a daughter."

Maybe this can work, Rene mused. *Maybe.*

* * * *

That night, when I came up to bed, Devlin was reading a book. I was surprised as it was clearly a young adult book, of the type teenage girls usually read. The cover showed a vampire and a swooning maiden.

"Just what are you reading?" I said in shock.

"A tale of love between human and vampire," Devlin said dramatically, quoting off the back. "Because their love was stronger than death, and his desire for her blood—"

"Okay," I interrupted, rolling my eyes. "But why? I don't usually see you read this type of book. Usually it's poetry, or sometimes about strategy, or other things like that."

"I find these amusing," Devlin said, giving me a fang-filled grin.

"Lash gets them for me, when he is out at the bookstores. He got one for me about twenty years ago, as a joke, and I had such a good time reading it, he usually gets me all the new vampire romance fiction that comes out."

"Why?" I managed, chortling. *A vampire reading teen romance?*

"Because I have to laugh, to see how many young girls want an old vampire like me biting them," Devlin said humorously. "It feeds my ego, to be so desired."

I didn't find this funny now. All those vampire books had one thing in common, besides the vampire being older by at least fifty years. "Do you want a younger woman?" I said hesitantly. "A twenty-year old, or a nineteen-year-old, someone who is fresh and new?"

Devlin looked at me in surprise. Then he tossed aside the book and came to me, wrapping me in his arms. "No, Love," he said tenderly. "I want only you."

Believe him, Rene said reassuringly. *He means his words, Sar.*

I was not mollified. "Your donors are all twenty-something. Just like the heroines of those novels."

"They give me blood, Sar. And in part, the truth is I read these novels, if they can be called that, because my donors read them. They give me ideas of what to say or do, to make my donors pleased with the experience." He kissed me gently. "You know I don't do more with them than kiss and hug, as Danial did. But I do need them, Sar, and I want to fulfill their fantasies. I need them to keep wanting to give me their blood, and this is an easy way to do it."

I was still very upset, though I wasn't sure why. "Why don't you want them?" I said, near tears. "I've met some of them, and they absolutely adore you. They can't say enough good things about you. They'd never ask you to be with only them, they'd let you do anything you wanted with anyone you wanted, if you'd only say you cared for them." I swallowed hard. "What made you love me, and not love them?"

There were a lot of things I expected Dev to give for his choice: my unique summer blood, or ability to birth V, his trust of me, or even because of what I'd done for Danial. But his surprising answer was none of those. "Because I could not love one so young," he whispered lovingly. "I have had many young lovers, even those that were sixteen or younger, back when that was not something viewed by society as wrong. I drank from all of them, and I loved feeling them beneath me. But they were lovers, Sar, no more than that. I never had a relationship with any of them, other than a sexual one. And even that was usually only for a night, or two."

I was still upset. "Why? I'm not special, Dev, even if my blood is."

"Because I like your hands," he whispered.

I blushed redder than I had in a long, long while, and blurted out, "Why? They are not pretty, Devlin. Though I heal fast now, I have many scars, from all that I used to do, before I met you, and—"

"Hush." Devlin held my hands in his. "Look at my hands, Sar."

I was a little embarrassed, as the rest of him was so spectacular I hadn't ever really looked at his hands before this moment. He had strong hands, not delicate ones like Danial. "I'm looking. You have nice hands." What did he want me to see?

"See the faint lines, Sar, across the fingers? Some of those are from old battle scars, but most are from sword practice. And the faint mark there on the back of my left hand is from an arrow that went through it when I was sixteen. I had to pull it all the way through, as the shaft was metal, and the tip was barbed. It hurt worse than anything I'd ever felt before, back then." He paused. "But that was only my first wound. There were a lot more painful ones I received in my later mortal years. After all my centuries now as vampire, my body only bears testament to the more serious ones. All my lesser scars have for the most part faded."

I ran my hands over the faint mark, feeling the ridge of scar tissue in an uneven circle on the back of his hand. When I turned his palm over, I saw that his palm was also scarred. But this was almost like a tiny sun, with delicate lines radiating outward from a much smaller uneven circle.

"The holes were similar once," he whispered. "The arrow hit the back of my hand first. But the wound was stitched, and I still had to practice, and fight. As the wound healed, the scar on the back grew bigger, from flexing my hand. The one on my palm stayed smaller." He paused. "Over the years, the scars have faded. They were much more noticeable when I was newly made. As you can see, all my time as vampire has made them shadows of what they were. But I still have them."

35

I brought it to my lips, and kissed his hands gently. "I'm sorry you were hurt. I've had bad wounds too before, though not so bad as yours."

"I've noticed you have a few scars from deep cuts," Devlin said quietly. "One of the deepest is near your forearm."

"It wasn't bad, just a burn, when I removed a brand from the woodstove. Or it could've been a baking pan from the oven, I can't remember."

"You have an inch-wide scar years later," Devlin said. "It wasn't trivial."

I shrugged.

"But the deepest is on your left foot, near the arch," Devlin whispered.

I hadn't ever mentioned that to Devlin, or anyone. "It was a stupid accident."

"Lash said it looks as if you stepped on a knife. He said the scar had to come from a blade, one that went deep."

"A razor blade," I said, wincing at the memory. "My grandfather was careless, and I was seven and barefoot. It went in all the way to the bone. I was on crutches for months."

"Why are you blushing?" Devlin asked.

"Because I'm embarrassed. I didn't know you saw these marks on me, and I feel as if I'm kind of, I don't know, flawed now."

"You are missing my point," he said, sounding chiding and sad. "I am happy that we have this in common." Devlin paused, as if looking for words, then began again. "I was thirty-five when I was made, Sar, and no longer a boy. Back in those days, that was near middle age, if not approaching old age. Now I am close to four hundred and fifty, or so. So what could I have in common with a girl who is still a child, who dreams of love, and knows nothing of true hardship, poverty, or war? She could never understand what I've gone through in my long life, or how it feels to be alive now having seen so much. To see everything I knew pass into history, and be replaced, and then even that also become history. To have that level of loss repeat over and over again, as the centuries passed." He rubbed his scratchy face against my neck. "I need a woman, Sar, one who has lived a little, and known some sorrow and loss, the kind of loss

36

you don't usually have until you reach thirty or forty, and feel your youth begin to fade. A woman who has lived, but is still young enough at heart to hope, to believe love is worth some pain. A woman who is willing to change her life to be with me, not because being with an immortal being is glamorous and exciting, but because she wants to share the short time she has to live with me. In short, someone who sees me for a man, and not just a sexy vampire, even if I am the very definition of the latter."

I blinked back tears, and embraced him, unable to say anything.

Devlin kissed me again. "You are that woman, Love," he whispered. "There is no other. And there never will be."

Chapter Four

The next morning, as I was dressing, I replayed the past night with Devlin, reliving how good his tender words had made me feel. Then I abruptly felt bad. "I'm sorry," I said aloud to Rene hesitantly. "You heard what Devlin—"

It's okay, Rene answered stiffly. *Don't think I don't know that he called to me for Anna's sake, Sar. It was one of the reasons I never revealed myself to him, over the years. I know what he feels for me is nothing next to what he feels for you.*

"I think he does love you," I said carefully. "He isn't a man who says those words idly."

I'm not saying that, Rene said, sounding put out. *I'm saying that I knew he loved Anna, and I know he loves you. I also know that if there was a choice of which long-ago lover Dev could have alive again, he'd have her back here, not me.*

I didn't know what to say, and I didn't want to agree. So instead, I got to business. "Let's go to Titus this morning, and ask him for his help."

Rene agreed. After brushing my hair and applying a quick dab of lip gloss, I teleported to Titus's house.

Leri was there reading a book, sipping a cup of what looked like coffee. "Hello, Sarelle," she said amicably. "I have some of the ingredients you'll need assembled. Titus is out, gathering the rest."

"You know what I've come here to ask?"

Leri nodded. "Devlin came last night after Lash and you got back, saying Tatiana was being uncooperative. He commanded Titus to do what he could, telling him of what she suggested. Titus was up all night, researching spells, and he found one he believes will work."

"Good," Rene and I both said with relief.

Leri gave me an odd look. "It's been a long time, Rene. I hope when you're flesh, we can catch up."

"Don't pretend we are friends," Rene said aloud in an icy tone, wresting control from me easily. "Last time we met, you said you'd see me dust. Your prediction came true, as I'm sure you're glad to see!"

"Do not bring up old quarrels," Leri remarked, annoyed. "Much has happened while you've been dead. I am a mother now. My concerns for Terian and my husband—"

Rene muttered something nasty-sounding aloud in French.

"—my concerns for them would make me give every effort on your behalf. My existence here as Hayden's resident witch has been a good one for more than a century now. Besides, this is clearly important to Devlin and Sar. So it is equally important to us."

Rene huffed more French in my mind, but said nothing aloud this time.

"Sar," Titus rumbled, appearing out of thin air. "I was just going to come looking for you. Please, follow me to the main house. I have everything assembled in the basement."

I nodded goodbye to Leri, and teleported with him. A moment later, we stood in what had once been his old workshop. Last time I'd been here, it had been more of a study, with most of his vials and ingredients moved to the house he shared now with Leri. But no more. Vials, sacks, ampules, beakers, and all manner of plastic holders were on every available surface, crowding one another for room. All held powder, or bits of things I couldn't identify.

"I'm sorry it's so jammed," Titus rumbled. "I got everything, though." He handed me a thick book, a long black ribbon through the end of it. "The spell is here."

"Thank you," I said gratefully. "Can you direct me, um, us?"

"I can do nothing further," Titus rumbled apologetically. "There must be nothing of demon in the finished product, Sar. If I taint the body in any way, it will not be allowed to enter holy ground. As it is, you'll be hard put to get Rene into her body and there before Shaker comes for her."

"Can you talk to him?" I beseeched. "I tried, but he refused to release her."

Titus shook his head. "He's right, he has to claim her soul. She traded him for his help, and he owns it. Worse, I must tell him the moment she becomes flesh, Sar. I've promised him to."

I blinked in shock, but Rene was not at loss for words like I was. "You bastard!" she swore aloud. "Wasn't it enough you killed me? Wasn't it enough you robbed me of being with Devlin?"

"I am sorry for dealing you your killing blow," Titus rumbled, not sounding sorry at all. "But you attacked my master of the time, and you knew the risks of coming against me, sorceress. You also knew what would happen through your glimpses of the future, that it would mean your doom to help Devlin, and you did it anyway. Take my help now, and let us leave our past in the past. I would be your ally now, as Sar is."

Rene nodded. "You are right," she said from my lips in an old, tired tone. "I will take your help gladly, and I thank you for it."

Titus nodded, and disappeared.

I sat down in a nearby chair, and opened the book. I saw with despair it was written in what looked like a foreign language, one that went on for pages solidly with no breaks. *We are fucked,* I murmured to Rene mentally.

"It's ancient Greek," Rene said aloud, after a moment of studying the text. "Don't worry, there are sentences written here, you just have to know the language to be able to see them. The Greeks did this to confuse their enemies, to make their language hard to decipher."

It worked. Can you read it?

"I can, though it's been a while. Let me have control so I can get us started, as you watch and listen."

Soon, Rene was gathering ingredients, and making a list in French in an elegant hand. I admit to my embarrassment that I was soon confused, as while she thought in English, or at least, I understood her thoughts, I couldn't read any of her notes. And the Greek was a complete mystery. Yet by the end of the day, I at least knew what French ingredient meant what physical thing. We'd done a little of the work needed for the spell.

"Tatiana was right, it will take weeks of working," Rene said tiredly. "There are ten stages to this spell, and we've done only a third of the first one. We can only progress so fast, or what we are making will not, um, grow properly."

"A month isn't so bad," I said, trying to be cheery. "We can use that time to show you more of how things are now in the world, so when you're your own person, you can move about with confidence."

Rene was silent. Then I heard her stifle a mental sniffle. "You are a good friend," she said aloud in a high, uneven emotional voice. "I did not expect it, Sarelle McGarran. Not for one I was sure you'd view as your rival."

"Come," I said, changing the subject quickly. "I haven't been to see V yet today. She'll be worried if I don't show up soon to walk Ghost with her."

* * * *

The rest of the day passed happily. Devlin had already told V of Rene's inhabiting of my body, and that it was my choice. To my surprise, my daughter told me she thought it was cool I was "possessed like that King was in *The Two Towers*." Rene didn't get why I was dismayed at that comparison, and I quickly got V onto less disquieting subjects, before my memory showed her the reason for my concern. Ghost by now was calm with Rene's presence in me, and our walk was nice. Spring had erupted for real in the last few days, the last of the snow melting, and most all of the early flowers had bloomed.

May 1st would arrive in no time, my favorite month to plant and to be outside. It was past time for me to truly enjoy summer again, my first real summer at Hayden. Ah, those words felt so good to say, and the experience would be even better to enjoy, knowing it was the beginning of my real new life, full not just of love and passion, but also stability.

* * * *

Later that night, sitting with Devlin as we watched an old thirties movie, I abruptly hit pause, and turned to him. "Why don't you have old paintings, or things like that? I know you like the arts and history, as V does."

Devlin laughed. "You're saying where are the antiques, because I've lived so long?"

I laughed aloud. "Well, yes."

"Because they tend to get destroyed," Devlin answered a little sadly. "Lash is my best friend, but he's none too gentle with his surroundings, as you've seen. True one-of-a-kind art should not be where it might be casually damaged." He ran his hand lightly down my bare arm. "As you know, I like music. I once had a very nice instrument collection, including a Stradivarius violin. It was destroyed when a demon attacked the outside of Hayden. I replaced only the piano, and that with just a recent model."

Ouch. "But why not enchant them, so they couldn't be damaged accidentally?"

Devlin shook his head. "Accidental damage is not the only destructive force. I had a collection of first editions of Poe, and other poets. Some hunters torched the box containing them on my way to America with mystical fire, thinking it contained me." His voice was sad. "None survived."

I touched his arm gently. "I'm sorry."

"I've been collecting one of a kind glass sculptures for the last fifty years," Devlin said, a wry smile that looked a twin of Danial's on his face. "They were all shattered by Leri fighting with Titus." He paused. "But I'd have lost them if I'd taken them with me. too, so it was meant to happen. Loss of things was and will always be inevitable." He hugged me tighter. "Things don't matter, Sar. Everything changes, and the longer you live, the more you tend to accumulate. And naturally, the more you have then to lose."

"I get it."

"I have only a few special prizes now," he said, grinning. "And they are more than enough for me to watch over, My Loves."

"I agree," I said lovingly.

As do I, Rene chimed in mentally.

* * * *

For the next week, Rene and I worked most mornings on her spell. Part of it was unpleasant, as Titus had indeed gone into her grave, and gathered what was left of her bones. They were mostly dust now, and I felt odd, putting my fingers into what had once been Rene. She told me not to be squeamish, that she didn't mind, and that it would be worth it, to be alive again. I gritted my teeth, and did it.

I also taught her a lot about life in this century. She watched and asked questions as I baked with V, operated my sewing machine and my tractor, or exercised on the gym equipment. I told her to be quiet the afternoon V and I met my mother at the mall for lunch, but I needn't have bothered. Rene was overwhelmed by the noises of the mall, and all the people, as well as the car drive on the highway through construction. She also had a few choice words to say about the way young girls were dressing these days. Much of what she did utter made me laugh, and my mother kept shooting me looks, wanting to know why I was laughing at nothing. I tried to keep a straight face, not wanting her to think I was losing my mind.

Elle also came back that week to visit Danial, and spent a few hours with me. She never gave a reason for why she hadn't come home over Easter, and I didn't press it. She seemed happy, and I was glad to see her getting along with V, though it was easy to see she still felt a little jealous of V's beauty. But there was something about her now, some new confidence and happiness that hadn't been there, back at Sun and Terian's wedding. I said nothing, resolving to ask Danial about it the next time I saw him.

T also came to spend time with Serena and to talk to Lash, and "met" Rene. He was a little unnerved to hear her words coming out of my mouth, but he handled it well.

Lash was still gone a good portion of the time, working. He was sorry to be away so much, and when he was home, he spent every free minute he had with me, after making sure Rene had really left us alone. He bitched a lot about hunters, saying that Peter and Hector had been causing a lot of trouble. "Akira caught a hunter in his jewelry workshop."

I remembered Akira, the Asian ruler of New York state, and his female companion, Chi. "He's a ruler, and he makes jewelry?"

"He makes it for special orders, only for non-humans," Lash said impatiently. "That ring you wear from Danial with the swirled colors, he made that."

"Did he make my choker?"

"Maybe Danial's, but not Dev's," Lash said thoughtfully. "But you're interrupting, Mate."

"Sorry, go ahead."

"Anyway, Akira killed the hunter. Chi called Devlin, all upset this evening. Later tonight, I've got to go there and inspect their defenses. I'm guessing it's mostly that they're new at having to watch themselves. They probably don't have any guards yet, either."

"Have there been any vampire killings?"

"A few. Nobody important, mostly a few newbies. The usual, you might say." He paused. "I also have greetings for you from Van and Erik."

I remembered the male duo from the Hallows party: tall, dark, and handsome. They'd helped Danial and I when Theo went missing, years ago. "How are they?"

"Good. They are ruling Pennsylvania now. Devlin told you he was going to change a few 'staties,' didn't he?"

I nodded. "Are they still, um, together?"

"You know, that's a good question," Lash hissed introspectively. "I've long wondered if they are intimate. Devlin thinks they are some kind of kin, cousins or brothers or maybe even father and son, but no one knows for sure. I've always assumed they are gay, though I've never been able to find out for sure. They never speak of their relationship or give any sign."

"How old are they?"

"Erik is about forty or so, relatively young for a vampire. Van, I'm not sure, he might be older. They keep to themselves, unless one of them is threatened. Then it's something to see." He grinned. "Anyway, I was down as a favor to Devlin, giving them advice. They've had some trouble with police in their state, as a newer vampire killed a few people in a bar messily. But they handled it okay, and Devlin's pleased. They said to say hi to you, and they hoped you were doing well. They'd heard of V, and told me to tell you congratulations."

"Say hi back, the next time you see them." I paused. "Lash, is there a reason that Devlin doesn't have any vampires around him, other than Danial? None visit him. The only other vampire I'd seen him be friendly with is Catherine. But there were many vampires buried in his cemetery with affectionate words on the headstones, even a very large monument for a vampire named Hamilton." I paused. "Are all his vampire friends dead?"

"It's lonely at the top," Lash hissed, his tone cold as he changed partway to snake. "We don't have any real friends except one another, and we wouldn't have any colleagues we know visit us here, either, Sar. Power and fame are both two-edged swords. They make you not trust anyone. I only trust Kyle because he's got no ambition. And Cain's a weenie, and no threat. Those two are Dev's only other true friends."

I took his hand in mine and squeezed it, trying to soothe him. "I'm asking because that wedding is next week. Devlin wants me to go with him to some kind of Oathing ceremony the week after. He said it may be an overnight."

"I know. I'm going with you, Sar. It'll be fine."

"You're sure?" I persisted.

"I wouldn't let you go, Sweetness, if I wasn't sure," Lash hissed in my ear, and then he tickled my lobe with his tongue. "But I do have to ask you something."

I braced myself. "What?"

"I need you as snake," Lash hissed, his tone unsure of how I would take his request. "It's been over three months, and I'm dying for a little coiling."

"That's not a problem," I said, after a moment. "V will be over at Sharon's tonight. I've already spoken to Samuel about it. Devlin will be on a conference call until midnight, easily. So we have all night." I kissed his cheek.

"Titus said that the potion may...may, um..." Lash trailed off uncomfortably, then began again. "That Rene...that she might not be able to wall herself off from you. A snake's body is smaller, Sar, even a weresnake's body. There may not be enough room for her to separate herself fully from you."

"You're saying Rene's soul has a specific size?"

Rene stirred, hearing me say her name. *Sar?*

"Titus just said it as a warning. I'm worried about us not being really alone."

"I'm not putting her somewhere," I said calmly, but firmly. "You know we've been working hard to make Rene her own body. We can't risk it, Lash."

"I know," Lash hissed uncomfortably. "I've tried to wait until you were done and she was gone from you, but I can't. It's got to be tonight, Sweetness."

"I'm okay with it," Rene said aloud. "I'll do my best to wall myself off, but I will not make myself known, if I can't."

"I don't want to have a virtual threesome, Rene," Lash hissed, irritated. "Yet I'm not going to last another three weeks, not with everything I need to do for Devlin."

"I will do my best to leave you two alone," Rene said quickly. "I'm going to wall myself off now. Say my name, Sar, when you are done, and I'll return."

I felt her sudden absence from my mind, and turned to Lash. "Where's the potion?"

* * * *

An hour later, Lash was coiled around me, contracting gently as he loved me, and I was hissing in pleasure, feeling his body around mine and inside mine. I came for perhaps the fifth time, shuddering, letting out a soft hiss. He hissed back to me that he wasn't done with me, not by a long shot, as he continued to move gently.

With sudden joy, a realization hit me: I could understand him as a snake.

I forgot to move in my surprise. Pleasure began to build in me once more then became a raging torrent of desire, as Lash moved faster, speaking to me in a sibilant tone of lustful possessive words. I hissed out eagerly that I wanted him, I wanted all of him, to squeeze me tight so I couldn't feel anything but his wonderful muscular body so strong and powerful around me, taking me as his own. Lash shook all over, and squeezed me so tight he cut off my air supply, even as he began moving faster. A moment later he came, squeezing me so tight I let out an "Urk!" sound.

After, Lash quickly uncoiled from me, and moved away, coiling himself up in a pile, facing me. I moved myself around with minimum difficulty to face him. *At least I've been snake now enough times that I'm better at moving then I was months ago.*

"Can you understand me?" he hissed, worried.

I nodded, then grinned lecherously. "You are fucking amazing," I hissed proudly. "Literally."

Lash ignored the compliment, still visibly upset. "Why now, suddenly? Is the sorceress in there with you telling you what I'm saying?"

"I don't know?" I hissed back, mentally feeling for Rene and finding nothing. "I just know I can understand what you're saying, as if it were in English. And when I speak, I can hear I'm hissing, but I can also hear the words I'm saying when I make the hissing sounds."

Lash vibrated, lashing his tail back and forth. "I like this, that you understand me," he hissed lustily. "I like it a lot, Sweetness. But there's guilt, too, like I'm somehow cheating. After all I said to Devlin about other sex partners, I feel like a fucking hypocrite." He flicked out his tongue, scenting the air.

I moved my body closer to his, and began wrapping my length around him. He let out a sigh of pleasure, and uncoiled, that I might better coil myself around him. I was soon twisted around the length of him, just in time for it to occur to me with embarrassment that I was in the wrong spot for connecting with him, my snake body being much shorter than his was. I tried to move at once, to better line our bodies up, and Lash grabbed me gently with his mouth, stopping me.

"That's okay," he hissed comfortingly. "It's just good to be held like this by you, and to talk to you. It's been hard sometimes to be intimate with you like this, knowing that once we were animal we couldn't communicate. I felt too awkward to mention it, when we were in human form."

"We can talk now," I hissed back to him, rubbing my scaly cheek against his. "We have two hours left, at most. Tell me what I can do for you, Mate. Let's not waste these hours."

"Screw it, I'm going to Hell anyway," Lash hissed roughly, and then he began to wriggle in my grasp a little, moving my body down the length of his. Soon, he was writhing in my coils, our snake bodies connected as they were meant to.

As soon as he'd come, Lash again separated from me, and faced me. "We're going to try 'The Knot' next," he hissed. "Lay in a loose circle for me, as I weave in and out of your circle. Then when I tell you to, wiggle a little all down your body."

47

I did as he asked, thinking it odd. Before long, we were in a knot, so much so I couldn't move well. When the time came, I wiggled a little, thinking it pointless. But when my orgasm hit me a moment later, as his body tightened around mine, the cry I let out was more rough grunt than hiss, it was so loud and full of pleasure. And Lash's cry was louder still.

We tried many positions, one after the other. I was surprised to see there were so many, and that they were so varied, and that some even had names, like "Hangman's Noose," or "The Lasso," or the weirdest, "Yarn Ball." I was further surprised to see some were for oral pleasure.

"We weresnakes are not just animal, we're human," Lash answered in exhausted satiation, while we waited for me to change back. "And it's natural for humans to like varied sex."

I sighed contentedly. "I was sure I was going to bite you by mistake, in that last one."

"All the motion in that one is done with your tongue," Lash hissed with a satisfied sigh, shivering as he remembered. "There's no risk."

I felt myself changing back, and Lash changed back too, pulling my human body into his embrace as our arms and legs formed. We hugged each other, as our bodies completed their change, our tails disappearing.

"I love you," Lash hissed, looking down into my eyes with his dark ones. "I feel stupid that I waited so long to tell you, Sweetness."

"I love you, Tryst," I said, clutching him hard against me. "Don't ever feel stupid with me."

Lash kissed me gently, as I slipped into a fatigued sleep.

* * * *

The next day as Rene and I worked in the basement, I asked her if she'd been there with me and Lash. "Did you help me to understand him?"

Yes, she admitted, sounding embarrassed. *I know some werelanguages, snake among them. I helped you make the connections, so you could both understand it, and speak it.*

"Will I understand him once you leave me?" I asked, feeling upset.

No, she said, sounding thoughtful. *But I'll see what I can do. There may be a spell of some kind.*

I wanted to ask her if she'd liked what he'd done, but I didn't have to as she heard my thoughts. *Of course!* she said, satisfaction oozing from her mental voice. *I've not made love as snake since my youth. Even then, it was not with such a learned and talented partner.*

I felt proud of Lash, though strange to be discussing his prowess with her.

I've never heard of more than one position, Rene said deliciously. *It was very good sex. Is he that good as human?*

"Yes," I said aloud, feeling proud again. "You wouldn't believe what he can do with his tongue when—"

"Who are you talking to?" Devlin said, coming down the stairs. "I can scent your arousal from here."

I blushed. "Just Rene."

"Lash told me of what happened with you and him," Devlin said, sounding irritated. "I told him next time you are snake for him, I am going to take the potion too, so I might join—"

"No," I said firmly. "That is our time, to be alone."

"As you wish," Devlin commented in an off-hand manner. "Please come to bed early this evening. I have something to discuss with you, before I meet my donors at ten."

I nodded and he left.

Something's up, Rene said in my mind. *Devlin was not jealous enough to push his will, and it's in his nature to do so.*

"I agree. Usually I'd have expected a fight, and he just gave in. Plus he didn't kiss me."

Let's get back to it, she said grumpily. *I'm sure he'll tell us later tonight.*

* * * *

About nine thirty, I joined Devlin in his bedroom. To my surprise, Lash was also there.

"I need to leave soon," he said, giving me a kiss. "Right after Dev's said whatever it is that's so important. But I'll be back tomorrow. I'll be with you that night you attend the wedding, Sar, so don't worry."

"Thank you." I turned to Devlin. "Please tell me what it is you have to say."

"I formally request your permission, as my Oathed One, for a new lover," Devlin intoned.

Rene took over, before I had a chance to say anything. "Devlin, do not do this from jealousy!"

"I'm not," Devlin said apologetically, looking uncomfortable.

"Then why ask for one now?" I asked, wresting control back from Rene.

"Love, I'd have thought you'd guessed by now," Devlin answered. "Part of the reason I go to Tiffany and Hillary is because I don't hold back with them when we have sex. I need some regular sex that isn't gentle, as I always must be with you. If I didn't hold back, I could hurt you accidentally, as I've said before. I don't want to hurt you."

I thought about what Lash had said back in January about how he was careful of me, but didn't say anything. Lash was beside me, but he made no comment, either. Yet somehow, Devlin seemed to know what we were thinking.

"I know Lash doesn't miss being rough," Devlin said carefully. "But I do like it, on occasion. And I need to—"

"You have my permission," I said heavily.

Devlin looked down at me, his expression carefully neutral. "You're sure?"

I looked up at him, and pushed away my feelings of jealousy, my feelings of hurt. I remembered Theo, remembered how he'd hurt me, when he'd loved me with all of his supernatural strength. I really didn't want that again, even if Titus could heal me after. Lovemaking was supposed to be enjoyable for both partners, or at the least, not painful. With Devlin's unbridled power, at least twice the strength of Theo's, sex would cause me a good deal of pain. "I'm sure," I said in a whispered voice that was no less sure, for being so soft. "But please, don't be with many others."

"I'll be with only one," Devlin said in a voice so happy it was a purr. "And it will take time to find one I can trust anyway, Love."

"Why not Tiff?" Lash hissed sarcastically. "I know she likes you to—"

Devlin cut him off. "She's half-human," he said with a sigh. "Even if the faerie blood in her does keep her from aging fast, it isn't strong enough to sustain what I'd do to her, Lash. You know that. Ebediah's blood was old, he was six hundred easy. I'm too strong now to risk it with any female even partly human. And Tiffany is too good orally to risk me damaging her."

Lash didn't reply.

"Would you need a vampire?" I said, thinking of Catherine and how surreal this was that we were discussing this so nonchalantly.

"It would be easiest," Devlin said with a sigh. "Except I don't enjoy bedding vampires usually, Love." He looked down at me. "Catherine was an exception—"

"Don't go into that," Lash hissed angrily. "I can smell her upset, even if you can't."

"I'm sorry," Devlin said immediately. "Forgive me, Oathed One, please."

"It's okay," I said absently.

"How about Jezebel?" Lash hissed, after a moment. "She'd agree, for a price. And you could trust her, especially with making it paid sex, like with the Oral Twins."

I wouldn't trust a woman named Jezebel, but that was just me. "Who is Jezebel?"

"Someone we've known a long time," Lash said cryptically. "A lover of Devlin's, one at least as old as he is."

"She's three hundred, not four," Devlin said, as if musing. "But you're right."

"What is she?" I asked.

"Goblin," Lash hissed in disgust.

I furrowed my forehead. "But goblins are pretty, at least Rosalyn is."

"They look nice, and smell like rot," Lash hissed nastily. "Not to mention they hold grudges and are hard to kill."

"Jezebel was never an enemy of ours," Devlin said, looking over to meet Lash's eyes.

"She wasn't a friend of ours, either," Lash hissed cryptically. "But you always said she was a good lay."

"She was," Devlin said, in a lustful voice that said he was remembering more than her face. "I'll call her, see if she's available. But let's get to sleep, I've got another call at noon tomorrow, and it's almost ten now. Some of my donors have likely arrived."

Devlin gave me a kiss and left. Lash followed, giving me a smile and a wave.

The door hadn't even shut, when Rene began talking. *Don't let him go to her.*

"You heard what he said," I said aloud, not caring if anyone overheard me. "He needs it."

He can come to me for that, Rene said flatly. *He doesn't need to see that whore.*

I blinked my eyes. "You'll be human, not strong enough—"

I can find a way to make my body more resilient, Rene said quickly. *I know I can.*

"Then you could just as easily have told Devlin you could do that for me, so I could handle his not holding back," I countered. "So why didn't you?"

You know why, Rene said guiltily. *Because I want to stay here, after I'm human. I want to remain his Oathed One, and his lover.*

I leaned against the wall, trying to sort out my feelings.

You've had his child, you won't ever be replaced, Rene said, sounding upset. *I want to mean something to him! This would work out so well!*

"You do mean a lot to him, Rene—"

For how long? I know Jezebel, she was a donor of his in France. Anna was very jealous of her, and Jezebel had designs on Devlin back then. He'd been her lover before she was his donor, back when he met her at a large estate festival. If he lets her into his life again, who is to say she won't ensnare him?

"You told me to trust him, that he meant his words to me," I said, angry and feeling as if I'd been manipulated. "Now you are saying that he can't be trusted?"

Anna was wise, Rene grated out reluctantly. *She saw Devlin was the kind of man who likes to be with someone. Some men cannot be alone.*

"He was alone for centuries, and had a ton of lovers."

He did, because his love of that time died! And if you, his great love of this time were to die, then he might be more receptive to a new lover! Jezebel has always wanted to be first in his affections! Do you get it, you dense woman?

"Are you threatening me?" I bristled.

You know I'm not! she spat out the words in my mind, making me cringe. *I'm trying to protect you! I tried to protect Anna, but she was stubborn, she just had to have a child! Listen to me!*

"Go," I said firmly, wiping my hands. "I need to think. We're done talking for today."

Rene cursed, but she left me, walling herself off. I walked upstairs, thinking of my few real options what was the best thing to do.

* * * *

That next afternoon, I spoke to Lash over a late lunch. V was beside me on the floor, brushing Ghost, who made little sighs of enjoyment.

"I'd understand," I said suddenly. "If you said that you needed what Dev needs, Sweetness."

Lash whipped his head around in surprise and looked at me. "Sar, I told you, it's okay."

I lapsed into an uneasy silence.

Lash's hand closed over mine. "What happened with Theo and you isn't going to happen with us," he said firmly. "I know what I need, Sar, and I don't change. And even if I did, you'd be the first to know, okay?"

"Okay," I said, mollified.

"The wedding is Friday," Lash said, changing the subject. "The thirteenth, if you can believe it. You'd think the werebats would pick another night."

"They must not be superstitious," I commented, not really caring. My mind was on Devlin and Jezebel, still wondering what was best to do. *Take Rene's warning to heart? Or trust that Dev could be with this old lover for sexual pleasure alone, with no emotion?*

"They aren't," he answered, finishing his burrito. "Most are very practical. If only most women were, too."

His snide tone got on my last nerve. "What's your issue?" I barked at him.

"That you're irritated about something Dev has no power over," Lash hissed, taking his plate to the sink. "This isn't a vice of his, Sar, it's a need. Devlin could easily make diamond from a piece of coal now with his hand alone, he's so strong. He's being honest about his needs, not sneaking off—"

"What's your fucking issue, Lash?" I interrupted, argumentative.

To my shock, Lash turned to me, upset. His snake features were forming, and reforming, over and over.

"What is it?" I said much more comfortingly, getting up and going to him.

"My last surviving sister died last night," he said, as tears slid down his face.

Chapter Five

I hugged Lash tight, as he sniffled. Then I felt V's arms hugging us both. For a while we just stood there, as Lash tried to get himself under control.

"She was ninety-two," he hissed finally. "That's old for a snake. Her name was Diane. She lived in Louisiana."

"I'm sorry, Lash. Did you still keep in touch?" V asked in her small melodious voice.

"No, not for years," Lash hissed sadly. "I became 'Lash' in part to keep her and my other family safe. But she left a letter that said when she was dead, the news of her death was to be given to me. One of my relatives called last night after you were asleep, and told me."

"You should've come to me afterwards," I said, hugging him tight. "I should've been there for you."

"I needed time to myself," Lash hissed emotionally. "I'm trying to decide what to do."

"What do you mean?" I asked.

"The relative's name who called was Diana. She was my sister's granddaughter. She told me when the funeral was. It's the same day as when I've got to be gone with you and Dev to that wedding, so I can't go. But the calling hours are tonight, and I think I should go—"

"We'll both go," I said firmly. "Let me go and get my black dress on."

"Should I go?" V said anxiously. "I don't know if I want to see a dead person."

"You'll stay here, V," I said, giving her a kiss. "Someone needs to walk Ghost, and make sure he's safe."

"I can do that—"

We must tell Devlin, Rene said in my mind. *He may not let us go.*

55

Do I give a fuck? No, I told her nastily, and she shut up.

Lash headed off, saying he'd be back for me in an hour, with directions on how to get there. Reluctantly, I headed up to Devlin, knowing that as much as I'd mouthed off mentally to Rene, she was right. I couldn't leave without letting my Oathed One know where I was going and why.

* * * *

"Neither of you should go," Devlin said, after I'd told him of where I was going. "It'll just bring attention to his family. Some may be hurt, if his relationship to them becomes known."

"That's all he has left of his blood family!" I said angrily. "You should understand, it's the same as how you feel about Danial!"

"He has more blood in common with me and you than he does with them now," Devlin said coolly. "He should send some flowers anonymously, and leave it at that."

"We are leaving in an hour," I said frostily. "Don't wait up for me."

"I won't be here, I'll be with Jezebel," Devlin said, his voice becoming the malicious one I'd heard so often in those first years I'd known him. "She's agreed to meet me tonight. Seems she's been pining for a little biting."

"You do it and you'll break my heart," Rene said, wresting control from me so fast I was left dumbfounded. "And you'll break your promise to me, to be faithful to me. I'm your Oathed One, Devlin. And I hold you to your promise you made to me, the night you took my Oath. I do not give you permission to be with anyone save Sarelle and myself."

Devlin looked shocked, then he snarled, "You died, Rene! That Oath is long broken!"

"Is it?" Rene said, her voice bitter. "I don't think it is, Devlin, not with me inhabiting a body now. But you'll prove it tonight, one way or the other, Lover."

Devlin looked at her with narrowed eyes. "What do you mean?"

"Titus brought me all of my body, Lover. That included my choker." Rene lifted my sleeve, to show him the bear with blue-green eyes wrapped around my wrist. "I fastened this on a few minutes ago, with Sar's help. I will wait tonight to see if the choker falls off with your

56

infidelity. I'll know if we were still Oathed, if it does."

Devlin exhaled furiously. "Why did you say nothing last night? You let me believe what I planned to do was okay with you, Rene."

"You didn't ask me, idiot!" Rene screamed at him, utterly furious. "How do you think it feels, to love someone for centuries, to be with them two days, and then go another two centuries of being alone? Then to be brought back not for yourself, but because of another woman, one who cheated on the man you loved, a man who never once came to your grave and apologized to you for not being able to save you?"

Devlin was staring at me openmouthed. But Rene wasn't nearly done.

"I loved you, me! I still loved you, even as a ghost! I love you now! How can you be so petty? Isn't it enough you have two women who love you, you've got to worry about not getting every little bit of satisfaction out of coupling? You should be glad you have a body to couple with! If not for me, you'd have been tortured, killed, and long in hell! And that was before you'd done all the shit you have since becoming Ruler!"

"I did what I had to—"

"Don't try to rationalize your actions, not to me! I am not some lovesick child, Dev! My God, you're as selfish and shallow as you ever were!"

"Don't say these things to me," Devlin whispered in a despairing tone. "You think it was easy for me, losing you, after losing Anna only days before? I didn't want to be Ruler, Rene, you told me I had to! I told you we'd go away together alone and make a new life—"

"That was bullshit," Rene interrupted, though some of her anger had left her. "You would never have been happy hiding out somewhere with me. You were meant to Rule, Dev. It's the one thing you're best at."

"I won't go to her," Devlin said solemnly, coming close to me. "I give you my promise, Oathed One. I'm sorry I hurt you. Consider the matter closed."

Rene sniffled a little, then she was bawling. Devlin held us, saying gently he was sorry, he loved her, and that he would honor the Oath he'd given her. I did my best to comfort her, too, but Rene was incoherent for a while. So I let her cry, and dozed, relieved she had succeeded where I had not.

* * * *

We arrived at the DeMonne Funeral Home about seven. Lash said he wanted to get there a little later, as he was worried that he would be recognized. "Family resemblance, you know?"

I assured him his goatee would help. "You look different because of my blood, remember?"

"I know I do," he said, squeezing my hand in thanks. "That's the only reason I felt I could come, Sar."

We got to the door, and he looked back at me. "By the way, I'm going to introduce you as my mate." He ducked in quickly.

I gave him a look of surprise, and then he was saying hi to the first person in the receiving line. "I'm sorry for your loss. I'm a distant relation to Diane. My name is Trystan Valeras, and this is my mate, Sar."

The woman looked at him and smiled, and hugged him. "I've never heard of you, Trystan. But thank you. It's good to meet you, Sara."

I resisted the urge to correct her, and nodded.

"Diane's surviving children are over there," the woman said. "I'm her granddaughter Diana, the one who called you."

"Can you tell me what other family is here?" Lash said awkwardly. "I've never met any of these people."

"My mom and her sisters are over there," Diana said just as awkwardly. "My aunts and uncles are all over here, and truthfully, I haven't been to a family reunion for ages, so I don't know any of their names, much less the names of all the cousins. Some of the relatives only speak Spanish. But my Mom's name is Giselle—"

Lash took in a breath quickly, nodding.

"—and I know one of my mom's sisters is named Raven." Diana said. "Please help yourself to some food in the adjoining room. There's alcohol there, too." She turned away from us, welcoming the next person.

"There's food at a funeral?" I whispered to Lash as we walked over to the casket. "And whiskey?"

"I'm not surprised," Lash hissed, sounding sad and also angry. "I told you about snakes, Sar. A lot of them have a problem with alcohol."

Ahem.

"And food is the norm at any werecreature gathering, even a funeral.

We might as well get a drink," Lash hissed, grabbing a bottle of Jack Danial's and pouring himself a shot. "They don't have any shiraz here, Sweetness. Want a glass of merlot?"

"No. But I'll get some food." I walked over, and dished up a plate of pasta, and some bread. There were no vegetables to speak of, but I did notice there was a lot of meat, or there had been, before it had been mostly eaten.

Lash got himself a plate of meat, and we sat down and ate at a tiny table. There were others around us, though most were absorbed in their own conversations. A few were dabbing at tears, some crying openly.

Ten minutes later, we were done eating. "Let's go," Lash hissed, getting up. "I want to see her, and then we'll leave."

We walked out to the casket. Lash and I stood there.

His sister hadn't ever been pretty, truthfully. But she'd been well loved, by all the pictures wreathed around her. Many had her in them, smiling, holding babies, working outside. There was also, to my surprise, a wedding photo of her from her youth, with two grooms.

"She was married to two men?" I whispered.

"Snakes mate females with more than one male sometimes," Lash hissed back. "Remember, Dev told you."

I nodded.

Lash looked once more at Diane. "Goodbye, sister," he hissed softly.

We headed outside. "Thanks for coming with me," he said, slipping his arm around me. "It was right I was here."

"Leaving so soon?" a dark voice asked.

Lash stopped in mid stride, whirled around, and drew his gun, pushing me in back of him.

"I've heard the rumors that you were young again," the voice intoned, still black as pitch, and just as thick. "But you're handsome now, too, aren't you? It's a miracle sometimes what can be healed with magic."

A figure stepped partially out of the shadows.

"And what cannot be healed."

To say the being was a monster wasn't fair. His face was burnt, his skin black as Devlin's had been, after he'd been burned by sunlight. But his eyes glittered in the poor light from the one streetlamp, and the blowing humid air wreathed his form in dewy mist, making his hair wave a little. It occurred to me there was something wrong, and then I saw patches of his hair were missing, where parts of his head were also burned.

Lash resheathed his gun, and drew his knife. "Stay here," he hissed, not taking his eyes off the figure. "When I go for him, run back inside. Stay there, until I come for you."

I opened my mouth to tell him to teleport with me, and Lash lunged for the figure, and a gunshot rang out.

The figure crumpled, and sprawled in the dirt. Another man stepped out of the shadows, a smoking gun in his hand.

Lash sheathed his knife, and went to the figure, rolling it over. "It's not a vampire," he said, something like relief in his voice. He looked up at the figure. "Who are you?"

"Name's Trystin Monteras," the figure said with a drawl. He looked to be about twenty, maybe younger. He had to be a relative of Lash's, they had the same eyes and dark hair, not to mention their body size. He also had the narrow face Lash had once had, his face having a cruel cast to it.

"You always go around shooting people, Tristan?" Lash hissed, changing partway to snake.

"You think you're the only one packing?" Tristan hissed back, also changing partway. "I'm working security here. I was told to watch for any trouble. This dude was trouble."

"He was, but I wanted answers out of him," Lash said, getting to his feet. "And now he's dead and worthless."

"You're welcome," Tristan said nastily, as he strode off.

"Asshole," Lash hissed under his breath. "He has to be related to me." He picked up the body, and together, we teleported back.

Lash took the body outside when we got back, and sent me for Devlin, who Seth said was in his study.

"Who are they afraid of?" I said to Rene, as I walked downstairs. "Did you recognize who that was? Lash thought it was a vampire, I think."

"He did," Rene mused. "I don't know, Sar. I don't remember any vampire enemy of Devlin's being partially burned. Yet vampires can always heal burning if they feed enough, even if it's bad. Still, this one acted as though his burning hadn't healed. It's a mystery to me."

Devlin was in his study, working again on his laptop. When I told him what had happened, he got up immediately, and raced out of the room, moving so fast he was up the stairs before I was out of the study.

I followed him as fast as I could, yet it still took me some minutes to get back to Lash and the body. Devlin was there, his expression deeply troubled.

"We were meant to think it was him," Lash hissed furiously. "I did think it was him, at first."

"Someone knows of what happened," Devlin said ominously, staring at the body. "And your part in what transpired. But this is very strange. If whomever did this knew who you really were, they would never have sent an actor, a mere human, to scare you. They'd know you'd kill the human, and torture him first. So it's just as well he's dead, as he probably had nothing to tell us anyway."

"Who are you referring to?" I asked. "Who did you think the man who attacked us was?"

They both ignored me.

"We must find out who is playing with us. And we have no time to waste chasing down ghosts." Dev began dialing his cell. "Time to call in a long overdue favor."

* * * *

I was making V and Lash breakfast the next morning when the doorbell rang. Jazz got it, and a moment later, my least favorite person stalked into the room.

"Morning, Cat," Lash hissed at Theo, making sure to slip his arm around my waist. "How's tricks?"

Theo gave Lash a nasty look, and opened his mouth, and then he looked down in surprise.

V was grabbing him around his waist, her gold eyes looking up at him. "You're Devon's father," she said a little sadly. "I remember you. Why haven't you come to see me ever?"

Theo looked at her, then he looked over at me desperately.

"He's been busy," I supplied quickly. "But why don't you dish him up some breakfast, V? He'd like that, I'm sure, especially as you helped me make it."

Theo took a deep breath. "Sure," he said in a cracked voice. "I haven't eaten yet."

V went and got him a plate, and loaded it with pancakes, bacon, eggs and sausage. She brought it to him, and he thanked her.

"I'll go tell Devlin you're here," Lash said in an odd voice. Then he left the room.

Theo didn't speak to me, but he talked to V as he ate, and she talked to him, telling him about what she'd learned yesterday from Caitlyn. I kept myself busy putting away ingredients and doing dishes. Luckily, there was a lot to clean up.

Just as Theo was eating the last of his pancakes, Devlin came in, followed by Lash.

"Sar, take V into the other room," Devlin said, his eyes on Theo.

"She can stay. I need to go see Caitlyn," V pronounced, giving me a hug. "It's time for my lesson, Dad."

"Go then, daughter dearest," Devlin said with pleasure. "Have a good day of learning."

"'Bye Mom. 'Bye Lash." V went to Theo again, and hugged him. "'Bye Theo. Come back and see me again?"

"Sure," Theo said, giving her a smile. "Now run along. You don't want to be late."

V raced out of the room, and abruptly the tension thickened to sludge.

"What do you want, Devlin?" Theo growled, folding his arms across his chest. "You summoned me here, never mind T phrased it as a request."

Devlin's reply was calm. "You told me that night I returned with you and Sar from PA over a year ago that you would help me, if I needed it. Tonight I am calling in that favor."

"You've used up whatever favors I owed you," Theo growled, pushing past him. "You've got lots of money, Devlin. Buy yourself another killer."

"I don't need a killer, I need some of your expertise," Devlin said

62

sarcastically. "That is, assuming you did learn something from my brother in those years you worked for him, solving your little human computer puzzles."

"Oh, I don't know, I can't seem to solve the mystery of how you're so old and powerful, and still such a putz—"

"Enough," Lash hissed flatly. "Theo, someone sent a human actor to us, to scare me. He was killed before we could question him. We need to know who sent him, and why."

"Any suspects?" Theo said, after a minute.

"Sweetness, please go," Lash hissed abruptly.

I thought briefly about fighting with him, but decided I didn't want to give Theo that pleasure. So I just nodded, and left.

I was walking out of the room when I felt cool arms encircle me.

"I was hoping I'd run into you," Danial said seductively. "I know you'll be busy in these next few weeks. Would you be in the mood for a little kissing?"

Hell, yes! I grabbed him and kissed him, and Danial kissed me back passionately, pushing me up against the wall.

"Come," he said, breaking away and taking my hand. "We'll go to one of the guest rooms, where we won't be disturbed."

Seth met up with us in the hallway, but he just nodded and stepped aside. Danial took me into one of the grey rooms, and shut the door.

I grabbed hold of him, and kissed him hard, and he kissed me back with fire and longing. Again. he pushed me to the wall, and I wrapped my arms around him, trying to devour him, trying to lose myself in him. Rene was yelling at me not to touch him, not to do this, but I ignored her.

Danial's tongue slipped into my mouth, probing me, and I let out a gasp. I pushed him back, and he half fell, half sat on the bed. I pushed him backward, and ripped his shirt down the front, popping a few buttons. I slid my hands over his chest, and he let out a groan. I straddled him, moving my hips on his. I could feel he was already hard beneath his jeans, and I pushed my hips down on him, and then bent my head, taking his nipple in my mouth.

Danial froze, and then I felt his hands on my arms, gently prying me away. "Stop," he said, breathing fast. "I don't want to do this, Lady. Stop, please."

I looked down at him, and wanted to scream at him to stop being such an ass. But I just nodded, and got off him, moving to sit on the edge of the bed.

Danial sat up a few seconds later. "This does not seem to be working," he said delicately.

No shit. I didn't look at him.

I felt his hand gently caressing my neck. I thought about smacking him, but didn't want to touch him. I was still excited enough to want him, if I turned and looked at him.

"I'm sorry," he said gently. "Don't think I don't want you, Lady, because I do. You can tell I do, by my body's response to you."

I lost it, and turned to him with tears in my eyes. "I love you," I said brokenly. "And you're right, this isn't working, because I want to be in your arms, I want to feel your skin against mine, inside mine! It's not enough to be bitten, and to have a few kisses, Danial!"

"That's all I have to give," Danial said apologetically, pulling me close to him, and resting his head on my shoulder. "Isn't it enough that my bite brings you some measure of pleasure?"

"It doesn't! It causes me pain!" I blurted it out, and then tried to get out of his arms.

He held me where I was. "I'm very sorry," he whispered, clearly upset. "I thought your movements were ones of pleasure."

"I'm resistant to your saliva, from all the exposure to it," I muttered. "I feel only pain."

"Then why let me feed from you?" Danial said in an agonized tone. Then he took a quick breath. "This is why Devlin asked that I bed you, if I took your blood."

I didn't reply.

"Why let me feed from you?" Danial said, making me look at him. His dark eyes were questioning. "Are you a masochist?"

"I was angry at Devlin," I lied. "I was angry at Lash. It was a way to get back at them."

"There is some new trouble? I saw that Theo is here."

I related to him the story of what had happened at the funeral home. "Do you recognize the vampire?"

"No," Danial said, after a thoughtful moment. "But Dev and Lash

64

have many enemies. And many of those were vampires. It could be any one of a hundred, at least."

That was a big help. Still, his next words surprised me. "But maybe it's not a vampire at all, just someone who is testing Devlin. Theo stopped doing assassinations for me, when he first got back together with Sar, when she was sick, and then pregnant. That led to him looking weak, and Robert's challenge. Perhaps someone is testing Devlin? By now all vampires in America know Devlin is Oathed."

I hadn't known all that. "For what purpose?"

"Some of it is just the politics," Danial said, still stroking my neck. "I remember when I first became a state Ruler. Garrett sent some police to check into my business. It was a major hassle: searches in daylight, all my things displaced, some of the foxes brought in for questioning. It went on for months. But I played along, and some months later it was over. Devlin may just need to play along, as I did, and wait for it to pass, or for a formal challenge to be issued. Assassins aren't the only ones who must face challengers. Vampire Rulers must as well."

Danial does not remember Ulysses challenging Devlin, their fight, or his own part in draining Ulysses afterwards. "Maybe."

Danial again raised my eyes to meet his dark ones. "I have noticed your bite marks, Lady. They do not match. One is surely Dev's, but who is the other vampire who bit you? Was it Nathan? Were you in bed with both of them, as you bed Lash and Dev sometimes?"

I was pleased to hear a little jealousy in his tone, even if I didn't know how to answer him.

"Tell me the truth," Danial said harshly. "Don't lie as you did a few moments ago, or I'll never speak to you again. Who was it?"

"It was you," I said, swallowing hard. "You don't remember it. And no, we didn't have sex at the time. We got some of that blue paste, to take the pain away."

"You're telling the truth," Danial said slowly. "Why do I not remember this? When was this? Where was this?"

I didn't answer, trying again to get away.

Danial held me tight. "Are you indeed sworn to me, as my brother tells me I am sworn to you?" he whispered. "Was I there, the night you swore to him? Did I consummate it with you? Please tell me."

"No, you were not there that night," I said honestly. "He included you in our Oathing, though. So if you and I were ever together, it's true my choker would not fall off."

"He must have done it for protection for you, in case something happened to him," Danial said slowly. "I can think of no other reason. I have been only with Sar for years now."

I cannot take anymore, no more! "Let me go," I said, struggling as hard as I could. "Let me go, Danial!"

Danial abruptly released me, and I staggered, steadying myself on the nightstand. But he grabbed my hand, and looked up at me searchingly.

"Give me time," he said, caressing my face gently. "I am still mourning Sarelle, Lady."

"I know that," I managed in a choked voice.

Danial gently pushed me back on the bed, and took my face in his hands. I was crying now and he tenderly kissed the tears away. "You know if I was to be intimate with someone, I'd want it to be you," he murmured. "I like you very much, Lady. I admit, I've fantasized about you—"

"Stop," I said raggedly. "Don't kiss me anymore, it just makes me want you more, and it hurts too much!"

Danial cut off my words with a long kiss, and then I felt him moving my legs apart, and laying his body down on mine. I felt his hard flesh pressing against my yielding body, and let out an agonized cry. Danial kissed me, and began rubbing his body on mine in rhythm. I held him firmly against me, burning up with desire for him. Before long, I felt an orgasm building from his body's motion on mine. I clung to him, scared he would stop, would deny me at the last moment. Instead Danial bore down against me, as I crested the wave with a groan. I came panting hard, moaning softly. As my orgasm ebbed, Danial sank his fangs into me, both upper and lower. Then I felt the pain abruptly leaving me, and knew he'd bitten himself, that he was healing me with his blood, even as he drank me down in long pulls.

I arched up against him, into him, and my control snapped. I reached down for his zipper, and jerked it down, sliding my hand in to wrap around his throbbing manhood. Danial let out a cry, and tried to pull

66

back, but I stroked him fast, rubbing the tip of him, and he convulsed almost instantly in orgasm, his semen jetting out, even as he pulled his fangs out of me. He went limp on me, still jerking and gasping, as his body emptied itself.

I held him to me in contentment, and then it occurred to me that Danial was crying.

"Shh," I said gently, kissing his cheek. "Don't cry. I wanted you to have some release."

"I didn't want to do this," he said raggedly, yanking up his zipper. "I asked you not to touch me, Lady!"

I opened my mouth to reply, but he was already through the door and gone, before I could.

"I told you not to do this," Rene said aloud in disgust. "You are going to have to change the bed—"

"Shut up," I said brokenly, wiping at my filling eyes. "Just shut up, please."

Rene fumed but went silent, thankfully. And I trudged to the linen closet and got a new bedspread, berating myself for pushing things when I could have just taken what Danial offered.

I'd just finished changing the bed, when Serena walked in. She sniffed once, then gave me a strange look.

"What is it?" I said crankily. "You want to tell me you're pregnant, and it's T's?"

"Stop being a bitch," she said calmly. "I'm the canine here, Sar."

"Sorry," I apologized. "I'm just being cranky. What is it?"

"Look, we haven't really talked for months. You ask me about V, pick her up from me, or bring her to me to babysit. But we don't talk or spend time like we used to, and I miss that." She paused. "Is it because I'm seeing Nick again?"

"It's not my business—"

"Fuck yes, it's not your business!" Serena growled. "But that's it, isn't it?"

I faced her. She was right, it was past time I stopped avoiding her and talked this out. "Look, you sleep with my son, and I know you don't love him. So as his mother, I'm worried he's going to get hurt."

Serena moved closer. "The truth is, we shared blood one night," she whispered. "T found it repellent, from what I deduced, though he never came out and said that. We haven't since that night last year, Sar. So what kind of a future could we have had? He's part vampire, and he can't stomach my wereblood. And he's been seeing less of me every month."

What she says fits, especially T's lack of emotion. It all fits. "I'm sorry," I said finally. "I didn't know."

"Nick and I...I don't know where that's going," Serena said hesitantly. "I'm not sure any longer where I want it to go, to be honest. I'm just happy that none of my lovers have died in a while."

I remembered the many graves in Devlin's cemetery, and nodded, not trusting myself to talk.

"Come watch a movie with me," Serena offered. "V's going to Sharon's again, just for a few hours. We'll watch *Thelma and Louise.*"

Who is Thelma? Rene put in questioningly. *And Louise?*

"It's too sad," I said to Serena. "Let's watch *Beaches* instead."

"Whatever you want," Serena said, breaking into a smile. "So long as you make some popcorn for us."

"You're as bad as a man," I said teasingly, as I followed her out.

Chapter Six

The next evening, I reluctantly dressed in an elaborate gown of green velvet, and slipped on the long over-the-knee leather boots Devlin had given me years ago.

Lash came in, as I was fluffing my hair. "Are you ready? Devlin's waiting."

I nodded and followed him out, noticing he was again all in black. But he'd been wearing more black again lately, for some reason. At least I thought so, reasoning that I hadn't washed his other colored clothes in more than two weeks. *Likely for his sister. Leave it alone, Sar, he needs time to heal that fresh wound.*

Devlin was standing with Titus. He was dressed in a black silk shirt, and a black suit, with some kind of gold streaks within the material. It shimmered when he moved.

"Only you could pull off that suit," I said appreciatively. "You look nice."

Devlin gave me a sultry smile. "Thanks, Love. Ready?"

A moment later, we were in Texas. Titus nodded to us, and disappeared.

I looked around. "Where are we?"

"We're near Eagle Flats," Devlin said, taking my hand. "Come, I can hear the music starting."

Devlin led me toward a lighted clearing, and Lash followed us.

I was surprised to see the ceremony was going to take place in a church, and not a cave. But Devlin whispered to me that the werebats had ties to the local community, and there were humans here in attendance. "You'll see no wings tonight."

"Then why were you invited?"

"I'm invited to all were weddings of note." His voice was arrogant.

69

"You're asking why I accepted. The reason is the werebats and I go way back, Sar. They came with me to this country, years ago. They helped me when I most needed them. I've been a friend to them ever since."

Devlin and I were seated in the second row, near the aisle. The wedding march began a moment later.

The wedding was a long one. It'd been a while since I'd attended a real church wedding. The werebat couple, Amber and Drake, had written their own vows, which took a while to say, as they were both emotional. Yet it was easy to see they were in love, and I said a prayer for them to be happy, as I listened.

An hour later, we were walking out, and hugging everyone in the bridal party. I expected to feel awkward, but Devlin was welcomed by both families as an old friend. After he introduced me, they gave me hearty hugs and big smiles, too.

The party afterward was held at a reception hall down the street. We walked there in a big crowd with the wedding party in the lead. The night was humid, almost tropical. In short, Devlin removed his suit jacket and tie by the time we got there. He put them back on as soon as we got into the subzero air conditioning.

"I'll be by the door, watching," Lash hissed, shivering a little, as Devlin and I went inside. "There's only one, and I don't think there'll be trouble, Dev."

For once, Lash was right. The evening passed swiftly, as Devlin and I danced, and listened to toasts, and talked to some of the bats he knew well. I wondered as I sat there why I was feeling so good. Then it came to me that every other time I'd been out with Devlin around people he knew, some if not most all of them had been saying nasty things about him. It was good to see that at least with some people, he managed to both get along and be liked.

Rene also enjoyed the party, though I only gave her control for one dance, as I was enjoying myself too much in my own body.

Close to dawn, Titus returned to pick us up. I was glad, as by that time I was tired, and Devlin was carrying me.

I was asleep before my head hit the pillow.

* * * *

That next week passed quickly. Rene and I were almost half finished with the spell, and it was odd, to see her body beginning to finally take shape.

"Will you look as you did when you were alive?" I asked her.

"I'm trying to do that," she said absently, studying a page of Greek. "But it's not said anything yet about how to make that happen. Fortunately, you are blond, as I was, and your eye color is close to mine. I was much thinner that you are now—"

I got irritated yet calmed myself, hearing her go on.

"—but I welcome the chance to have a more rounded body, as I know Devlin likes that, as do most men. I do not want to make a body or face that's identical to yours. But I do hope my new body will have your resistance to the vampire virus, Sar." Rene seemed to gather herself. "I would like to try with Dev for a child, as you did, if this works."

I didn't know what to say. I couldn't begin to get my mind around my feelings.

"It probably won't," she said quickly, feeling my unease. "I am faerie, and it's hard for us to have kids anyway, as you might know. Your body is also much closer to a vampire's now than it was, so you may not be as fertile as you once were."

"What?"

"Let me finish," she said. "There's no guarantee I'd get your resistance anyway, even if this does work, and I don't get sent to Hell, and that's if I could get pregnant at all. It's such a long shot that this'll work that I don't intend to mention it to Devlin, Sar. But I'm mentioning it to you."

"What do you want me to say?"

"Tell me you won't get angry, if by some miracle this all works."

"I won't get angry. Or I'll try not to. Okay?"

"Deal."

* * * *

That next Friday, Lash again teleported with Devlin, Titus, and I out west. But this time, we travelled to New Mexico.

Again we'd gotten dressed up, though this time Devlin hadn't shaved, and his outfit was a white suit made of leather, with a silvery-cream shirt under it, complete with white Western style boots. I was also in white, but my dress was white lace over a silver-underdress in a simple style. I had on some white leather boots to match his, though the heels were obscenely high, and difficult to walk in except very slowly. It was fair to say I was envying Lash in his black jeans and black cotton shirt very much, even with the heat of the night.

"David rules New Mexico," Devlin said as we walked down the well-manicured driveway. "You may have heard of him, he's been a kind of friend to Danial, over the years."

"David….um, Helm?" I said, racking my brain. "The one who helped Terian?"

"The same."

"Is he a friend of yours?"

"Not really. He's more like Danial, very proper. But he's a good manager. There have been no complaints of unfair treatment in the time he's ruled this state."

That hadn't been what I'd asked, but I left it alone.

Soon we came to the door. It opened to us before we got close to it.

"Greetings, Master," the man opening the door said, bowing low. "Please come in. David will be out momentarily."

Devlin nodded, and walked in, leading me. Lash followed.

We were led to a formal sitting room, where we sat. "Do you wish any refreshment?" the man asked. I saw he had a young woman with him, in a low cut dress.

"I'll be drinking soon enough," Devlin said, the double meaning in his voice loud and clear. "I can wait a few moments. But my man may like some."

The woman recoiled, but the man grabbed her arm, and brought her close to Lash, who changed partially, baring his snake fangs at her. She let out a scream, and ran, jerking free from the man. He turned red, and ran after her, apologizing to us loudly.

"Why'd you do that?" I hissed at him.

"Shh," Devlin said curtly. "Lash has a part to play here, as do we all. Just do what I tell you, Oathed One."

I made a face at him, but I didn't say the smart remarks I wanted to.

Soon enough, the man came back. But he wasn't alone. There was another man with him, a man I recognized from one of the vampire parties I'd attended over the years.

"Greetings, Lord Dalcon," he said, bowing. "I am very pleased to see you've arrived."

"Thank you, David. My man wishes some blood. Can you see to that?"

"Of course," David said smoothly. "I apologize for the delay." He motioned to his serving man, who came out with another woman, this one who looked scared but determined. She offered her wrist to Lash hesitantly. He grabbed it and sank his snake fangs in. She flinched, but didn't pull away. After a minute, Lash withdrew his fangs, licked his lips, and thanked her. She walked away with the man, trying to look serene and calm as she put pressure on her bleeding wrist.

"May I present my Oathed One, Sarelle?" Devlin said graciously. "I believe you've met."

"Twice," David said, kissing my hand gently. "Once at Danial Racklan's party, when he was formally acknowledged Ruler of the States, and the other in Canada, when she was introduced as the mother of Theoron, Danial's son."

"It's good to see you again," I said, grateful he'd remembered all that, so I didn't have to dredge it all up from memory.

"I'd have stood by you," David added, his dark blue eyes meeting Devlin's golden gaze. "If it had come to a fight that night. I want you to know that."

"Trying to curry favor?" Lash hissed nastily. "I didn't see you beside us, when the guns were being pointed, and the knives were out of their sheaths."

"I was not beside you in body, I was getting ready to create a diversion," David said, his voice strained. "I had only one guard with me, so muscle wasn't an option. But setting off the fire alarm would've emptied the place out—"

"Good thinking!" Lash hissed, sarcastic. "Why didn't *we* think of that?"

David was silent, his eyes looking at Devlin, who'd said nothing and was just staring at him.

"I love Krystin," David said emotionally. "That's why I asked you to turn her, so she doesn't die. She's already sick, Devlin, even though we've spread out the times we're together. It's my blood, it's killing her. I want her with me, even if we can't share blood anymore."

"I'm here to turn her," Devlin said formally. "As I agreed to. You know my terms?"

"I do, as does she," David said. "She is waiting for us."

"Then lead on," Devlin said coolly. "You do not have to explain yourself to me, David. And you should've run and not stood with me at the gathering. Samuel could've shredded you with his bare hands."

"It matters that you stood up for Sar as your Oathed One," David said, not moving. "What's the point of living forever, if it's not to enjoy those you love? And it was wrong, what they were going to do—"

"You are upsetting Sarelle," Devlin hissed at David, his eyes red. "She was terrified that night, David, with good reason. Now apologize, then be quiet and lead us to your lover."

"Forgive me, Lady Dalcon," David said smoothly. "Please follow me."

We followed him, ending at an opulent room at the western end of the house with a long mirror along one side. A woman was sitting on the bed there, in a white robe. She stood, when we came in.

"Krystin, this is Lord Devlin," David said gently. "Devlin, this is my love, Krystin."

"Enchanté," Devlin said seductively, kissing her hand. Krystin made a little sigh, and I could see she was indeed enchanted.

"Leave us," Devlin said. "Go with David to the viewing chamber, Oathed One."

David motioned to me, and I followed him out, feeling weird. Soon we were in an adjoining room, and I saw that we were going to be viewing the whole thing, via the one-way glass. I wanted to ask David if was uncomfortable with this as I was, but I didn't need to. His eyes had a red cast to them, and his hands were clenched as he stalked to and fro, staring through the glass.

I turned back to watch the room, at Rene's insistence.

Lash had pulled up a chair, and was sitting near the end of the bed, his elbows on his knees, facing the door. His back was to David and me, as well as to Devlin and Krystin.

Devlin was getting undressed; at least, I thought he was. But I saw he'd just taken off his shirt and coat, and hung them up.

"Get on the bed," he said in a commanding voice. "And drop your robe."

Krystin shot a look at the mirror, then obeyed. She was pretty, but her body was thin, a little too thin, as her breasts were non-existent and her hips narrow. But her long brown hair looked healthy, and shiny.

Devlin took her face in his hands and gave her a gentle kiss. She relaxed in his embrace, as he kissed down her throat. Then he bit into her neck deeply, burying his fangs in her completely. Krystin let out a loud moan and clutched him to her, her lips parting as she pushed her body against his.

David was pacing rapidly now, clearly upset, but he made no noises.

Devlin drank her down quickly, and soon, Krystin was lying on the bed, her movements feeble and weak.

Devlin withdrew his fangs, then unzipped his fly, looking down at her, his golden eyes hot with passion. He sat on the bed, and pulled her astride him, and began drinking again. Then I saw Lash hand him his knife, and Devlin pulled his fangs out of Krystin with a gout of blood, using the blade to nick his neck, before handing it back to Lash. He pushed Krystin's face into his neck, and resumed drinking.

All of a sudden, Krystin grabbed hold of Devlin, her face burrowing into him. Devlin bared his fangs in a movement of utter pleasure, removing them from her neck. Then I saw him grab her hips, and shove them forcefully down on his, as he let out a sharp cry of satisfaction. He moved atop her, then pushed her back to the bed, prying her off his neck with his hands to hold her down beneath him.

"Please!" she cried, struggling wildly. "I must have more, please!"

Devlin sank his fangs into her again and began thrusting hard and fast into her. Krystin screamed in pleasure, and Devlin roared out his orgasm, his muscles spasming as he came.

Devlin took a few breaths, and then sat up, zipping his fly. Then he looked down at Krystin.

"Lord-mmph!"

"Shh," Devlin said gently, touching her lips. "It will take time for you to learn to speak around your fangs, Krystin. David waits for you.

Can you stand?"

She nodded. He took her hand, and helped her to her feet. Lash handed Krystin her robe, which she belted around herself. Devlin gathered his shirt and coat, and then they moved to leave.

I turned to David, but he was already out of the room. I followed, to see David already embracing Krystin.

"She was sick, as you said," Devlin said to David. "It took only a little of me to turn her. But she will be fine now."

"Thank you, Lord," David said emotionally, not letting go of Krystin. "Please go with my man. A room has been prepared for you, to your request. He will come for you in an hour, two at most, depending on how long it takes her to adapt to her fangs to speak her vows. The ceremony will take place directly after."

Devlin nodded, and then strode after the man, Lash and I following. We were led to another opulent room, where Devlin began to undress.

Were we supposed to have sex? If so, I wasn't in the mood.

"I'm going to shower, not try for you," Devlin said, rolling his eyes. "I can smell your annoyance from here, Sar."

"I'm not annoyed," I said, shrugging. "You were right. It was nothing like we share."

"Told you," Devlin remarked in passing, as he turned on the shower, and stepped in. A few moments later he got out, and began to towel himself dry. I could tell he wanted me to come and help him, but I knew he didn't need my help, so I ignored him, despite Rene's attempts to cajole me.

When he was dry, he belted a robe around himself, and lay on the bed. "Come and lie next to me," he said, his tone relaxed. "We will be up till dawn again, so take this opportunity to lie down, Love. Lash will watch."

I crawled into his arms, and lay there.

"Penny for your thoughts," he whispered in my ear five minutes later.

"I'm thinking about you turning her."

"Are you jealous?"

"No," I said reluctantly. "But I thought there would be more ritual. It was 'get on the bed, let's exchange bodily fluids,' and then it was over."

"What else would there be?" Devlin asked, turning his head and giving me a questioning look. "I was merely turning her, Sar. David will be doing all the rituals tonight, when he Oaths her."

"You seemed to like it a lot."

"I always come when I turn a woman," Devlin said, shrugging. "I usually use that as the last bit that's needed to push her over."

"I saw that."

"I liked it," Devlin said, looking into my eyes. "I won't deny that. It's one part of my duty as Ruler that I truly enjoy, Love. Nothing else feels like it. But it's not a substitute for making love, though I used it as one for many years, just as I used all kinds of sex."

"Tell me you love me."

Devlin smiled tenderly. "I love you, Oathed One."

"Tell me it will always be like this between us."

"It won't be," Devlin whispered, a shadow passing over his face. "Much has already changed in the years I've known you. But my feelings for you won't change, that I promise."

Screw it. "Make love with me?"

Devlin turned to me eagerly. "I thought you were never going to ask."

* * * *

An hour and a half later, there was a knock at the door which woke me, but not Devlin.

"What?" Lash hissed at the door.

"David requests your presence, Lord Dalcon."

"Five minutes," Lash hissed.

Devlin and I were already dressing by that time. Five minutes later, we left.

I was glad I'd quickly fixed my makeup and hair in the mirror before leaving the room. When we arrived at the ballroom, everyone was waiting for us.

"Master," they all murmured, bowing their heads. Devlin didn't look at any of them; he went to the front, where David and Krystin stood, both in white. Lash and I followed him.

Devlin stood between them, back a few paces, and I stood to his right, Lash to his left.

"We come here today to witness the Oathing of David and Krystin," Devlin intoned in his rich voice. "David, speak your Oath."

"I, David Helm, give you my heart, Krystin. I promise to be faithful to you, until there comes a time you wish for others to join us. I promise to respect you, and love you, and ensure you are taken care of, and nourished, body and soul—"

Must be something to do with blood?

"—This I swear."

"Krystin, speak your Oath," Devlin said, turning to her.

"I give myself to David," Krystin said very slowly, wincing a little as she spoke around her fangs. "All I am is his. So I swear."

"By the authority given to me as Ruler of these United States, I pronounce you Oathed," Devlin said, giving them a faint smile. "I wish you happiness, David and Krystin, on behalf of Sarelle and myself. May you know the happiness that we know in loving one another."

Everyone clapped and cheered, as David and Krystin carefully kissed.

The party was a grand one. It was close to how Danial's parties had been, save it was all non-humans, excepting me and what I surmised were a few other Oathed humans, by their silver collars. Devlin and I had a good time. Lash and I even sampled a little food from the platters out for those guests who weren't vampire.

More attention was paid to Dev than the couple. Every single person there wanted to talk to him. Their behavior was as Lash had accused David of acting: they all seemed to be trying to curry favor with Devlin, flattering him and me, telling him they were so glad he was Ruler again, congratulating him on Venus.

Devlin handled it well, acting very aloof, and removed. Lash glowered at everyone. And I nodded, and tried to be regal, but it was hard, as I was used to being friendly, not scornful. But after being told by the tenth man that I was incomparably beautiful, I got why Devlin didn't often spend time with vampires. *I'll take the werebats any day over these lying flatterers.*

The night dragged on, and around two a.m., Devlin took me aside. Lash was in the bathroom, taking his first break of the evening. "Did you eat enough?" he said with concern. "You look tired, Love."

"Are they always so fake?" I murmured in his ear.

"Most of them, yes. But they are right to want to stay on my good side, Sar. As tiring as it is, it's best they act this way. The other option would be to disrespect me."

I nodded, and yawned.

"Lash is over there, speaking to another guard. Tell him we are going. We've stayed long enough to be remembered."

I walked over to Lash. He saw me coming, but turned away.

I wasn't offended. Devlin had said Lash had a part to play, and that was of the badass guard, not my loving mate. At least I felt that way until I heard him talking.

"So she's a good lay?" the other guard hissed eagerly. "She looks cute enough, anyway."

"She's okay," Lash said in an offhand manner. "I've had better."

"But word around is you're just with her now," the other were said excitedly.

"For now," Lash said, and grinned.

"Doesn't that suck, her not being snake?" Then he grinned. "Or not suck?"

Lash gave him a look. The man looked back, waiting expectantly.

"She sucks just fine," Lash drawled, baring his fangs in a leer. "Though her movements as snake could use some work. But hell, John, it's free! Dev likes the arrangement, so I get my needs met, all of them, whenever I want! It's fucking great."

"You mean great fucking!" John said, and they both laughed.

"She seems to like you," he added, glancing over. "She's been watching us for a few minutes now."

"She probably wants me to do something for her," Lash said irritably. "Wait here."

He strode over to me, swaggering. "Need something, My Lady?" he said mockingly.

I gave him the most disinterested look I could, which wasn't hard, considering the mood I was in after hearing how he'd referred to me. "Not from you. Dev sent me to get you, no rush."

"Okay," Lash hissed turning away. "Tell him one minute."

It was then I noticed with shock that Lash's old girlfriend Lys was there, talking to the other snakeman.

I went back to Devlin, trying hard not to stalk all the way to him and failing miserably.

"What's eating you?" he hissed, his tone pointed. "Relax, before others notice."

My smile came out a forced grimace. "Lys is here. What's she doing here? We're not in the Northeast."

"So she is," Devlin said with disinterest, casting his gaze over the room. "She's probably that other snake's date."

A crash rent the silence. I turned fast in fear, worried. Lys was holding onto Lash, trying to hold him back. The other snakeman was on the ground on his back, in the middle of two broken halves of a table.

"Don't ever call her a cunt!" Lash hissed in a dangerous tone. "Not in front of me, Brad. Now leave, before I kick your ass."

Devlin restrained me as I moved toward Lash and Lys, pulling me into his embrace. "Do not go to them, Sar."

"Let me go," I grated back, still trying to smile.

Brad got to his feet, then cast a hateful look at Lash and Lys before shoving through the exit door with a loud bang. David headed toward us, his face worried. Before he was even halfway, the screaming started.

Chapter Seven

Devlin grabbed me in his arms, pushing me in back of him. I fought him a little, wanting to know what was going on.

Fire roared in an arc through the door, brilliantly glowing as a blast of heat hit me like a blow. Sweat immediately beaded on my face.

Vampires were running and screaming, as various weremen tried to push through them, trying to get to the source of the fire. Another blast of fire arced through the air, catching a woman. She fell to her knees screaming, her long hair afire, her dress melting into her skin. Even as I watched her body tried to heal her, but she was hit with another blast of fire, and she convulsed, collapsing backward.

A figure dressed in black came through the door, a military issue flamethrower in his hands. He sprayed the female vampire again for good measure, even though she was mostly ash anyway by then. More figures in black ran in behind him, armed with crossbows, and assault rifles, machetes strapped to their waists.

Vampires were backing away as fast as they could as the figures advanced, the lead one guarded by his fellows. But there was utter panic. All the exits were being covered with other figures in black who began spraying the crowd with bullets. Vampires were yelling and pushing, and Rene was screaming at me to teleport us out of there. I concentrated, and then the vampire next to me stumbled, hit by a bullet. The movement knocked me to one foot, and I lost my grip on Devlin.

I screamed for him, but all sound was lost in the cacophony. I looked up in fear to see the various weremen guards were fighting with the figures in black, fighting hard, but they were losing.

Then Lash waded into them.

I hadn't ever really seen him fight, and to say he slaughtered them wasn't fair. He moved so fast he was a blur, and whomever he hit stayed down. He punched one black figure so hard the man was knocked off his feet, his gun releasing a burst as it flew from his hands. Another man shot him, but Lash didn't even flinch, knifing him smoothly, and knocking him off his feet with a kick to the stomach. He ducked another spray of bullets, and let fly with his whip, knocking the flamethrower out of the lead man's hands.

I felt Devlin's arms envelop me tight. Turning to him, I tried to burrow into his arms. Yet instead of comfort, he turned my back to his chest, resting his head on top of mine. "Watch."

Everywhere the figures in black were going to their knees, holding their ears and screaming. Some vampires were running past them out the doors, but others were cowering back, as the figures tore off their masks and hoods, exposing contorted human faces, some male, some female. Their eyes were crazed, and they were shaking as if they were hearing something that was so painful they were dying from it.

There was only one not screaming, the lead man. Lash had him, his whip wrapped around the man's neck, the man cursing and fighting him.

"Enough!" Devlin said in a rich voice that carried, still cradling me in his embrace. "Enough, Titus!"

The figures went to their knees as one unit, gasping. Then the exit door opened to admit two stumbling figures in black, Titus levitating behind one of them. He moved through the air, his feet a good three feet off the ground, until he was before Devlin and me. The figures in black crawled after him, again looking as if they were in terrible pain, their faces contorted, though none of them made a sound.

"Do you wish them killed, Master?" Titus rumbled, his red eyes on Devlin.

Devlin bared his fangs. "Bring him to me, Lash."

Lash strode over to us, shoving the man he was holding in front of him, though the man was twice his size. The man had gotten within three feet of Devlin and me when he lunged for us, a switchblade in his hand. I recoiled with a shriek, but Lash had hold of him, and he shoved him down on his knees before Devlin, so the man went sprawling, the snap of his left wrist breaking audibly in the sudden silence.

Devlin looked down on him, unruffled. "It's Peter, isn't it?" he said in a cool tone.

The man didn't answer, his eyes looking up at us with hate and fury. But he looked too young by far to be the Peter I'd spoken to on the phone. *Was this the leader of the vampire hunters, the man who had threatened the life of my daughter?*

"You have the look of your mother," Devlin purred, letting go of me, and moving closer, his steps almost a glide. "You are Old Peter's grandnephew, aren't you? Yes, I remember your mother *well*—"

The man spat at him, but Devlin moved aside deftly, the spittle missing him. "Now, now," he purred. "Let's be civil. Don't you want to plead with me for your life?"

"Go ahead and kill me," Peter hissed, still struggling in Lash's grip. "Others will come!"

"How about I turn you?" Devlin said with malicious pleasure, raising the hair on my arms. "You have the balls to face me and still be defiant, Peter. With that bravery you might rise high in immortal status, provided you learned some respect for your betters."

"Fuck you!" Peter shouted. "You're going to die, you evil vampire!"

Devlin let out the most bloodcurdling laughter. It started out small and unsettling, and rose in volume, rising and stretching and growing until it was all encompassing, until it drowned out everything like the black shadow of forever night descending like a curtain fall.

The hunters were watching him now with fear-filled eyes, though some were still trying to be brave, their faces stony. But most were shaking and quivering, especially the women.

"Want me to kill them?" Lash hissed, grinning. "Or should we have fun with them first?"

"This is a celebration," Devlin said, baring his fangs completely. "Fun is the obvious choice!"

The vampires behind him roared their assent. Lash cackled as Peter struggled in his grip, cursing.

Devlin held up his hands for quiet, and silence descended again utterly, except for the sound of praying and crying. "There is to be no rape of any kind," he said in a cold voice. "Out of respect for Krystin and David." Then he grinned, and reached down, grabbing hold of the nearest hunter, a woman. She screamed and struggled in his grip.

He turned to the crowd, baring his fangs in an evil grin. "But their blood is forfeit, all of it. Who wants one?"

The vampires roared and pushed forward in masse, and Devlin threw the hunter into their midst like he was tossing a ball. She landed in arms that caught her and held her, bearing her down under a sea of bodies, still screaming as the vampires began to drain her.

Devlin turned, grabbed another, a man, and tossed him. Waiting hands again grabbed hold of him, and bore him down. Bared fangs sunk into him and drank from him even as he tried frantically to get them off of him, screaming loudly.

Devlin laughed maniacally, and grabbed another. The hunters were all screaming now, and climbing over one another trying to get away from him, but he caught them easily, throwing them like candy to the waiting grasping hands that eagerly caught them, and pulled them down.

I shuddered. Titus's arm grabbed hold of me to support me. Grateful, I leaned into him. Rene was silent within me, though I could feel she was as nauseous as I was at the carnage unfolding all around us.

Five minutes later, the screams had died. The vampires began carrying the remains of the hunters outside, their bloody faces exultant in their triumph.

Devlin turned to David, Peter still untouched at his feet. "By victor's rights, Peter is mine. But it is your party that was attacked, your bride that was threatened, and your guests that were killed. So I'll share him with you, if you wish."

"I accept," David grated out. The polite host he'd been only minutes ago was gone. The man who stood before me now was angry, killing angry, as he gently pushed his frightened vampire bride away and came toward Devlin with resolute eyes of solid crimson.

Devlin turned to Lash, even as I saw his fingernails began to lengthen. "Set him free."

Lash flicked his wrist, and stepped away, the whip sliding off Peter as if it were alive. But before Peter'd taken a step, David hit him hard in the jaw, knocking him across the room. Peter slid across the floor, but even as he did he drew an exploding bullet gun. He fired at David, and missed, blowing a foot-sized hole in the wall. Devlin raked him across his gun hand, sinking his talons in. Peter dropped the gun with a cry of pain, and faced Devlin. Devlin grinned widely, crooking his taloned finger at him, and Peter stopped still as a deer in headlights, and then he turned and ran.

Devlin and David were on him before he'd gotten ten steps. They bit him together, Devlin at his throat, and David on his arm. Peter screamed, and David gripped his mouth hard, muffling his cries, even as his feet kicked, still trying to fight, while they drank him dry.

Titus squeezed my arm comfortingly, and I leaned into him, unable to look away though I wanted to.

Devlin withdrew his fangs and let Peter go, licking his lips. David gathered the body closer, still drinking, even though I could see Peter was unconscious by now, if not dead.

"Found another one!" a cheerful voice called. I looked up to see Rip leading another man into the room, though he was pulling on his hand so hard I thought he'd surely dislocate it. "He was hiding behind the coats. Like that was going to work!"

"He's all yours, David," Devlin said nonchalantly. "Dispose of him."

Everyone held their breath, looking at David. I was afraid to breathe myself. What act of punishment could be more intense than what I'd already witnessed?

"What do you want me to do, Lord?" David asked respectfully. "I'd like to honor you, if you permit me to."

"Yes, honor an old custom," Devlin said with a faint smile. "You are newly Oathed, and you are both vampires now. You know of what I speak: the Red Blessing."

David nodded once, and beckoned for Krystin. She came up to him. And as she joined him, David reached out delicately with his talon in a smooth motion and cut the hunter's throat.

The spray of blood from the carotid artery hit him and his bride, spattering them like light rain. It also hit Devlin, standing behind them, though it was only on the left side of his face.

Rip gathered up the dying hunter, and walked outside with him, his blood still flooding out of his slit throat.

Devlin beckoned to me, and I walked up to stand beside him, glad I was on his right side, and that I still had Titus's hand in mine. "We are leaving," Devlin said smoothly. "Have a good night, David. And be wary, as Peter will know of what happened here. I'd advise more guards, and getting a demon, if just an imp-sized one."

"I will be, first thing tomorrow night. Thank you again, Lord. Travel home safely."

Devlin nodded, took my hand, and we left, Titus and Rip trailing behind us. I was just beginning to get over my shock when I received another one.

Lash was outside, waiting for us. I was livid to see Lys still with him. They were holding hands!

"I need to take her home," Lash hissed, looking at Devlin. "She has her car here. Send Titus back for me here, say in four hours?"

"Sure," Devlin said, nodding. "See you at home."

Lash grinned at him, and then Lys was leading him away towards the parking lot, a big grin on her face, too.

Fuck playacting. I wasn't going to stand here and watch him leave with her.

I went to go after them and in the next moment, we were at Hayden. Ghost raced in, barking and growling, and I grabbed hold of him, hugging him tight. He wagged his tail and licked me.

"Be vigilant," Devlin said to Rip, and Titus. "Peter's sure to be pissed."

"You couldn't do other than what you did," Titus rumbled. "Not without looking weak, Though you should've saved one for us, Devlin."

"I did," Rip murmured in a low voice. "That last one. I've got him downstairs, and he's still breathing, though we should hurry if we want him to be alive—"

I told myself not to think about what they meant. But Rene did anyway, and she imagined them eating him together, the man still alive as the other hunters had been, feeling his body being eaten. I pushed away the images, even as I knew I had to leave right then or I was going to have a psychotic break.

"I'm going to shower," I said as calmly as possible, and ran from the room. I made it to our bedroom before I felt myself breathing hysterically fast, almost hyperventilating as I turned on the shower, my hands slipping on the knobs.

Rene was also frantic in my mind, her thoughts jumbled, the images of her thoughts mixing into mine, vivid images of fighting hunters and demons long ago, interspersed with some kind of orgy she'd attended, where she and another witch had raised a demon and it had ravaged them both.

"Stop," I screamed at her. "Stop! Go Rene! Go!"

I felt Rene try to pull back, but her thoughts bombarded me, showering me with pictures of red skin on pale skin, and brick red and black horns, and desire, so much desire! And then the other witch being eaten alive, as the demon wrested control back from her as she orgasmed, and Rene trying to save her, trying to help her, and screaming helplessly, and the demon laughing as it ate her friend piece by piece!

"RENE, STOP! STOP IT! GET OUT!"

She was alive, Rene screamed in my mind, and I screamed back at her mentally to get out of my head, and then I felt her wall go up, and then there was just blessed silence. The feeling of relief was so strong I went to my knees, my hands still holding my head.

God, that had been so close.

I heard a faint, almost inaudible sound. It sounded like meat ripping. There was a faint cry of pain.

My breathing went back into hyperventilation, my heart racing so fast I had chest pain. I yanked off my clothes, tearing the lace of the gown, and stepped to the shower, almost falling. I put my hand on the door, and then a cool hand gripped me, and spun me around.

I looked up into golden eyes that were no less dark for their light color. Blood still adorned his face in a spray. There was more blood on Dev than I'd first noticed. Crimson drenched his collar, the moist beads like small round glistening jewels on his leather suit jacket. He gazed down at me, his face serious, his bearing one of the utter alpha male.

I put out a shaking hand to him, and touched his stubbled face, letting out a sound that was part crumbling reason and part fear. His skin was warm, the blood wet. *So wet...*

Dev shuddered under my touch and then he lunged forward, kissing me roughly. The moment his lips met mine, something that had been strained for years to the verge of breaking finally snapped inside me.

I grabbed him forcefully, kissing him so roughly I was almost biting him, and he groaned, lifting me in his arms and turning to push me up against the nearest wall. I heard the sound of his zipper, and then I felt him pushing into me almost brutally, despite that I was already slick for him. I felt his skin on mine, felt the wetness of the blood as it smeared onto my skin, and then the strokes of his tongue as Devlin licked it off me. I let my head loll back with a moan, and Devlin pushed his head into my throat, kissing me passionately, almost trying to eat me in his intensity as he pistoned in and out of me.

"Fuck me, Dev," I breathed in his ear, my eyes shut tight. "Oh God, I want you to, and I know it's wrong, and—"

Devlin cut off my words, kissing me roughly. He drew back, and grabbed my wrists in his hands. With a clench of his muscles he pushed himself into the hilt, as I writhed helplessly, trapped there against the wall.

"I'm going to fuck you!" he said in a guttural voice in my ear. "Fuck you the way you dream of being fucked and never dare speak of! You've wanted this as much as I have, Sweet Sar! You were made for me! You were made for this, we both were!"

I convulsed at the raw power in his words, letting out a desperate soft cry of need. He grabbed a handful of my hair, and made a fist. He pulled sharply, and I opened my eyes to see his hot golden ones an inch away from mine.

"But it's not wrong!" he hissed, baring his fangs at me, his eyes tinged red. "And don't you dare say it is! Not ever! What you and I have is the only Goddamn thing that always makes sense to me! It's worth killing for! It's worth whatever I have to do to keep! Anything I have to do!"

He kissed me again and I whimpered in raw wanting. He let go of my hands and pushed frantically into me, rubbing me. I met him thrust for thrust, my only thought the crescendo that was rapidly building inside me. I came screaming, wrapping myself around him, trying to get him deeper into me.

Devlin came in the next moment, his head thrown back as he screamed out his release, his cry so raw it was almost like pain.

We were both breathing hard, the air tearing out of us. I held onto him, feeling afraid, tears in my eyes. What we'd shared had been so raw, so animalistic. Part of me had never felt more satisfied. The other part of me was horrified and terrified that I felt that way.

"Hold still, Love," Devlin murmured gently, cupping my rear with one hand as he eased us away from the wall. "I'll move us to the bed. But I don't want to leave your body right now, not for anything."

I nodded, and held onto him. Carefully he turned, leaving his pants on the floor, using one hand then the other to shuck first his suit jacket, then his shirt.

"I could have unbuttoned it," I whispered.

"No point, with the bloodstain," Dev said. He eased me back to the bed, cradling me close to him, wrapping me in his embrace.

For many minutes we didn't speak, we just held each other.

"I was afraid," he said softly, kissing my shoulder. "That few seconds I lost your hand. But a few bullets hit me, and it took a moment to heal them."

"You called Titus through a mental link?"

"Of course. He and I both knew there might be trouble, me being away from Hayden. Peter still hasn't learned that time and space is relative to a demon. As I expected, he thought it was a good time to catch me out of my roost."

"You killed his relative. Will he come for revenge?"

"Possibly. I still don't know what he thought to do. David's guards were no match for Peter's men, yes, but Peter had to know Lash would be with me, he had to know that Lash would mow them down like grass, even if Titus was not there."

"Why'd he do it?" I whispered. "Go home with her?"

Devlin kissed my shoulder again. "You know why. Word is getting around he's seeing only you, and this makes it look like he doesn't have feelings for you. Lys is going to be pissed though, when he gets her home and then tells her no sex."

"Maybe he won't," I said bitterly.

"He will, and you know he will," Devlin said chidingly. "You just like to hear me say it aloud. But really, is there a question in your mind that he would do anything else but refuse her?"

"No," I said, leaning back into him. "Honestly, no."

"Good," he said. Then he got up, separating from me with a little groan. "Come, we need to shower. Dried blood is not a pleasant thing to wake up with on your skin, take it from me."

* * * *

Lash arrived home sometime that evening, but I didn't see him until the next day. He came to me hesitantly, and it was obvious he was worried I was angry. But I told him I understood why he'd done what he had, and gave him a kiss on his cheek, which of course led to sex in the nearest available room. Afterwards he held me and told me in a halting voice that he had kissed Lys a little, though it hadn't gone beyond that.

"I have to admit...she got me hard, Sweetness," Lash admitted. "And for a moment all I thought about was how good she used to feel, how good it would be to fuck her, and how easy it would be to cover up."

I looked at him questioningly.

"What stopped me was knowing I'd have to come home and admit it to you," Lash hissed gently. "And I couldn't face the look of hurt you would give me when I did. So I told her to watch herself, and that I was going, and then she bit me."

My eyes widened. "She bit you?"

He nodded, the rueful smile slightly bitter. "And injected a little poison, until I managed to pry her off me. But at least she's staying out there. I left her shouting at me that she was going back to Brad that very night. Who knows, maybe he'll take her back."

I could hope, anyway. If I saw Lys ever again, it would be too soon.

Chapter Eight

The coolness of early spring gave way to warmer weather, as the month of May slowly passed. I spent many afternoons out in the sun riding Annabelle Lee, or lying with Lash on his rock overlooking Hayden's big pond, sometimes accompanied by V and Ghost. Devlin missed me staying inside with him, but he said he understood my need for sunlight after the long winter. My vampire also still had his hands full with Ruler duties, even though our scheduled appearances were done for the foreseeable future.

I still spent most mornings with Rene working in the basement on her new body, and a few evenings too, when my guys were out with one another on business or doing the male-bonding thing. Rene's body was nearly fully formed by this point, though she advised there would easily be two weeks of finishing touches to follow the last steps of the main spell. But we agreed that if we worked hard, we could likely finish by May 31st.

I was glad of that. As much as I liked Rene, it was getting hard to have her with me all the time. I was no longer sure she was really leaving me during my intimate times with both Lash and Devlin, even though she said she was and that I allowed her to have her own private time with Dev every other day. We also hadn't spoken at all of the night she'd gone a little crazy after the David and Krystin's wedding, either. I kept trying not to think about the images, pushing away the thoughts and focusing immediately on something else whenever that night came to mind.

I had not seen Danial since that day together when I'd touched him intimately against his will. Devlin told me sadly to let him be, that he still had healing to do. I nodded, but inside I still felt torn. Part of me wanted Danial back, wanted him badly. Yet the rational, sane part of me knew I'd dodged a bullet when he'd all but told me to leave him alone. It was better this way; having him back could only cause more jealousy with Lash. So I avoided him at all costs.

* * * *

Another week passed of hard work, and longer nights, as I pushed with Rene toward completion. Happily, we finished early, a fully formed female body resting as if sleeping on the lab table after she murmured the last lines of the spell. Its chest was rising and falling with long, slow, even breaths. There was only one unnerving aspect: Rene's new body was the mirror image of mine.

I'm sorry, she said contritely in my mind. *But there's nothing here in the spell to modify the body that grows in any way. It must look like you from the tissue and blood that you donated to help me.*

"This spell might also have been designed for someone who'd been badly hurt, and wanted a new whole body, instead of taking time to heal?" I offered aloud. "Something that would be exactly the same?"

Rene assumed control of my body, and begin looking through the beginnings of the spell we had used. Ten minutes later, she finally answered me aloud. "You're brilliant," she said. "Yes, the spell was for victims of blue fire, and other non-healable injuries. It looks like it was designed for those that were immortal, so they would not have to go through eternity with terrible disfigurements."

I wrested back control from her, thankfully telling myself that this would be one of the last times I had to do that. "Does the beginning part say anything about how to modify the existing body?"

Rene read for a while, then easily took control back from me again. "Sorry, but no," she said, closing our eyes and rubbing them with her hand. "But I know enchantments that I can use to modify my appearance, Sar. Do not worry. You will not have a twin."

That's a relief. "So another few weeks."

Maybe less, Rene said in my mind. *I promise to work as fast as possible, Sar.*

Thank you, I said tiredly, as I headed up to bed.

* * * *

That spring, several new guards joined Hayden's ranks, all

werebears save one. Devlin had finally conceded that another Canadian would be allowed at Hayden, on the condition that it not be a werewolf. Thus, Bobbie the werewolverine came on the next flight from Toronto, Ontario.

Hearing his name, I expected some jolly-looking, salesman-type person with a short haircut in a suit. Alternately, knowing the animal he was, I anticipated some scruffy guy with long sideburns and a plaid shirt to arrive, uttering sarcastic comments.

Bobbie was neither. He was medium in every way: medium brown hair of medium length, medium height, medium weight. There was nothing scary about him at all except his eyes, which had an alien look to them, as if there was no rational mind behind them, just an animal, one whose reason wasn't functioning beyond food, sex, and sleep. The animal he became resembled nothing more than a large dog whose fangs were much like Ghost's.

To say no one liked him was putting it moderately. Everyone disliked him, and it didn't help that he only spoke French. But Bobbie oddly didn't seem to mind or care. He kept to himself, mostly roaming the forests of Hayden at night as a guard, and sleeping during the days outside on the grounds. Devlin explained when I asked that this arrangement was a way to keep Bobbie out of any serious defensive fighting, and still make it seem as if he were helping. "This appeases the were groups in Canada, Sar. Trust me, this is best."

I never asked beyond that, though I found the hungry way he watched V and I disquieting.

* * * *

Finally, the evening of May 31st arrived. Rene and I had put the finishing touches on her body the day before. Now it was finally time for her to leave me.

Devlin waited anxiously while Rene said the final words. A glittering mist showered over us like dew from our hands, and then I felt her leave me with a wrenching searing pain, as if my very soul was being torn out of me.

I let out a loud shriek, going to my knees.

Devlin lunged and grabbed hold of me, asking what was wrong, as

Rene let out a shriek of her own, her new body's chest expanding as her body arched up off the table, her hands gripping its sides as her eyes opened for the first time.

A black feeling instantly enveloped the room, along with the smell of sulfur. I lunged for Rene, grabbing her hand, just as Shaker appeared, baring his teeth, his clawed hands reaching for her. Devlin tackled him, and Shaker turned to catch him, struggling, as Hayden's basement faded away to be replaced by the walls of the convent. I shoved Rene hard, and she fell through the wrought iron gates, as Shaker appeared behind me, snarling.

He grabbed hold of me, his touch burning my skin through my clothes. "You should not have interfered, human," he rumbled, his red eyes an inch from mine. "We are kin now, so I can do nothing to you, which you well know. But I will remember this, Sarelle. And know that there will come a time when you'll beg me to help you, and I will laugh as you crawl at my feet."

I pulled my hands out of his grasp. He turned to Rene, who stood watching us from the safety of the hallowed ground. Nuns opened the door behind her, several of them hurrying out with a candle, calling to her in French.

"And you, witch," Shaker rumbled. "You are safe among the nuns, for now. But take one step off that blessed ground and I'll harvest your soul." He laughed evilly. "You don't have the will to stay celibate for the rest of your life." He faded away, still laughing.

I entered the gates and went to Rene, hugging her, trying to overcome how strange I felt, as she still looked almost identical to me. "It's okay. We made it."

"He's right," she said with her French inflection, resigned. "I'm not going to last here long. I was never good at following the rules. I hope this works."

"It will." I let go of her, my eyes catching the herd of nuns that was fast approaching. "Mother Olga expects you, so just tell her you're here." I handed her some money. "This is from Devlin, in case there is anything you need."

"I need him," she said, tears beginning to fall from her eyes. "I miss him already, Sar."

I pushed down my feelings of jealousy, then let them alone, feeling relief that my thoughts were once again my own personal domain. "Here," I said, handing her a prepaid cell phone. "Dev said to call as often as you want to. He said he would write, too, and so will I. This isn't forever, just until we figure out a better solution."

"Come to see me, as often as you can," she said, hugging me tightly. "It's already odd to be here, to be by myself, and not have you in my mind to talk to."

"I'll miss you, too," I said, trying not to sound as relieved as I really felt to have separated from her. "Please call me."

She nodded and let me go, turning to the nuns. I hurried outside the gates, then immediately teleported back.

When I returned, Devlin was there waiting anxiously on the upstairs couch, nursing a rapidly healing clawed up chest and arm. He bolted up, taking hold of my shoulders in a desperate motion. "Did you make it?"

I nodded. "She's safe."

Devlin let loose a sigh of relief, his hands letting go of me. "And you gave her the phone?"

I nodded. "Why don't you just sneak in to see her?"

"It was a condition of the sisters agreeing to take her in, that she not have any male visitors," Devlin snarled angrily. "You'd think with the donation I gave them to rebuild their chapel, they'd bend the rules a little for me. But they were unyielding and insufferable as a chastity belt. They warned if a man was found even close to her during her stay, she would be expelled instantly."

"She's safe, and she's no longer a ghost, alone and forgotten," I comforted, sitting down beside him. "We found a way to save her, Dev. And she'll be back with us soon, Love."

Devlin looked over at me, and then hugged me. "You're right," he whispered. "We must be thankful for the things we've got."

* * * *

The next day was unreal for me. Not only was there no one in my head but me, there was no magic work to be done. So within a few hours, the same feeling of being boring settled in me, until I remembered that I did have some unfinished work to do.

I spent the rest of the afternoon in the basement, attempting to finish the filing of Devlin's important papers that I'd begun over a year ago. The work was as I'd left it so many months ago, except there was another box of tax records from this year, along with some of the files from the guards who'd died in the fall, and the newer files from others like Bobbie that had been hired.

Being my usual curious self—and as there was no one watching—I looked through Bobbie's file. I was shocked to discover his real name was Armani Roberto Bonne. No wonder he went by Bobbie. But other than that there was nothing interesting in it, at least to me.

The next day was the same. And the next. Five days later, I finally made myself grab the last file that needed to be stored, the file of my good friend, one who'd happened to be a werewolf and been murdered by Ulysses last fall when he'd declared war on Devlin and all who lived at Hayden.

I sadly stored away Robin's file, and closed the drawer with a click. I'd made some of her recipes in the past few months and liked them, as had Lash. *She really knew how to make good Borscht. I didn't know beets could taste that good.*

"Sarelle, phone," Jordan said hesitantly from the doorway. "It's your mother. She said you were meeting her for dinner after your doctor appointment today?"

Shit. I ran out of the room without replying, grabbed a purse from the hall closet, and teleported to the doctor's office. I apologized to Dr. Camlyn as he led me into exam room one, and he said it was okay, this was just a physical, and added that he'd been busy all morning on an emergency call, anyway.

The way he said it made me look at him. "Who was it?"

"By law, I really shouldn't tell you," he said, his blue eyes looking into mine worriedly. "I know you're divorced. But you haven't signed the privacy papers for this year yet, either of you, so technically—"

"What happened to Theo?" I hated myself for caring, for needing to know.

"He was shot someplace down south," Stephen said. "The bullet went thought him with no problem. But on it was some of that poison he'd run into before—"

Oh God. "Is Elle okay?"

"She's away at college, I don't think he even told her. But it was pretty bad, Sar, as the poison didn't just get on his skin, it got inside him. Adding to that, Theo refused to call Titus for help, saying he didn't want to owe him any favors. Terian helped him, but you know his healing power is limited. I did what I could, once they got him here. But he's going to be laid up for a while."

That damned secret business of Lash and Devlin's. "So he's going to be okay?"

"Sure," Stephen affirmed. "He's already healed the wound. But he'll have to rest for a while. You know how much he hates that."

I smiled. "I do. Thanks for letting me know."

"But I do have to have you sign these today, I'm afraid." Stephen handed me some papers, and I signed them, taking off Theo's name as emergency contact, and adding Lash's, and Devlin's, and then Titus's for good measure. I left my mother's name untouched.

My physical was completely normal, and Stephen said everything looked good. After the medical physical, Stephen gave me one of his magical ones, getting out the silver wand that he hadn't used on me for a while. I knew by the way his eyes widened then narrowed in concentration that something was wrong. "What is it?"

"Sarelle, I don't know how to say this, but…it looks like a bit of your soul is missing."

Well, now I guess I knew what the tearing feeling had been when Rene left me. "Will it grow back?"

He nodded. "In time, sure. It's a miniscule piece. My question to you is what happened. Something did, as you aren't the normal hysterical mess you should be, hearing that kind of news."

I explained about Rene, what Devlin had done, and what I'd helped her do. Stephen was livid by the time I was finished. "Do you know how bad things might have turned out?" he said in barely contained fury. "You could've been possessed for real, Sarelle! Not to mention that if she had the power to take control from you, she must've had the power to take your body from you, to force you out! You would've been the ghost!"

"Look, she didn't," I said defensively. "I wanted to help her."

"Think about this," Stephen said in an ominous tone. "You keep risking your life to save people, Sar. So far for you, that's worked out okay. But you keep sacrificing yourself, and sooner or later the price isn't going to be one that you can pay. Some things can't be healed. Or survived."

"You might be right," I answered, feeling very old. "But what's my choice? Do nothing, and tell myself I had to, because there was too much to risk, that I had too much to lose?"

"People aren't bad for wanting to hold onto what they have, or for taking care of themselves. Sometimes it's best not to help, Sarelle. Adults should understand and embrace the consequences of their actions—"

"And I do," I said, forcing myself to smile. "Thanks, Stephen. I understand you only want what's best for me."

"I do," he said, laying his hand on my shoulder in a fatherly gesture. "You've become more than another patient, Sar, you're a good friend. I don't want to get that call one night saying something bad has happened to you."

I squeezed his hand briefly, then released it. "I hope you won't."

"Me too. Take care, Sar. Please make an appointment with the nurse for next year. You should be okay until then, under normal circumstances."

I cracked a smile at that and so did he, and then we were laughing. "Normal circumstances, sure! When does that ever happen?"

"We can always hope," he said with a laugh. "Have a good day."

When I got back to Hayden, Jordan met me at the door. "Devlin wants you, right now."

I forgot to tell him I was leaving. I hurried upstairs. Devlin was in bed reading.

"I'm sorry I left without telling you," I said, taking off my sweater to change my clothes. "I forgot I had a doctor appointment."

"Are you well?" Devlin asked with concern, putting down his book. "You've not said you were feeling poorly?"

"It was a yearly thing. I'm fine," I said, as I pulled on a more elegant sweater. "But I'm late to meet my mother for lunch."

"Is everything as it should be?" Devlin said meaningfully. "Did you have Stephen check you inside?"

I rolled my eyes, and made sure he saw me do it. "If you're asking if I'm pregnant, I'm not. I'm due soon for my period."

"You know what I meant," Devlin said as charmingly as he could. "I wanted to know if you're still fertile, Love. I know we spoke about you checking on that—"

"As far as I know," I said curtly. "Though I do have this for you. They were offering samples at the checkout." I handed him a packet.

"What is it?" Devlin said in surprise. "Total BlockTM? You got me sunscreen?"

"It's supposed to block 100% of UV rays." I shrugged. "I thought it might be worth a try."

"Interesting," Devlin said, turning the packet around to read the back writing. "Thank you, Love. While this would not be effective enough to walk in the sunlight, as my hair and my eyes would still burn, perhaps I could feel the sun just on my hands. I will try it in a few days."

"I thought it was worth a try," I said again, feeling a little like I'd broached a sore subject and then put my foot in it, too.

"Take Bobbie with you when you go," Devlin said, picking his book back up. "Lash is out doing an errand for me. And you need a guard."

Eww. "Can't I take someone else?"

"Sure," Devlin said. "Pick whomever you like. But I wouldn't advise Nick. Lash is jealous of him, even though I know you've never done anything more than watch his ass with longing as he strolls past you."

I flushed guiltily, and Devlin chuckled. "I don't mind, Love. I know you enjoy the male anatomy. I just mention this as good advice."

I leaned over and gave him a kiss. "Want to come? You can guard me, Love."

"Your mother would not like that," he said, his tone sarcastic. "She's just like you, immune to my charms—"

"Shh," I said, kissing his earlobe. "No woman's immune to your charms, Love. I'm smitten. See you in a few hours."

Devlin didn't look up again from his book but I felt satisfaction emanating from him at my words.

I walked back downstairs to run into V. "Want to go see Grandma?"

"Sure!" she said, smiling. "Is this a shopping trip?"

"Sure, we'll stop at a store, while we're out," I said, feeling guilty I hadn't gone out with her much lately. "Get your coat."

I went into the living room, then the hallway, and then the ballroom, but no guards were around. I was heading back outside to get Bobbie via the kitchen door when I bumped into Kyle. He looked embarrassed, but then he should've been, with two handfuls of cookies, and two in his mouth besides.

"Hi. What are you doing here?" I asked curiously.

"Hiding," he said, taking one cookie out of his mouth and eating the other. "I got found again by that demon hunting me. So I'm going to stay here for a while, while Leri works on a few spells to alter my appearance."

"Want to come meet my mother?" I offered.

"Sure," he said, and laughed. "Does she cook?"

"She does, but we're eating out," I said, smiling. "I'll even treat you."

"Then I'm ready."

"Okay but no bawdy songs," I cautioned. "She'd laugh, but I'd hear about it later."

Kyle laughed. "Understood," he agreed. "I'll be on my best behavior."

* * * *

Kyle, V, my mom, and I had a good time out. We had pasta plus a little wine, and told jokes. I was surprised that for all his morality and promise to behave, Kyle had a raunchy sense of humor, though he told his jokes in a way which kept the true naughty meaning from V. But his mix of intelligence and articulateness coupled with a filthy mind explained why both Lash and Devlin liked him so much. To my surprise, in spite of his wicked witticisms, my Mom liked him, too.

After lunch, we shopped some. Kyle wasn't ill at ease as we took our time looking at clothes and shoes, and he helped us carry some of V's purchases out to the cars. There were a few moments when V and I said goodbye to my mom where he looked a little sad, but other than that he seemed like he had an okay time. V also enjoyed herself very much, except when I told her that we had to head home because there was no more room in the car for just one more stop. Instead of the tantrum I expected, though, V behaved herself well, and reluctantly gave in after only a few shrill protests.

We returned home about ten. Kyle helped me carry V's things up to her room, and we left her there talking to Sharon on the phone.

"She's a good kid," he said, as we walked downstairs.

"She is," I agreed. "Though I'm not looking forward to her true teenage years."

"I heard you were back," Lash hissed, looking up at us from the base of the stairs, his eyes on Kyle. "I thought I told you to call me if something happened."

"It happened before I had time to dial," Kyle said in disgust. "He was just there, Lash. I got away, but barely. I headed directly here. Titus put a block on me, so no demon can pinpoint me. But he says he has to renew it daily…" he trailed off.

"Stay as long as you want," Devlin said from behind us. "There's a job for you here, if you want it."

"I'm a guard, not a killer," Kyle said, looking back at Devlin. "But thanks."

"Are you a savior?" Dev countered. "I need someone to watch V, just her, as Samuel employs men for his children. Lash is occupied with Sar and I, and Titus needs to watch over Hayden, with Rip as backup. You're qualified for the job."

"You know if you need me, I'm yours," Kyle said seriously. "So do you need me?"

Devlin nodded. "Yes."

Kyle smiled. "Then I'd be glad to. She's a good kid."

"One who has death threats from all the hunter groups," Devlin replied solemnly. "As my daughter, you can imagine the threats that are yet to be made against her. I need to know you will not fail in this, Kyle."

Kyle's smile disappeared. "I won't fail."

"Good," Devlin said. "Please work out with Lash the particulars. I'll pay your going rate, plus overtime, plus room and board, with Titus's block as a bonus."

Kyle nodded. "Agreed. When do I start?"

"Tomorrow," Devlin said. "Days only, plus whenever V leaves the premises, and the few times Sar, Lash and I are gone together during the night."

"Thank you," Kyle said, offering his hand.

Devlin took it, then hugged him. "Thank you, my friend."

* * * *

The next night, Lash and I entered the ballroom to get Devlin. He was singing Elton John's "Daniel" while playing the piano. I'd never heard him play that particular song before, and so I stopped for a minute, and listened.

Lash gave me an odd look, but he paused, too until the song was done. "Ready?" Lash asked as the last notes faded. "We need to go get the wine, Dev."

"I've never heard you play that before," I said, running my fingers over the keys and sending a few notes to break the sudden stillness. "Did Danial go to Spain?"

"No," Devlin answered. "But I made the mistake of asking him to take more blood, to increase his power. He accused me of wanting his blood for Lash. It escalated from there."

"He's such a fucking jerk," Lash said. "I wouldn't take his blood if he offered it to me!"

Devlin set down the key cover with a sharp clack. "You would if you were dying again," he said with a sneer. "Danial knows that you are my reason for asking him, that with Ulysses dead, he's my only other source for blood for you besides myself. What if we need it?"

"I told you both about what Roslyn said, about how there are other potions we can try," I interjected. "She said just to let her know, and she could direct Titus to them, remember?"

"I don't trust her," Devlin said seriously. "She's hated me for a long time."

"Lots of people hate you," Lash hissed. "But what could it hurt, Dev? She's not going to make us anything, just point us in a new direction. Maybe it's worth it."

"We should go," Devlin said, striding to the door and changing the topic. "It's already eleven. We need to get there before they close."

"Tell me again why we're going to pick up the wine?" I asked. "And not have it delivered like usual?"

"Because my birthday is very soon," Lash hissed proudly. "I want to see if there's something special we could get to celebrate, Sweetness."

"What would you like for a gift?" I said teasingly. "Dev, what do you usually get him?"

"We usually go out," Lash said in a casual tone. "We'd get a few women, and party until dawn."

"Is that the plan this year?" I said bitingly, feeling put out.

"Yes," Devlin answered. "But the women will only striptease for us onstage in a private show, nothing more. After we've had our fill of visual stimulation, drink, and conversation, we'll come home and celebrate with you."

That was fair, though I made a resolution that if Rene was allowed off her convent grounds by my birthday, we would do the same thing to celebrate with a herd of male strippers, and Lash and Devlin could deal with that. "Okay."

We arrived at the liquor store, and went inside to the counter. The cases of Groom Shiraz Devlin had ordered had arrived. Under Lash's direction, the store staff loaded them into our Hummer. When that was done and we knew how much room we had left, our trio went back inside to look over the many bottles stocked on the shelves.

Devlin was friends with the owner, so we sampled a few wines that looked interesting to him. I liked all of them, but allowed that I wasn't as particular as he was. We did pay for the ones we'd sampled, and they sealed them for us, to take home.

"Dev, Sar, let's try this." Lash was coming toward us with a bottle. I was surprised to see it had two snakes on in, intertwined.

"Red Black Underbelly," Devlin mused. "Sure, let's try it."

We sampled it, and I found it good, even a little unusual.

"My vote is yes," I said.

"This might be my new signature wine, the way that Groom Shiraz is Devlin's," Lash hissed, taking a large sip. "I like it."

"You've always preferred scotch," Devlin said in a droll voice. "You never much cared for wine, especially red. Now you have a signature wine?"

"Maybe I'm going to start at this moment," Lash hissed irritated, giving Dev a nasty look.

Devlin laughed, and turned to the shop owner. "Add in a case of that, too."

* * * *

Later that night, Lash prepared again to go out on a demolition job. I decided it was time to say something and spoke up, asking him not to go. This started a mini fight.

"I have to. The client expects me."

"You've been gone at least once a week for months now," I said, trying not to sound ungrateful. "And when you are here, you're very busy with making sure Hayden's defenses are running well. Enough is enough."

"It's my job. You know that, Mate."

I've asked you not to call me Mate when we fight. "I know you said we needed the money. But I need to know if it's always going to be like this."

"I know I've been gone a lot this year so far," Lash said haltingly. "Believe me, it's not going to be like that for much longer." He let out a breath. "This isn't easy for me either, Sar." He looked at his watch. "I need to go, Sweetness. I'll be home tomorrow."

I hugged him goodbye, and went to the room where my books were stored, hoping to lose myself in a good fantasy tale. I stopped still with the door open only an inch. Danial was in there, reading. I saw with a little careful maneuvering that the book in his hands was one of his books that I'd been given by Theoron.

I watched him for a few moments. Part of me wanted to go to him, to tell him that I was his Sar, that I remembered the night we'd read that book together, when I'd been pregnant with our child. How he'd read to me until I'd fallen asleep, and then kissed me awake the next morning, telling me he'd gotten about an hour's sleep as he'd felt T move all night.

I wiped away my sudden tears, then noticed that Danial wasn't reading, he was sleeping. The book was propped up in his hands, but it was almost out of his grasp. I took a step inside the room, meaning to grab the book before it fell, but then stopped, knowing I'd wake him if I took the book from his hand. Then what would happen? *Another fight for sure.*

With a sigh, I retreated and left him there sleeping, quietly shutting the door behind me.

Saddened, I hesitantly went downstairs to Devlin, who was working in his study. "What is it, Love?" he said, turning as I opened the door. "Why are you not asleep?"

"I needed to talk to you," I said, ill at ease but also determined.

"Come in, and sit, then," he said, patting his lap. I sat down and he put his arms around me. "What is it?"

How to say it? Better to work up to it. "I'm still upset about Cain," I said finally. "It bothers me, that I wanted him."

"Why?" Devlin said, furrowing his brow. "He's a good-looking man, and he wanted you. It's normal to want him back. And you did restrain yourself, Love, like the good little girl you are."

I frowned and hit him lightly, and he laughed. "I'm worried I did it because I miss Danial."

"Maybe you did," Devlin allowed, by his tone still confused. "So what, Love? He does resemble Danial strongly. I know you love my brother, and it hurts you, that he doesn't remember you."

I nodded.

Devlin studied me, then he nodded once. "Are you requesting me to be him for you?" he asked, an odd note in his voice. "To make love with you as he did? I admit I know enough of his fancies to give it a solid try."

"No," I said, flushing. "I was with him for years, Dev. I could not pretend you were him in bed, ever, even if I wanted to, which I don't."

"Then what?" Devlin said, giving me a look. "I do not understand what it is you need from me. But just say the words, Love, and I'll do my best to give you what you are asking for."

"I need to forget how things were with him and me, Dev. I need to stop thinking of how much love I feel for him, to distance myself from him like he's distanced himself from me. Because I can see that Danial is finally beginning to stop grieving so much for his Sar. And it's making me depressed, when I should be being happy for him. I want him to move on, I know that's best for him. But being here and watching it every day, it makes me feel like when he took up with Monica. I know he can't leave, or he might be hurt—"

"Shh, Love, I get it now," Devlin said, thoughtful. "I think I can come up with something." He kissed me quickly. "Go back to bed, Sar. I'll be up shortly."

I went up to bed, and before long, I was asleep. Devlin woke me two hours before dawn.

I looked at him blearily. "What's wrong?"

"Sar, I went to Titus, to check on a few things. He said he thinks some of your reaction is from Danial's blood. You have given it to him whenever he asks, correct?"

I nodded. "Yes, as I told you, though it isn't often. When he first awoke, and then maybe four other times at most, over these past two months."

"And he healed you each time?"

I nodded.

"Do not give him any more," Devlin said a little sadly. "I'll talk to him as well, tell him you are close to turning, so he does not ask you."

"Dev, it's not the blood he's given me that's making me feel like this. I love him."

"I can't help your love for him," Devlin said, caressing my arm. "But I can help your blood tie to him. Titus gave me a charm that will draw what can be drawn of his influence out of you."

I looked at him skeptically. "How is that possible? His blood is part of me, isn't it?"

He fastened a charm around my neck on a thin delicate chain. "This will bring most of what can be drawn from you into your carotid artery, Love. I'll drink from you for a minute, heavily. Then I'll give you back some of my blood."

Don't see how this is going to help, or how it is even possible. "You're sure?"

"Trust me," he said softly. "You're suffering. I will do all I can to make you able to let him go."

I nodded, and lay down with a sigh, suddenly tired.

I lay back against the bed, and Devlin lay beside me, kissing me. I kissed him for a while, until I fully relaxed, almost dozing.

Devlin felt me relax, and struck fast, sinking his fangs into me. I gasped, because we were not making love, and it hurt. I went to move away, but Devlin held me down, drinking in long pulls.

Already I was lightheaded. Was it an effect of the charm? "Dev, stop, please," I said weakly. *God, why is my voice so weak?*

Devlin held me down, still drinking, groaning in pleasure. He moved his hips against my thigh in his excitement, though he made no move to have me.

"Stop," I whispered. "I'm asking you to stop."

Devlin took his mouth off me, swallowing down a last mouthful of blood. "By the way, that was bullshit, about drawing out any influence," he whispered. "I'm just taking your blood. The charm is to make you compliant, and heighten your pleasure while it lessens your pain, My Love. I want you to want what is going to happen to you tonight."

I felt the first tremor of real fear. His tone was as dark as it had ever been, dark as that night he'd tried to kill me, years ago. "Dev, please, don't do this."

"Shh," he whispered back, his voice again loving. "Acting afraid is not enough, he must sense it. Follow my lead." His tone switched back to evil sadism. "I hear someone at the door, Sweet Sar. Could it be someone's come to see you?"

Devlin got up off the bed. I was unable to lift my head, drowsiness and tiredness overwhelming. There was the sound of the door opening.

"Why ask me here?" Danial said in annoyance. "I was napping."

"Because I have need of you," Devlin purred.

"I don't want your woman," Danial said mockingly. "Though it's true, her blood is tasty." His voice turned malevolent. "Has she told you how she let me feed from her, in spite of the fact that she is Oathed only to you? Has she told you how she's tried to seduce me time and time again? She'd do anything I asked her to, without question. How does that make you feel, brother?"

Danial had used me. He'd used my love and desire for him to try to hurt Devlin, as he'd used Anna all those years ago. Pure anger flooded me. I seized on it, and held, feeding it as much as I could, remembering

Danial's sweet words. *You played me. Fuck feeling fear, I'm going to make you pay for that, Danial.*

"She admitted it to me, along with her love for you. I need you to have her, as a favor to me," Devlin said, sounding sad.

Danial gave him a narrow-eyed look. "Why? You're giving her what she's asking for."

"She came to me this very night, and told me she wanted you, that she cannot get over her feelings for you," Devlin explained. "So I want you to bite her, and have her, so she can understand clearly who she is Oathed to, and to whom her allegiance should be confined."

"As punishment?" I expected Danial's voice to be sarcastic, and disgusted, but instead it was eager. I felt a chill, which dampened my fury.

"Yes," Devlin said just as eagerly. "I need to get you out of her system. Even if you don't like her, she's attractive enough that you shouldn't have trouble getting erect." His tone became mocking. "It was not only her who was aroused in your secret meetings, dear brother, or so she has told me. Oh yes, Sar has told me all about them! And you really think I did not know?"

"Did you put her up to it, all of it?" Danial asked in fury. "The dress, the things she said to me? Was it all to torture me just that extra bit, you bastard?"

"No," Devlin said, his tone again seemingly sad. "She feels genuine love for you. And that must end tonight." He paused. "I know you want her. This is your one chance. I will not offer again, Danial." He paused. "Unless you are so out of practice that a real woman to fuck would be too much for you to handle?"

"As if I ever had that problem," Danial sneered. "It was you who had to relearn fucking, after Ulysses all but gelded you." He paused. "Are you going to watch me have her?"

I managed to raise my head, enough to see the two brothers facing one another.

"Of course." Devlin leaned on the wall, his golden eyes glowing faintly red.

"Ever the voyeur." Danial moved towards me, unzipping his pants. "You sure, brother?" he added in a low voice, as he removed them. "If you're looking for me to do anything more than fuck her and drink her, it's not going to happen. I'm not going to draw it out for your pleasure."

I dropped my head, my feelings conflicted. *I get to have Danial one last time, for what it's worth. Do I want him like this, though? Not unless I can move.* I carefully concentrated, moving my head until the charm resting on my neck was in my mouth. I bit down on the delicate chain, severing it, then spat the charm out discreetly onto the bed beside me. Immediately, I felt my strength returning, though I was still weak from blood loss.

"Do anything to her you like," Devlin said casually, then his tone hardened to iron. "But don't attempt to hurt her or turn her." His voice turned conniving. "And by the way, it was her who asked me to get that dress of Sar's out for her to wear, after I told her the story of how you met Sar. She had a fantasy of you seeing her in it, and loving her instantly, which she admitted to me tonight."

I mustered my strength, angry again at Danial and Devlin both. *If this is goodbye, yes I want Danial one last time. But afterwards I'm going to knee him in the balls.* I grabbed hold of the bed, and pretended feebleness to drag myself away, but Danial grabbed hold of me by my hair, pulling me with a yell back towards him. "So you thought to wear Sar's dress, to draw me to you?" he said in a low menacing tone. "You are nothing like her, Lady. Or should I even call you a lady, after what you did to me?"

"You wanted it," I hissed at him, my green eyes glittering with anger. "You wanted me. Deny it all you want, you and I both know the truth."

"So you want me, do you?" he said, his cool breath on my neck. "Well, I aim to please."

Danial slid inside me with a grunt. I let go an involuntary sigh when I felt him enter me, because it was him, and I loved him, even if he was being a prick.

Danial heard me groan, and immediately withdrew. "You desire me, even like this?" he said, incredulous. "No wonder my brother's so taken with you."

"You desire me, even like this," I retorted. "Or else you wouldn't be rock hard, would you? Take me, vampire, if you have the balls to."

Danial took a sharp intake of breath, and then he rammed himself back into me, thrusting hard. He slid his hands under my clothes, gripping my breasts. I reached up and gripped his hips hard as he bent his head to my neck, and bit down. As he swallowed, Danial began to groan, his hands no longer hurtful as they caressed me, his thrusts deeper and less frantic.

I pushed the pain away with effort, trying to concentrate on Danial's body in mine, on his hands squeezing my breasts, and the sounds of sheer need that was long denied suddenly being fulfilled that he was making for me. I felt my climax building, and relief flooded me, as the first orgasm washed through my body, a moan tearing free of my lips as I clasped his hips to mine hard.

A second later, Danial came with a soft gasp. He collapsed on me, still drinking, even as he finished, his body contracting a few times as he spent himself in me. Immediately, he pulled out of me and rolled off, then came an audible snap of rubber, as he removed a condom.

I let out a long satisfied sigh, keeping my eyes closed even as I felt my anger return. Danial hated condoms and had no reason to wear one, other than to put another layer of distance between us.

Danial leaned down over me, resting one hand on the bed to brace himself. "You've had me now," he whispered in a satisfied yet bitter tone. "All of me you'll ever have, Lady. Don't worry, your snake lover won't know this happened, unless you tell him yourself. And I wouldn't advise it, knowing how he feels about me." He leaned in so I felt his breath on my ear. "I hope it was everything you wanted it to be."

"It was good, but brief like usual," I said mockingly, not opening my eyes. "Don't worry, Dev can take it from here." I opened my eyes, then sat up and faced him, fury flooding me as I looked into his beautiful yet cold dark eyes. "Goodbye, Danial."

I saw sudden hurt flash in his eyes before they bled to red, then he left, the sound of the door slamming loudly behind him.

It registered suddenly that Danial'd had me, and not let me enjoy it, to the best of his ability. *And you hurt him, too, with what you said in parting.* Tears formed in my eyes, and I brushed at them. Devlin lay down beside me, naked, and gathered me into his arms. "Shh, Love," Devlin said quietly. "I'm here." He kissed me gently, then opened his mouth on mine. My lips parted in surprise, and I tasted warm maple sugar on my lips.

God! I grabbed his head with both hands, my mouth feeding at his. Devlin groaned, and rolled onto his back, moving me to straddle him, his organ hard as steel against my clit. I swallowed him in long pulls as I begin rubbing my wet center against his thick hot shaft, as he moaned loudly beneath me in time to my thrusts. When he slipped inside me, I barely registered how good it felt to be filled, I was so close already to climax. *His blood is everything, better than chocolate, or love, or sex, or anything!*

Devlin ripped free from my clutches, throwing his head back as he arched his hips up to meet mine. "Ah, Sar! God, please! My Love, take me, drink me, love me!" Devlin's words were full of yearning, desire, and need, so much sheer need. "Take everything of me you want!"

I moaned then pressed my torso closer, fitting my head in the hollow of his neck and shoulder, kissing his neck. Suddenly my kiss became a light love bite, then a true forceful bite as my teeth slid through his skin and I found more of what I craved. I bit his throat harder. Dev convulsed under me, arching his back again, even as more of his blood flooded my mouth. I orgasmed hard, drinking deep as we came together, Dev's screams of pure satisfaction almost deafening. It was as if I'd exploded with desire, the climax was so strong. *I need more!* I bit down still harder, trying for more of his blood. Devlin gasped, and came again, another loud scream of pleasure breaking free of him as he arched up into me, his hips pumping wildly.

Then he pushed me back from him forcefully, even as I fought him, snarling. "Stop, Sar!" Devlin shouted. "Please, Love, stop!"

I fought him, and he shoved me back, holding me down. I struggled, my heart beating wildly, my one thought that I had to have more of him. *I don't want to stop, not ever, not until—!*

"Stop or you'll turn!" Dev shouted. "Stop, please, Love!"

I went utterly still, looking up at Dev, my eyes went wide with fear. With a trembling hand, I reached up for my teeth. I cut my hand immediately. My teeth weren't just unnaturally sharp, as they had been last time I'd had a lot of vampire blood. They were longer, and curved. They were fangs.

I had fangs.

Chapter Nine

I burst into tears. Devlin got up from beside me, and when I saw he was dressing, I bawled harder. *This is it, I'm a vampire, I've lost the sun forever and all because I couldn't control myself. You're so fucking stupid Sar! You know better! Why didn't you stop?*

He came back to me fully dressed, and gathered me into his embrace. "Shh, love. You are not vampire, though you are closer than you have ever been, it's true. But please, calm yourself. You are still human and safe."

"Why?" I got out, then cut my tongue on my teeth. I swallowed, and probed the wound with my tongue, feeling it rapidly healing as the sharp pain receded. In ten seconds, I was healed.

I looked at Devlin in depression, as he handed me a pen and paper. "Don't try to talk, Love," he advised. "Your teeth will revert soon, as your body handles my blood. Tell me what you need."

"Why did you dress?" I wrote.

"To give you an impediment, if you tried to bite me again." he said, brushing away my hair. "I thought you might, and you should have no more of it for a good while." He went to the back of the door, and grabbed my robe, helping me put it on.

"Why did you do this—what you did with Danial?" I wrote.

"I needed help to draw out your blood."

I gave him a "try again" look.

"Sar, if I take more than a certain amount, I become as you did, almost crazed. Then I want to take it all, the drive is strong, terribly strong to do that. You saw me with Krystin; the desire doesn't ebb until the change is complete. And doing this with you, I knew it would be walking a fine line already. I knew I wouldn't want to stop you drinking from me. I knew I'd have to wait to love you until I gave you my blood,

113

or risk losing control. I couldn't risk taking any more than I did. Danial's arrival was timed to help me remember to stop—"

"Why not Lash, then?" I wrote. "Lash, not Danial?"

"He would not have let me do this with you, knowing how risky it is. He does not want Danial to remember you, as you've probably already deduced, or for him to be your lover again. And it had to be Danial, as you wanted him."

"Bullshit! Try again," I wrote.

"I wanted it to be just you and me," Devlin said, a little sadly. "I share so much of you with Lash already, Love. I wanted to experience this with you, just us sharing blood."

Liar! "And?" I wrote.

"And I can not give you Danial as he used to be with you, Love. But I knew if I made it seem a punishment, he would have you. I knew also once he began sex with you, his body would remember yours, that the experience would for you be close to how you two were together. You once told me you enjoyed sex even if you didn't climax every time. I also knew that no matter how angry he was, Danial at his worst wouldn't hurt you."

"He did hurt me," I scribbled. "He was like another man. He didn't care about me at all. He was so cold!"

"That is the man he is now," Devlin said, hugging me. "That is the man he always was, with every woman he didn't love. You have never seen it before personally, but likely got glimpses of his behavior with other women like his donors: polite, but cold and self-absorbed, even in his lust. Danial was this way with most women, over the years. This is the way he was with Angelica. I was there, and saw how he treated her. She often did not come during sex with him, as he didn't care enough for her to wait for her."

"Don't say her name." I wrote, and underlined it.

"I thought doing this, hard as it might be to experience, would help you forget what you had with him, and see him for who he is now." Devlin sighed. "He's back to the way he was before he met you, Love. I know he still loves Elle, and T, and even his cat, Briar, but his despair has hold of him as if it never left." He reached out for me, and I recoiled, so he took his hand back. "I was wrong to hope he'd begin a new relationship with you, when it's clear he only wanted to use you to hurt me, as he used Anna years ago."

"Did you suspect that?" I wrote.

"No," he replied. "I believed him to be falling in love with you slowly." His eyes narrowed. "But as he was not, it is better this way, Love. Now, he'll stay away from you, and you will be able to let him go." He paused. "I only wanted to help, to give you a last coupling and a means to let Danial go."

I felt a wave of tiredness, mixed with hopelessness. Yet it was pointless to wish I had never come to Dev with my pain, or went along with his plan to heal my heart. What we had done to Danial had just given me another new hurt that needed healing. And I had my own stupidness to blame for going along with his plan, and giving into my frustration and anger. "You hurt me, doing this," I wrote, and underlined it a few times. "It doesn't matter how much I liked the sex with you after, Dev! What you did was wrong."

"Then I'm sorry, Love," Devlin said quietly. "I'd hoped to make you feel better about losing him, and give you some good sex in the bargain. I tried my best to give you what you asked for. You do see that, don't you?"

I stared at him, incredulous.

"Sleep," Devlin said, helping me to lie down near him. "I will remain dressed, though I believe you are past any uncontrollable urges."

I nodded and closed my eyes, resolved not to sleep in spite of my exhaustion. As soon as Devlin slept that night, I went into the bathroom and called Lash. He had left me a number, in case of absolute emergencies.

He picked up on the first ring. "Sar?"

Talk slowly. Very slowly. "Lash...where...are...you?"

"Why are you talking so slow?" Lash hissed, worry and anger in his words. "What's wrong?"

"Where?" I said a little desperately. "Please!" I winced, as I cut myself again on my teeth. *Fuck!*

"That motel in Penn., where you stayed with Theo," Lash hissed, still upset. "What's—?"

I hung up and teleported, arriving outside in the parking lot, just in time to avoid being run over by an exiting car. *Fuck!*

I walked to the side door entrance. Lash there behind the glass, waiting for me. He let me in, and I grabbed hold of him, crying hard.

He pried me off him. "What's wrong?" he shouted, his words panicked and loud. "Damn it, answer me!"

A door opened behind him. "What's going on?" an irritated voice asked.

"Fuck off, before I fuck you up!" Lash retorted. The door closed with a sharp click.

He turned back to me, opening his mouth to yell again. I bared my fangs to him, and Lash froze. He closed his eyes, shifted halfway to snake, and put out his forked tongue, tasting the air for several long seconds, his snake eyes staring at me. "You smell strongly of vampire," he hissed finally. "And close to turning. But you still smell of human, Sweetness."

I nodded, relieved again at the confirmation.

"Come with me." Lash led me to his room. When we got there, he closed and locked the door. He brought me to the bed, and kicked off his shoes, putting his weapons in their usual places. Then he brought me under the covers with him, his clothes still on, and hugged me. "He gave you too much of his blood, because you were having sex?"

I nodded.

Lash swore, paused, then swore again. "Shh, I'm here, Sweetness. Rest and relax. In the morning, we'll go back."

Comforted, I held him tightly and fell asleep.

* * * *

In the morning when I woke, I was relieved to feel my teeth had reverted to normal, though they were still a little sharp. But at least I could talk again.

I touched Lash gently on his hand, waking him. "I'm sorry for scaring you," I whispered.

"I'm sorry you were scared," he hissed irritably. "I was worried he'd do this, when I wasn't around to help pry you off him. Someone has to be there who is not feeling like it's too good to stop, or next time he will turn you, Sar. Because there will always be a next time. And each time

116

it's going to be harder to stop."

"I don't want there to be a next time," I whispered. "Not without you right there."

"Then why did you agree to do it?" Lash asked petulantly. "Why didn't you wait for me to come back?"

"I didn't know what he was going to do," I admitted, not wanting to go into Danial's role. "I thought it was going to be something else. But it wasn't what I wanted, not at all."

"Dev is twisted, when it comes to sex," Lash hissed in resignation. "He always has been, at least a little. Just refuse him his games, Sar. That or get him to tell you exactly what will happen, all of it. He will tell you, if you ask him. It's an unwritten rule, that he not lie."

There was something dark about this, something in Lash's tone that spoke to a pact of some kind between Devlin and him. "What do you mean?"

"Never you mind," Lash said sternly. "Just do it."

Don't ask more. It's just going to be another thing you'll want to forget, once you know it. "Okay," I whispered.

"You know, even if you were vampire, I'd still love you," Lash hissed quietly. "It's okay, if it's something you want, Sar. Nothing would change between us, even if you turned."

"No," I said, shivering at the thought of my fangs of last night being permanent. "I like the sun, Tryst. I like walking with you, and the dogs. I like that I'm warm for you. I hate the feel of fangs in my mouth."

"Good, because I like kissing you like this," Lash hissed gently, and then his tongue slipped into my mouth, and stroked me gently. I kissed him back, feeling like it had all been a bad dream.

His cell phone began to ring. Lash broke the kiss, and answered. "Yes, Dev?" Pause. "She's here, Dev, and she's fine. She was just scared." Pause. "We'll be coming back soon, as soon as we get some breakfast." Pause. "Okay."

He handed the phone to me.

"I'm sorry I left," I said, trying to muster an apologetic tone in my voice. "I panicked."

"It's okay," Dev said soothingly. "Have some breakfast, and return. It was good you went to him, otherwise you might have bitten me again as I slept—"

Ass! I clenched my teeth together, lest I say anything condemning him for his irresponsible actions.

"I was too relaxed afterwards, and I apologize, for falling asleep so fast. I'm sorry, too, if I scared you, Oathed One," Devlin said gently. "My intentions were good ones."

"I know they were," I lied. "I love you. We'll be home soon." I clicked the off button, then tossed the cell phone over the side of the bed to the floor.

"Why did you lie?" Lash hissed, getting up and grabbing the phone from the floor. "I heard it in your voice, that you weren't telling the truth. And you're throwing things, too. He didn't mean to hurt you."

I said nothing.

Lash grabbed hold of me roughly. "What else did he do or say, that made you think he meant to hurt you?"

I didn't need to hear the anger and worry in his tone, or see the venom as it spattered off the end of one of his forming snake fangs to know Lash was upset. But to admit what I'd wanted with Danial was sure to hurt him, just like Danial had alluded it would. "I just…I never meant…"

"What happened last night, Sar? Tell me, and don't leave out anything."

I told Lash what had happened, all of it, in a flat tone. The truth was I had been scared last night. While I was certain Devlin wouldn't ever do something to me that would scar or kill me, that left a hell of lot of leeway, because Dev's definition of what was allowable pain wasn't my definition of that word. There was much he could heal, with just a bit of his blood.

Lash hugged me after I finished, remaining quiet for a minute. Then he said reluctantly, "Do you want me to go away with you, help you leave him?"

"No," I whispered. "I need to be with V. Everything we have is there, Lash."

"All I care about is you, Sweetness," Lash hissed, his arms tight around me. "If we are leaving him, there is no better time than this one. I've been paid in cash for this deal, and together with what I've saved

118

from working this year, we'd have enough to hide ourselves, and to live on for at least a year or so, until I got another day job."

"No," I stated. "We have to go back. I need to go back, for V, for my pets. I gave my word, Lash; I can't break it." I took a breath, willing myself to be resolute. "I know that deep down, he really didn't mean to hurt me. I was just scared."

And you and I need him, or I'll be hunted down and killed by hunters, or taken by someone else for worse purposes. Without his blood, I'll age. And without drinking my vampire-tainted blood, you'll die.

Lash glanced at me, then looked away quickly, before my eyes met his. "Ok," he said, and sighed. "Ok, Sar."

* * * *

We arrived home a few hours later to find Devlin waiting for us, with V. She ran into my arms, and I picked her up.

"You're getting too big to pick up," I said lovingly.

"Where were you?" she said angrily. "I wanted to show you something, and you weren't here! Dad said he didn't know where you'd gone!"

"Show me now," I said with a smile. "I'd love to see."

She took me to her room, and showed me a massive house she'd built, all of wooden blocks. It was good, and I told her so. For a while we played together, and then we took Ghost for a short walk. After that, we went to visit the horses in the stable, bringing them some apples. About noon, we had some lunch. Devlin joined us, as we ate.

"Are you okay?" he said, coming to me, but not touching me. "Lash gave me an earful this morning, and then a few fistfuls."

Great. "I'm okay," I said carefully. "I was just scared, Dev. If I'd known what you were going to do ahead of time, I wouldn't have done it."

"I can't take it back, Love," Devlin said seriously. "Tell me what you'd have me do to make it up to you."

I remembered Lash's words. "Please, tell me your plans, when we roleplay, or do a fantasy. Tell me everything, so I can decide for myself if it's something I want to do."

Devlin nodded. "Ask, Love, and I'll always tell you. I promise."

119

I knew my choker had heard his promise, and so I relaxed some, as his cool arms encircled me. "I'm glad you're back," he whispered. "I was going to have to send Titus to track you both down, I was missing you so much. I knew when I awoke that you had to be with Lash."

By his tone, he was smiling. I smiled back at him, but felt a chill at his possessive words. *He means it, literally.* "I was just scared. But Lash talked me through it, until the fangs faded." Which brought me to a question. "Do you cut yourself, when you talk?"

Devlin smiled ruefully. "Often, if I'm angry. That is why my words are so measured, Sar. It is not all of it just that I'm used to another style of speaking. But they heal easily, being small cuts."

"But they hurt a lot. The fangs are so sharp. Does it get easier?"

"Fang cuts always hurt," Dev said sadly. "But with practice, it becomes easier. Singing was hard, for a long time. Kissing was hard to re-learn too."

"How do you kiss me, and not hurt yourself? Because you have never cut me, at least, when you didn't mean to."

"Most of my kisses are gentle ones," Devlin said, smiling widely. "And truthfully, when I'm feeling passionate, or making love with you, I don't care if I cut myself a little. It heals, as I said, and much faster than yours do. But I do take care not to cut you."

"How?"

"The same way you take care not to cut me or Lash with your teeth, if you kiss us intimately."

I flushed a little, nodded, and changed the subject.

Later that night, I went into the reading room that was mine, and sat for a while, thinking. I had a lot to think about.

Lash had asked me about ten months ago if this was what I'd wanted from my life. And when I'd Oathed to Dev and he, I'd thought I'd finally decided what I wanted. When I'd held Lash in that hotel room back in January, I'd been certain of it.

Yet I'd understood something clearly last night. Devlin was still the person he'd always been. That person had a good side, sure, and I didn't doubt his love for me. But I was always going to have to be careful with him, to only trust him so far, because if I gave him free rein, he was going to hurt me, because that was the kind of man he was.

And Lash...Lash was the same. I could call him Tryst, sure, but the truth was that no matter who he'd once been, Lash was who he was now. He'd been living in Devlin's shadow for decades, and it had warped him, changed him from the good-hearted and innocent boy he was to a decisive assassin. Having heard the story of his childhood, I wondered that his father hadn't begun that with all he'd done to him, trying to make his son another copy of himself.

Lash wasn't going to stop drinking. He wasn't ever going to be anything more than what he was right now. Neither was Devlin. They were never going to grow up, and stop partying.

Part of me had gotten a thrill that long ago day with Devlin, thinking that making love with me had changed him, as he had vowed that it had. But I hadn't changed him at all, just as my being with Lash later hadn't changed him. Love could only do so much, even if our first months of being in love had put them both on their best behavior for a while.

But we were Oathed now, which was something like married. None of us were going anywhere anytime soon, and the three of us knew that. So the real people that we had always been under the good behavior were starting to emerge again.

Yes, honestly, I was the same as they. I was always going to set free live animals I knew were destined for Lash's gullet, and I was always going to be bothered by Devlin's sexual appetites. I was always going to worry about V, and Elle, and wonder if I'd done the right thing, by staying with Devlin, and not trying to be cougar, as Theo'd wanted me to do. I was always going to remember I killed more than one person in cold blood and feel bad about it, even if they'd deserved it.

I couldn't change them, either of them. But I could change myself, if I wanted a life with them. I could tell myself that this was who they were, and accept it, and stay with them. Or I could tell them it was over, and try to leave. That was one decision that couldn't be put off any longer.

Chapter Ten

I thought about my situation for several more hours, and didn't come to any big epiphany. I thought about calling Rene, but decided against it. I knew she'd try to convince me to stay with Devlin, no matter what.

I went into the living room. *Enough thinking for one night. You need a break. Maybe there's something good on...*

V ran in, looking panicked. "Bobbie said to tell you there are strangers in the backyard. He's running to find Lash! He said for us to run!"

Fear enveloped me in a rush. I lunged at V and grabbed her, just as a bullet smacked into the doorframe, making a crater where her tiny head had been a moment ago.

V let out a scream, and I pushed her behind me, as an angry looking woman came through the doorway. She was dressed in camouflage, her face painted black and green. "I have orders to kill you," the woman said, her dark eyes angry, training her gun from V to my chest. "You must be mom, the bitch who is lover to that fiend—"

I tried to teleport V and myself, and failed. *Fuck!* "Stay back!" I said, keeping a whimpering V behind me desperately. "Get back!"

An explosion rocked the room from underground. There was an awful scream, then muted guttural roaring. The woman took a step, went rigid, and then collapsed.

Lash appeared behind her body, his gun smoking. "Come, quickly!" he hissed. "Dev is waiting!"

We ran outside. The clash of fighting bodies and sounds of automatic weapons, and bears roaring echoed through the air, the cacophony rising as the smell of burning wood deepened, the dusky air around us turning murky with smoke.

We ran to the edge of the pond, and Devlin emerged quickly from behind Lash's rock, when he saw it was us.

"Dev, get out of here!" Lash hissed, pushing me towards him. "Take her and V and go! I've got to get back and fight!"

"Daddy!" V shouted, reaching for him.

"Shh! No!" Devlin said, grabbing V from me. "I need you to guard her, Lash. I can't guard them both, and there is something blocking teleporting, or Sar would already be gone!"

"I tried, he's right," I gasped. "We need to run! Where is Danial? Serena?"

"He got out, I think," Devlin said. "They would have him out here nailed on that cross, waiting for the morning sun, if he hadn't, then erected another one for me."

I looked. A huge cross was impaled into the front lawn of Hayden. What chilled me most was that right beside it was a smaller version of it. I knew who that tiny cross was meant for. *God, the monsters!*

"Okay," Lash hissed. "We'll split up. Dev, you and V go through the forest. Sar and I will follow the tunnel, then we'll meet up—"

"What about my pets?" I shrieked. "Ghost is in there! My cats! I can't leave them! I won't!"

"Damn it! Take her!" Lash hissed angrily. "I'll get the dog, if I can!" He turned and ran back towards the house.

"My cats, they'll kill them!" I went to go after Lash. "I can't just leave them behind to burn!"

"Phantom has his own escape route," Devlin said quickly, pulling me with him. "Did you never wonder how he seemed to come and go outside at will? There is more than one. Your cats have learned to use it in the past year, Sar, most likely they are all in the forest safe. But we can't go back for them, or we'll die. The hunters aren't here for our cats. You know who that smaller cross was for. Come on!"

I cried and blubbered, but I ran with him away from my burning home and into the forest, towards an old stonework wall. Devlin moved aside a few stones, and passed his hand over the opening. The stonework abruptly vanished, leaving a black hole into the earth full of darkness. We went in, and then Devlin crouched over, setting V down. I huddled next to him.

We waited in silence for about ten minutes. Then someone approached, running fast. Lash appeared, with Ghost at his heels. I hugged my dog, briefly checking him. There was more than a little blood on his flanks and wagging tail.

"It's not his, though a bullet meant for me clipped his paw," Lash said, grabbing up V, and handing her to Devlin. "It's cauterized. Now, run!"

We ran down the tunnel, Devlin and V first, then Lash and I, Ghost following. Soon we passed dead werebears. The odor of burnt flesh was strong.

"They used fire," he hissed angrily. "They trapped them in their animal forms, and burned a few. And the rest ran."

"Why?" I asked. "They heal easily."

"All animals are afraid of fire. These bears are in their twenties, the oldest thirty-four or so. They used flamethrowers, Sar. The bears had no training like I had; they couldn't steel themselves and fight on while their flesh burned."

I cringed as I followed him through the dark earth. Suddenly, I felt a sharp stab on my ankle, and stumbled, letting out a cry. Ghost growled fiercely, and Lash whipped around and fired in a split second. I saw a dark form fall, and saw it was a woman, her braided hair shiny and blonde. She was dead, a bullet hole right between her eyes.

"Are you hurt?" Lash asked, helping me to my feet.

I tried to put weight on my ankle, but it wouldn't hold me. "There's no pain."

"She sliced your tendon, with poison on the blade," Lash hissed. "Hold still." He tried to support me, and I managed a few lurching steps before falling. Lash grabbed hold of me and threw me up on his shoulder, his gun still in his one free hand. "Hold onto me," he said sharply. "I have to have my one hand free, to shoot!"

We made it out of the tunnel a half-minute later, me gripping him the best I could, my muscles already protesting and my blood rushing to my head. Lash took off into the forest after Devlin, following twists and turns, Ghost beside us. We reached a tree that leaned slightly to one side, and stopped. We waited a few minutes there, catching our breath and me trying not to be dizzy, before we started off again.

"Think the emergency Hummer is still there?" Dev said wearily to Lash.

"Most likely," Lash hissed back. "Shut up and save your energy."

We took two steps and then I was abruptly jolted from Lash's arms. I landed on my injured leg, and let out another shriek, as pain ripped through me.

Everyone stopped. Lash looked around for a target, his gun in hand. But there was no one around.

What the hell happened? It was like something had grabbed me. I tried to get to my feet, but couldn't because of my ankle. I crawled forward, and abruptly bonked my head. I put my hands up, and they met something my eyes couldn't see. There was some kind of barrier in the air.

Dev was on his cell, but he quickly flipped it shut with a curse. "I can't raise Titus." He came to me, and tried to reach me, but the barrier held him out. We were what appeared to be opposite sides of an invisible glass wall. "Can you teleport, Love?"

I tried and failed. I shook my head. "No!"

"Stand back, Dev," Lash hissed. "Sar, get down."

I lay flat, and I heard him fire. The shot hit the barrier, and ricocheted, clipping a nearby branch. Leaves showered down.

"Magic," Devlin said bitterly. "A magical prison."

"Go, Dev," Lash hissed suddenly. "I'll stay with her. Go!"

"No!" Devlin said stubbornly, his hands splayed on the glass, V beside him, clinging to his leg. "I won't leave her!"

"They're after you most of all, you and V! They'll kill you! They don't know Sar can teleport! When they get here, I'll have her teleport us to Florida, or somewhere, as soon as they take the spell off to access her!"

"I'm not leaving her!" Devlin said again, his talons growing. He raked at the barrier but it held, even when he pushed at it with all of his strength.

"Go," a worn voice coughed out. "They're right behind me!"

I looked over to see Kyle come up, breathing heavily.

"Who's coming?" Lash hissed. "Who attacked us, Hector or Peter?"

"Both of them, and a shitload of hunters," Kyle said, shooting a look behind him. "That's why they acted so stupid when they attacked you before, Lash! They'd been planning this since V was born! They were testing you, to see where you were weakest!"

The futile scouting party in the fall, the attack on David's wedding party! It all clicked into place. *God, he's right. Just like Terian and Ulysses, Hayden's weak link had been Titus, on whom all Hayden's defenses rested. Peter had even sacrificed his own relative, just to get the means to kill Devlin.*

"Go, Dev!" I yelled. "He's right, they'll kill her! Take Ghost and go!"

Devlin gave me an anguished look, picked up V, and ran. I saw the gold of her hair, and her wail for me as he carried her into the trees, Ghost running after them.

"I'll protect them till my last breath," Kyle said to Lash. "You have my word." He ran into the trees.

Lash looked after them in worry and I could see how much he wanted to go with them, to make sure they were safe. Then he turned back to me, and put both his palms on the prison, and pushed. He leaned into it, grinding his teeth with effort, pushing, and then with astonishment, I saw his hands push through. The rest of his body and his weapons followed slowly, and then he was inside with me. He went to his knees, and brought me into his lap. I clutched him like a liferope, and he hugged me tightly.

"How did you do that?" I asked.

"It was meant to keep you in, and Dev out. But I'm neither vampire nor human." He paused. "I was carrying you when it hit you, and was inside with you. That's the story you tell. Got it?"

I nodded. "I'm scared," I stated, even though it was obvious.

"I'm right here, Sweetness," Lash hissed gently. "Anyone wanting to hurt you is going to have to go through me to do it. Be ready to teleport. I'm good, but I'm no match for fifty men or so. And by the sound, there's an army coming towards us through the trees."

He was right. First came light from searchlights, then a large group of armed men and women coming, two men leading them. They had not only guns, but also crossbows, and huge devices with tanks on treaded large wheels that I guessed were flamethrowers. They gave shouts when

126

they saw us huddled on the ground, and began to run toward us. Then, everything froze.

I gave a sigh of relief. "Thank God, Titus—"

"No," Lash hissed angrily, tightening his grip on me. "Not Titus."

Chapter Eleven

A familiar voice said, "Sarelle?" Michael appeared near the edge of the prison, his clothing dirty and in disarray. "Are you hurt?"

"Release us!" Lash hissed, baring his fangs at Michael.

"Certainly," Michael said. "Cyrus?"

Samuel's sorcerer, who had been ready to force me into a life of breeding female on command. The same sorcerer who had bespelled Theo to make him love another woman, and changed my life forever, along with Elle's. I turned, feeling a wave of hate, and saw my old nemesis. The wizard was ancient, as withered as an old brown flower in February. He looked like Merlin out of the fables, with a long white beard, a staff, and a small winged demon-looking thing perched on his shoulder, dressed in a brown hooded monk's robe. He cut a door in our cage with a few gestures of his staff, and Lash carried me out.

"Hold still," Michael said. He pulled out one of my head hairs, and gave it to Cyrus. The wizard used it to make another of me, some form of doppelganger, and soon I was looking at my twin, right down to my hurt leg and torn dress.

Damn, what I wouldn't have given to know that spell to have helped Rene. I shivered, knowing that for Cyrus to have done it so easily, he commanded a much greater power than anyone else I'd likely ever known, maybe even Titus or Shaker.

"Come," Michael said, extending his hand to me. "We'll take you to safety."

"No," Lash insisted. "We must find Devlin and V first."

"There is no time!" Michael hissed at him. "Bring her! She is hurt, and we must leave!"

"Have your sorcerer kill the hunters!" Lash hissed back at him. "We are not leaving without Devlin."

"They need to think they caught her, and killed her!" Michael replied. "This attack was aimed at her and her child, Lash. You know that!"

"Stop arguing!" Cyrus said with effort, even as he healed my cut tendon unbidden, sealing the wound as if it had never happened. "She must be found, Lash, she was their goal. Dev and V are gone, and if the mob is not sated, there will be hell to pay. You know killing Hector and Peter, not to mention all their men, will lead a trail straight to Devlin's door. One murder can be covered up, but not the murder of hundreds in a single night."

"And making martyrs of both of those 'heroes' would mean riots, and many more dead vampires, and humans," Michael added. "There would be war, and maybe the world we live in would be exposed—"

"Fuck them!" Lash hissed. "Fuck everything! We've held the truce for years, and not just obliterated them, as we should've. What's it gotten us? They're changing the rules and attacking Rulers!"

"No, Sar and Danial changed it," Michael said softly, reaching out to touch my hair. "She and Theoron changed things, but even then, it was passed off as a fluke, when Harriet couldn't replicate what happened, and her children didn't look human, even if their blood said they were dhamphir. The discovery of Venus's existence was the breaking point. That his old enemy could have a child that looked so beautiful, that could walk in the daylight...Peter went mad." Michael took my hand. "Come, Sarelle. We must leave now."

He began leading me away toward the forest. Lash grabbed my other arm, and followed, Cyrus walking behind us.

Michael guided me. "The humans think if they kill her, they'll set the status quo back to how it was, that things will go back to the way they were, when only those with a century or more of living as changed men were strong enough to make more of our kind—"

"What?" I asked.

"It takes the virus that long to mature in our systems," Michael explained. "We have the superior strength and weaknesses right away, as soon as we're turned. But true power takes longer to generate. The exception is drinking older blood of a mature vampire, and even then, the power is not the same. In fact, often a young one dies trying that, as the old blood is too potent a mix for them to—"

"Enough with the vampire history lesson! Get us out of here!" Lash hissed angrily.

"Yes, we must leave now," Cyrus intoned. "My strength is rapidly ebbing. I cannot hold time for much longer. We should teleport now."

Michael turned to him. "Then take us back now, please."

We were suddenly in an unfamiliar room. "Rest," Michael said, and he and Cyrus walked to the door. "I'll contact Devlin and leave word that you are here—"

Lash is right, fuck that! I went after them. "I need to speak to him, make sure he got V out! My phone was left behind—"

"Rest now, please. I'll call immediately, and come to you when he responds." Cyrus and Michael left, shutting the door behind them. I went after them and tried the door, but it was locked. I tried also to teleport to my mom's house, but was blocked.

"I can't teleport," I said, turning to Lash. "Do you think Michael will make the call? Something's off about this."

"Fucking yeah, something's off. I'm calling Dev right now," Lash hissed. He took out his phone, and a moment later he was leaving a message, saying we were with Michael, and to call ASAP. He made several other calls, but got no reply to Titus, Kyle, Shaker, or even Rene's phone.

For a while Lash and I paced, not talking, too nervous to be still. Yet as the night wore on, exhaustion overcame us, and the large bed was comfortable, and inviting. Once I sat down, I lay down shortly after. Then it was morning, Lash shaking me awake.

"Dev called. He and V are safe. Ghost has been healed by Titus—"

"What about—"

"Hayden was partly burned. But most of it's intact. The bears rallied, under Seth and Nick. Bobbie got through to them, he raised the alarm—"

"Danial? My God, what about Serena?"

"Serena spent a good portion of the night in the dungeon hiding, but she's okay. Danial also made it out, and he's fine, too. Except for some singed fur, all of the cats are okay too."

We saw dead werebears on our tunnel walk, at least ten. I knew there had to have been more casualties, and swallowed. "How many died?"

"Thirty, including three females. The hardest hit was the bear quarters nearest the deep woods, where the hunters attacked first. Valerie was the only one I think you knew—"

I closed my eyes and said a quick prayer for her, bitch that she had been. "Is Jazz?"

"Coping," Lash said flatly. "And of course, Peter and Hector were not among the hunters killed. But over fifty hunters died, which is easily half their force. Thirty more were wounded and captured, and according to Titus, Devlin is working his way through them today, with Danial's help—"

Ugh. "So they are back at Hayden?"

"No, they are staying with T, until they're sure that the tunnels are shorn up. Some were blown apart, in the fighting, when a burning guard ran into an ammunitions storeroom. Leri is working on that, with help from Rip, while Titus rests. The other guards are too busy helping them to guard V."

I breathed a sigh of relief. Everyone I cared for was safe. My pets were safe. *Whew.*

"Devlin said to stay here for now. Michael was right; from the hunters he's tortured and killed, they were after you and V. In fact, V is now staying with Terian at all times at T's house."

"I'm glad things weren't too bad—"

"They were bad, Mate. Nick is badly wounded. And Titus got forced into hell."

"You said he was resting! Is he okay?"

"Leri got him out, with some damage. But it was bad enough that he's resting now in bed."

"How could vampire hunters manage that, sending him to Hell?"

"They had an old priest with them, Leri said. Maybe more than one."

"What priest knows enough magic to banish Titus?"

Lash looked uncomfortable. "Dev said he wasn't sure. There's some debate, with what Leri told him, that the Devil might have had a hand in this."

Shudder. "Why?"

"Because Titus is happy here, he's living the modern demon's fairytale, complete with family, sex, and lots of dead bodies. He's not supposed to eat them dead, Sar, that's against Demon protocol—"

I felt my stomach roll. "Skip that. How could the devil do it?"

"He's Titus's original master. He can recall him back anytime to Hell, Sar, within certain parameters. And it's fact that Titus is not doing what Hell would prefer him to be doing, and hasn't for a long time—"

Shiver. New topic, quick! "But Devlin's okay?"

Lash handed me his phone. "He asked that I have you call him, as soon as you woke up."

Did that count, when he'd been the one to wake me? I took the phone.

Devlin was already on the other end, saying hello. After that, he wasted no time. "Be on your guard, Love," he hissed. "Danial and I are working on finding out if this was Peter's plan or Hector's."

"Danial is helping you?"

"In contrast to how he's been lately, the attack pissed him off in the extreme," Devlin said, sounding pleased. "It's the first emotion besides grief he's displayed, since coming back to us." He paused. "Hayden should be secure by the end of the week. But I am coming to get you tomorrow, Love, and take you to T's. V's already missing you, and I am as well. Now hit speakerphone." His voice got darker, as I hit the button so it echoed in the room. "Lash, when she's safely there, you are going after Peter. I've had enough of his bullshit, no matter if this was his plan or someone else's. Complete demolition."

Lash gave me a sidelong glance, then looked back at his phone. "Everyone?"

"Yes. Every blood relation, and those by marriage, too; every man, woman and child, even his newborn great-granddaughter. Kill them all. And then burn everything with blue fire until there is nothing left but ashes and smoke."

Lash gave me a final look and then away. "Okay, as soon as Sar's safe with you, consider it done."

"We didn't kill humans like this, not ever!" Devlin rasped. "But if he wants a war and blood, I'm going to give him blood, blood enough to drown in!"

"Enough, Dev," Lash said quietly. "Sar doesn't know of everything that's gone down, over the years. This is upsetting her."

"Know this, Love: the reason that everything had happened for the last sixty years is because when I had a chance to end it cleanly, I didn't. That I balked at killing two children, and it has caused me misery ever since. You can't afford another sentimental mistake by me. V can't afford one. Understand?"

"I understand," I whispered.

"Take care, Love," Devlin said gently. "Please, take care of yourself."

I said that I would, and then Lash took the phone back, and hung up.

"Come lay here with me," he hissed softly. "It's barely dawn. You've only slept for a few hours. I'll stay awake, and watch."

Relieved and exhausted both physically and mentally, I fell asleep in his arms.

* * * *

When I awoke, it was late afternoon. Lash was no longer beside me, but in a chair reading across the room. He closed his book, *Grimm's Complete Fairy Tales,* when he saw I was awake. "Are you feeling okay? Does your ankle still hurt?"

I moved it a little. "No. I'm fine. Cyrus did a great job."

"Michael's so flakey," Lash said, sneering as he gestured to the pile of books beside him. "I told him I wanted a book, and he brings me this crap about the enduring mystery of religion. Where's his horror and sci-fi section? Even a good western would do! Who gives a shit what some backwater tribe in the jungle thinks about how man evolved? Someone needs to show them the fucking theory of evolution!" He exhaled deeply. "Thank God at least he had this."

Did the theory of evolution apply to weresnakes? They can't be descended from apes, right? I shook my head to clear it. "We'll be home soon," I said groggily. "Won't we?"

"Yes," Lash hissed. "Another day or so, and Titus will be done with the repairs. But we are going to Danial's tonight, Sweetness."

I had some late breakfast with Lash, though he himself refused to eat

133

or drink anything. The afternoon passed calmly, with us dozing.

But that night, a call from Devlin changed our plans and my outlook. "Don't come back for a few more hours," he said frantically on speakerphone. "There have been large scale attacks all across the world, Sar. Samuel's estate was burned, and though he escaped with the children, Harriet didn't make it."

I swallowed hard and said a prayer for her. "Who else?"

"Perseus was burned, but he got away. Zane managed to kill all of his attackers, though it's only because the smallest force came for him—"

"It's true," Michael interjected, as he entered our room. "My estate was attacked in Asia roughly ten hours ago. It isn't an accident I'm visiting the United States right now. My men have killed them, but they didn't come just for glory, Dalcon. They came for wealth, and for vengeance."

"This has never happened, that Rulers were targeted." Devlin's voice was restrained but furious. "Part of me thinks this is because they are trusting us not to retaliate."

"I've already retaliated," Michael said bitingly. "There is one hunter left alive in all of my lands. And he was appointed by me to keep control of vampires and hunters alike, to ensure a balance between them. He will report to me alone, and I will decide who hunts and whom is hunted. And that is how it will stay."

"You and Zane do not have as large a vampire population as I, Perseus, or Samuel do, Michael," Devlin remarked in a frank tone. "I cannot control a thousand vampires with just one hunter, no matter if he was very good, even among the Ranked. Too many vampires come into being accidentally, or arrive on my shores, to have just one—"

"You could if he was both were, and sorcerer, yes?" Michael interrupted.

"Maybe," Devlin allowed darkly. "Maybe not. Most of the vampires that need to be put down are young, not old, but that doesn't always mean they are stupid—"

"Then you'll have to get off your immortal ass and control them," Michael said sarcastically. We looked at him in surprise, and by his silence, Devlin was shocked too, that Michael has spoken to him like that. "You are a Ruler, Dalcon. It is time you started acting like one, and not like an immortal Hugh Hefner. We must emerge victorious in this struggle. This is too important for us, now that we have Sarelle to protect. She must survive unharmed, no matter what must be done."

"I agree," Lash hissed loudly. "We should strike back fast, and hard. I'll leave for Peter's as soon as Sar is at Danial's."

"Go tonight, immediately," Michael commanded. "Sar will be safe here at my hotel."

Both Devlin and Lash ignored him. "Bring her to Danial's tonight, Lash," Devlin said. "And leave immediately after for Hector's home, and thrash him within an inch of his life. I will go with a few of my constituents and Danial, and punish Peter and his nearest kin myself. It's fitting they should be drained anyway, all of them."

"You are making a mistake, Devlin," Michael said mildly. "Sar should remain here, until you make sure Danial's home is safe. As I understand, it was compromised only months ago."

"Terian is there, and Theo as well. She will be safe enough," Devlin retorted. "We'll leave for Hayden when Lash returns. And I might add that Sar is my Oathed One, my woman to protect, not yours. As much as I might be happy for your assistance, Michael, do not overstep your bounds."

"As you wish," Michael said calmly. "As you say, she is your Oathed One."

"I'll see you in about five hours, Love," Devlin purred. "Lash, watch her."

"Will do," Lash hissed, and hung up. Then he turned to Michael. "Will you bring Sarelle some food? We last ate hours ago."

"Of course," Michael said. "Do you need meat for yourself, as well? I can provide beef or chicken, raw or cooked."

"No," Lash hissed coldly. "I'll eat at Danial's. Thank you."

Michael nodded, and left. Soon, food arrived, mostly comfort food—fries, hamburgers, several glasses of great Shiraz, and even chocolate cake. God, was there nothing he hadn't found out about me? I ate my fill. Lash looked hungrily at the food, but he didn't touch it.

"I don't trust him," he hissed softly in my ear, when he came close to make a show of embracing me. "He will not do anything to you, Sar,

135

but it's better for us if I wait to eat."

I hugged him, and didn't reply, because I thought he was right.

* * * *

The hours seemed to drag while we waited for night to fall. Lash showered briefly, for about a minute and a half, but otherwise he just paced. And my dear mate, who could easily go without food, water, and sleep, reached his breaking point with the one thing he could not go without for long. "Want to do it?" he said, stroking my neck with his tongue. "I really want you, Mate."

"I don't have my pills," I whispered back to him apologetically. I'd been ready to start a new pack two days ago, but with the fighting and problems, I'd not started on time. I knew better than to think Lash wouldn't get me pregnant, if I didn't take them, and risked being with him.

"There are some in the bathroom," Lash hissed softly. "I saw them earlier, when I was in there, among all the other toiletries that Michael provided. And they are your...our brand, Sar. You can start wherever you left off."

I got up, and went to look. Sure enough, there they were, along with several brands of leave-in conditioner, shampoo, conditioner, toothpaste, hairbrush, hand soap, mouthwash, a tray of hair clips and associated hair bands. More toiletries crowded the drawers of all kinds, some brands I'd never heard of before. Other drawers had clothes in the brands I preferred and my size, though not all were in the colors I favored. But I left them alone, and began to brush my teeth, even as I discreetly looked at the pills.

The dream. The nightmare I had just before finding Rene. The pills were part of it. Like the dream, the room I was in was a prison of sorts. While Lash was with me, something was very strange.

Michael might be thoughtful, but this was outside the norm. I felt a cold shiver seeing that rectangle plastic container. Something was not on the level here. No matter that Michael's words had been nice, and he'd been the perfect host, my danger sense was going into overdrive. There was only one logical conclusion: Michael had some plan of his own for me, and it involved me not getting pregnant by Lash.

Yet an easier way to assure that would have been to leave some condoms for Lash. If he was planning to claim me, having me be on the pill would mean he'd have to take more time, waiting for them to clear my system so he could impregnate me himself. Could he be planning to trade me to one of the other Rulers for something?

"Sweetness, what are you doing in there so long? I'm dying out here!"

Michael wasn't supposed to know I was still fertile. He was supposed to think, like everyone else, that I'd had irreversible surgery after birthing my twins, that I couldn't have any more children. But he clearly did know, by these pills being here, and he wanted me not to conceive. Somehow, he'd spied on me, and found out. It wasn't an accident that although there were several different choices for everything a woman might need, there was only one pack of pills. *Michael didn't offer me more than a single brand, the right brand, because he didn't want me to make the wrong choice. Birth control pills come in cases that look nearly identical to one another. Hell, he is probably watching me right now to make sure I take them, maybe even to find out how close I am to the end of my cycle.*

I broke out in a sweat, but kept still, and didn't move, trying to think.

"Do you not want to?" Lash asked hesitantly, from behind me. "I can wait, if you want me to."

Whatever Michael's plan was, I wanted no part of it. And there was only one way not to be part of it, here in his hotel, surrounded by his men. *Get pregnant right now.*

I turned to Lash, and kissed him roughly. He kissed me back, and tried to drag me to the bed, but I pushed him away with a smile. "Not yet! I want to take a shower, Mate. And I need to take my pill. I already missed one this month, last night."

Lash nodded. "Okay. But what were you doing in here so long?"

"Trying hard to remember where I left off!" I responded with a laugh, hoping it didn't sound too brittle and fake. "It's not easy for me to remember. I've had a lot to think about. But get in bed, and I'll be right out, as soon as I shower."

Lash left, and I heard him undressing rapidly. I took off my clothes, and selected the right pill for two and a half weeks ahead of where my schedule really was, after putting the sticker with the days of the week in the right position for my lie to work. *Anyone watching will think I've been taking them for a month, and so missing one isn't a big deal, as I'm at the end of my cycle, almost ready to have my period instead of my reality: having missed the first crucial two 1st week pills after a week of not taking any. If I miss the first week entirely, I'm sure to get pregnant.*

I grabbed the pill I needed to take, while ejecting the rest in the garbage to further enforce my lie. I put it in my mouth, and swallowed, even as I held the pill between my incisor teeth, trying hard to not get any saliva on it.

I turned on the shower, and grabbed the brush, brushing my hair a little frantically, as I waited for the water to heat up. *I should have waited to put the pill in my mouth when I got in the shower! What if I accidentally swallow it?*

As soon as the water was lukewarm, I got in the shower, and let my hair fall forward, covering my face and head. I put my hands up toward my face, brushing my hair back slowly, and spat the pill into my cupped hand.

I stood there under the water, holding the pill in my fist, and trying to make it seem I was luxuriating in the water. Slowly, I felt the pill dissolve. It took more than a few minutes to disappear completely, as I made it seem I was scratching an itch. I felt odd, thinking I was being recorded in here, but better safe than sorry.

I paused as I did my normal routine of conditioning my hair and putting on lotion and deodorant, remembering Michael's comments at the last Hallow's party Danial had last fall. Michael had alluded then that he knew I could be pregnant, that the surgery Dev told everyone I had was a lie. *Am I completely overreacting? If I do get pregnant by Lash, I'm in for another pregnancy that will likely be really hard, maybe even life-threatening.*

I bit my lip. *Anything is safer than having another dhamphir, especially with one of those horrible vampires. And Lash said if we had an accident and I got pregnant, he would want it. I have to trust my gut feelings. And I have to trust him, that he meant what he said.*

Resolved, I went into Lash, who was practically beaming at me from beneath the covers. As usual, his weapons were beside the bed, his knife on the end table.

That first time with Lash, I was a little nervous. I'd thought to be done with children, and here I was getting ready to make another. But it was far better for me to have Lash's child than a vampire's dhamphir. One hadn't really been enough for either Danial or Devlin. If I got pregnant by any of the Rulers, I would never be free again. They would keep me like Harriet had been kept, like a treasured possession for as long as I lived, having child after child. I'd be the brood mare Lash had spoken of the night I'd met him. *No way.*

"Make love to me now, Lash," I whispered seductively. "Please."

Lash shot me a look of surprise. It was not that I'd asked, but that I hadn't waited for him to make the first move.

Lash began kissing me gently. Soon he was kissing me harder, reaching down to move me into position beneath him. He slipped inside me with a grunt, and I felt him kissing up my neck, as he moved in and out of me. "Do you want me to bite you?" he murmured lustily.

By now Lash had likely guessed why I'd wanted him to take my blood, though we never spoke of it. I couldn't ask him if he wanted to, because he'd say "no," that he didn't want to hurt me. As far as the sex went, it didn't do anything for me sexually to be bitten by him, now that The Lust wasn't present. But it had been a week since he'd last had my blood. *I need to give it to him.*

"Please," I said, kissing the side of his face.

Lash slid his slim hooked fangs into my upper shoulder, and I felt a little prick, as he bit me, then him swallowing me down as he loved me. His hands caressed me gently, just as I caressed him.

God, I never got tired of him loving me. Maybe that was the best sign of our love. That no matter how much we knew of each other, he could still surprise me, and I him. That I still wanted him that much, even though we'd made love so many times now, at least once a day since we'd been mated.

Lash moving in me, groaning, as I ran my hands over his back, feeling him contracting on me. I remembered him telling me how much he wanted me to have his child that long ago night, though he had never spoken the words to me again, or even alluded to them. Because of that, I wanted badly to tell him what I was doing, but I couldn't risk it.

He sped up, and soon he was coming hard, spurting into me as he loved me, moaning my name. I held him to me, holding his body so he stayed as far inside me as he could get, until he was done, hoping that his seed was still as potent as it had been months ago. Lash looked at me a little oddly as he grinned at me happily, but I just gave him a smile in return and kissed him chastely, sliding my hands up off his behind to his back and onto his shoulders, to hold him.

"Are you finished with me?" I teased.

"All this time, and you have to ask? You know better! Of course I want you again, my Sweetness," Lash said with a grin.

"Then take me, I'm yours." I kissed him gently, as he began to move in me again.

Sometime later, he grew soft, and then he eased off me, with a contented hiss. "I wish I could stay near you, and just sleep," he said. "I'm exhausted. But we need to leave in an hour or so. You rest, Sweetness. I'll wake you, when it's time to go."

I gave him a kiss, rolled over, and went back to sleep.

* * * *

Sometime later, I woke up alone. I groped for the light, but it would not turn on. Scared, I rose and went to the window, which was oddly not where I remembered it being. It was full dark outside. I ran back to the bed, finding it empty. *Where is Lash?*

I eased towards the bathroom, then stumbled over a low table and cursed.

There was a soft noise to my left.

Scared, I called out softly, "Lash?"

"He's otherwise occupied," a courteous voice said.

"Michael?" I said softly, trying hard not to let my voice tremble.

"It is I," he said gently, as he switched on a light near the door, then came toward me, his long pale robe shining dimly in the gloom.

"Where is he? Why are you here?"

"He's sleeping off the sleeping potion he ingested that was in your blood," Michael said gently. "As for why I'm here, I'm sure you know the answer to that already, Sarelle. You are a smart woman, not a beautiful object that's only purpose is to be admired."

I faced him, livid. "I will not Oath to you. Devlin is expecting me to be at Danial's tonight, and he'll come for me, the second he realizes I'm late!"

"You will not be there for him to find," Michael said loftily. "And neither will I. We are no longer even in the United States. We left earlier tonight by plane, as soon as you both fell asleep. You are in my domain now."

He flipped on another light switch, revealing an unfamiliar and much larger room than the one I'd gone to sleep in. Aside from a large bed and dressers, there was a sitting room, a large TV, and another two doors that were shut. There was a pile of bags and boxes which I assumed was luggage near the door Michael had been standing near.

Michael moved across the room towards me, making it obvious he wore only his robe. His body was thin but well-built, close in build to Danial's. *Perhaps all vampires are like that? No, Samuel hadn't been.*

I attempted to run, but he caught me within a few steps, the touch of his warm hand on mine sending a shudder through me. I withdrew my hand from his with a jerk. "Don't touch me!"

Michael stopped, stepped back one pace, and didn't try to come any closer. "I know you're healed inside. You know how much I want a child of my own, Sarelle. Please agree to let me try with you to make one."

"I will not agree," I said, my voice trembling. "No matter what you do to me."

"You and Devlin think you have decades to think about this, to have other children," Michael said calmly. "But did either of you ever think that through?"

"What are you saying?"

"That a woman is born with all her eggs already created. No matter how young you look, those eggs are going to be older, even if like your body they don't show your true age. And that the more vampire-like you become, the less fertile you'll be." He paused. "I sired a son on my betrothed, when I was only twenty-six. But when I became vampire at thirty-one, I lost the ability, as soon as my fangs grew. It's only with magical help that I will be with you, and have something come of it. Your window is closing fast, Sarelle."

"You can't know that."

"But it's logical, is it not?" Michael's tone was persuasive, but also non-argumentative. "Your child with me will lack for nothing, Sarelle, not even if he or she should outlive me by centuries—"

"I don't want to have a child with you, Michael. Find some other woman."

"Sarelle, I do not want a version of a dhamphir that cannot hide its nature. Elijah, and his sister are not as Theoron, or Venus! You are the true and only source of a child that could live in the human world, as well as in mine."

"I'll not cooperate!"

"Then I'll take you by force," Michael said simply. "But I wish you would reconsider. I've no wish to be anything but gentle with you. I'll give you anything you ask for in return."

"I'm Oathed to Devlin, and specifically barred from having any vampire lovers but him and his brother, Michael," I said softly, pleading with him. "Don't make me break my Oath."

"Devlin can have you back, when I've a child of my own," Michael said softly. "I'll not make you Oath to me. And I will not keep Lash from you either, Sarelle, so long as you don't fight me, and that you make him use protection when he has you. This room has cameras everywhere. If I suspect he's had you without a condom, as he had you earlier tonight, I'll make you take a morning-after pill. I don't want you having his child." His reasonable tone turned deadly. "Also know that he won't be waking up tonight if you don't cooperate. He'll be killed if you do anything that might cause you to lose the baby I'm going to sire on you. I'll use him however I need to in order to get what I want from you, Sarelle. His life is worth only what currency it buys me in terms of your cooperation."

"Please don't do this!" I pleaded, crying. "Please! I believed you, when you said you'd protect me."

"I will protect you, Gentle Sarelle," Michael said softly, hugging me as I pushed at him. "I'm a man of my word. You won't be hurt, and you will be much safer with me than you would be with Devlin. He may need the next few months or years to deal with hunters, and the backlash of vampire and human murders that will surely occur, when it becomes known that the majority of the hunters in Canada and the United States are dead by his order. He is right, there are too many to control in his lands with only one hunter." He paused. "There are others who will also press their advantage, with the hunters out of the way. You are safest here."

"I won't do this! I won't become some cow for breeding, to be used at your will!"

"I'll try with you only once a night, for this next week. Two weeks from now, I'll have a doctor check you, and we'll repeat the procedure only if you aren't pregnant. I don't want to traumatize you, as Samuel and Perseus did to Harriet. Lash can spend all other hours with you, and be with you as much as you want to be with him. You want anything special to eat, or drink, or read, or wear, anything, anything at all, you have only to tell me you desire something, and it's yours."

"Please don't do this!" I screeched at him, fighting free of his hands, and fleeing to the nearest corner, where I backed against the wall, looking in vain about me for anything to use as a weapon.

"I've removed your pills from the bathroom," Michael said gently. "I know you've been taking them every day for months now, but you're going to stop tonight. I've also left some condoms for Lash. There should be enough there for a day at least, but just tell me if you need more, and they will be provided."

I was beginning to pant. His eerily calm voice coupled with the things he was saying was making me hyperventilate.

"There was a fertility potion in your wine you drank earlier tonight, just as there was with the water you drank at breakfast," he said quietly. "You should be ovulating in a day, as the pill's effect wears off. I disliked having you take the one, but there was no other way, until Lash was under control." He gave a faint smile. "At least you were near the end of your cycle, so any delay in ovulating should be minimal."

"Don't do this!" I shrieked, bolting away from him again.

He grabbed hold of my arm, his hand like a vise. "Calm down, and lay back for me, Sarelle," Michael said gently. "It will be over soon."

"No! You'll hurt me!" I cried quietly. "I can't! I won't!"

Michael gave me a look, then he shook his head slightly. "You do not understand," he said softly. "The deed itself is already done."

I grabbed for my choker at my throat, and felt it was missing. I let out a loud scream.

Michael grabbed me. "It was as you slept, Sarelle," he said calmly. "I am not Devlin. I take no pleasure in forcing you. Now lay back and relax, or I'll tie you in place forcibly. Do not fight me, or it will go badly for Lash. Say you understand that."

"I understand," I cried, tears running down my face. I crawled onto the bed slowly, cursing myself for my foolishness, for my being trusting, and for my stupid summer blood, that I had been so proud of these last few years. *I wish I hadn't been special, that I'd stayed a simple country woman with no knowledge that there was anything supernatural in the world. I wish I'd never heard of vampires, or witches, or demons, or werecreatures, any of it.*

My choker with the bear lay on the bedside table. Even if I tried to refasten it now, it probably wouldn't refasten. I curled up in a ball, crying and feeling utterly hopeless.

"I'm sorry," Michael said finally, after some moments. "I wish there was another way, but there isn't. I don't want to give you any more fertility drugs than I already have, and artificial insemination doesn't work with vampires."

How in hell did he know that? I stopped crying and looked up at him through my tears.

"Samuel tried it with Harriet, when she couldn't get pregnant the first time," Michael explained. "With no success. His sperm died in seconds outside his body. There was no reason they could find, but it happened over and over. The best doctors couldn't fertilize even one of the many eggs they took from her."

Michael reached out for me and I recoiled. "I won't touch you any more than I just did," he said quietly, withdrawing his hand. "Though if there is something I could do to make it less upsetting for you, please tell me, and I'll do it."

I shook my head, crying again. "Get out," I managed. "Get out, get out, get out."

Michael got up, adjusting the belt of his robe. "You are not to shower, or get out of bed for an hour after I have you, to give my seed time to find your egg," he said softly. "After that, you may shower, or do what you like to get clean. And you will not see me when I come to you, or remember my being with you, if you are careful to drink all of the wine you are served with dinner."

I cried harder.

"I'll have my men bring Lash in," Michael said gently. "He'll sleep until dawn, but having him near you should make you feel better."

"Please," I got out in a croak.

Michael left. Soon after, his men brought in Lash, and lay him down next to me, unconscious. He was fully clothed, his weapons gone. I breathed in the scent of him, and calmed myself. I fell into an exhausted sleep curling my body around his.

Chapter Twelve

At dawn, Lash shook me awake. His eyes were scared, and questioning. He'd scented Michael's spoor on my body. He looked in my eyes, then looked at the choker on the table beside us.

I burst into tears.

He held me to him tightly. "I'm so sorry," he hissed sadly. "I'm so sorry, Sar."

I cried, and he held me, telling me over and over he was sorry. Finally, I quieted, and he took me into the shower, stripping off his clothes and my robe. Then he was cleaning me thoroughly, much as he had when we'd been together in the Everglades. When I was clean, he wrapped me in a towel and dried me off first, then himself. Then he led me the veranda, to sit outside in the sun.

Michael had taken us somewhere tropical. Vibrant blue water was below us, unlike any sea I knew, stretching to the horizon. The climate was very wet, almost like a jungle. Palm trees dotted the landscape, but mostly there was a lot of rock and vegetation.

"Where in the hell are we?" I couldn't think about what Michael had said or done or might do. I didn't want to think of anything right now except getting out of there.

"I don't know," Lash answered. "But I will find out, Sweetness." He wrapped his body around mine, and sat with me silently for a while. I was glad of it, and just held him, relieved to feel he was here with me.

"Did he hurt you, having you?" he asked finally, with reluctance.

I shook my head. "But it's going to happen again tonight, and every night, until he gets what he wants."

"I'll kill him for this," Lash hissed softly. "Even if it takes my life to do it, or decades, I'll find a way, Sar. And the stake I drive into him won't be through his heart, at least not horizontally."

I said nothing. Who cared about the future? Lash was one against many, and I wouldn't endanger him. Michael was smart, very smart. He'd broken my will to fight without landing a blow, and there was no way out, as I saw it. The one man I'd have been hoping to rescue me was here with me.

"I'll fight them tonight, when they come to take you," Lash hissed vengefully. "But I'm going to lose, Sar. They took my weapons, they'll be tiger, and they'll be at least ten of them—"

"How do you know?" I said almost absently.

"Because Michael's no fool," Lash hissed ruefully. "He's been planning this for more than a year, I'll bet. Probably from the first time he saw you, back before you were Oathed to Devlin. I knew that he had to have planned at least some of it, to have all those things you preferred right there in the hotel."

"Don't fight then," I said softly. "I don't want you hurt, and there's no point."

"I can't not fight them, knowing that he plans to rape you again, to get you with his bastard," Lash hissed angrily. "Because that's his damned agenda. But I'll try to kill at least one a night, Sar. Michael's going to pay for this with his life, but the lives of his guards will be enough for now."

"No," I said, hugging him. "Get out. Get away from here, and find your way back to Devlin, Tryst—"

"No. I'm not leaving you here at his mercy."

"He used my love for you to get my cooperation," I said as tactfully as I could. "If you are free, I'll fight him—"

"And he'll just force you anyway," Lash said roughly. "If I leave you here, I may never see you again! Michael obviously had resources he kept hidden to get us here so quickly, so secretly. Devlin probably doesn't even know we're gone yet. Michael also has power, magic power through Cyrus, or another sorcerer. You can't teleport, Sar—that's no accident. Someone of Titus's magical level or greater is stopping the tracking spell on you from working. But that's probably still on you; it's likely not gone. Even if I escaped with you, they would find us, use it themselves to track us down. Not to mention we don't know where the hell we are anyway!"

"You have to leave me, get out and come back with help!"

Lash's tone turned hateful. "I'm as Theo was, Sar, without papers or money in some foreign place. I'm wanted for questioning by Interpol, from a job that went bad just this year. I have no way to contact Dev. But that I could handle, Sweetness. I'm not leaving because I have no way to find you again!"

"You just said the tracking spell was still on me."

"They'll remove it if I leave, if they haven't already," Lash hissed, scales forming on his hands. "I can't risk it. I can't risk losing you."

I hugged him, despondent. Everything he said was true.

"I waited my whole life to love someone like I love you," he said, holding me. "I'm not leaving you here. I'll get us both out, or I won't go."

* * * *

Every night, I drank my wine with dinner and slept very heavily, not waking until morning was half-gone. When I woke, my first thought was that Michael had been with me as I slept. The bastard left not a single sign that he'd been with me. But the knowledge of my violation alone was upsetting enough. As the week went on, I began to feel like it was happening to someone else. I began to pretend nothing was happening, telling myself he was impotent and that he hadn't touched me at all.

Lash did kill a guard of Michael's those first three nights, first with stolen weapons, then with his hands, and finally, with his poison. But it didn't stop what happened to me from happening.

When the week was over, I breathed a sigh of relief. There would be no more nightly visits.

Lash was hesitant about being intimate with me in the mornings afterward. But I wanted him badly, irrational as that was. There was the feeling if I could only make love with him enough times, I could forget what had happened to me, erase it, block it out. In that next week, we made love over and over. Even though he bitched, he wore the protection as Michael had requested, even though I knew he wondered why I insisted on it.

As long as there was a slim chance Lash had gotten me with child, I couldn't risk terminating it with a morning-after pill, one strong enough to kill a supernatural fetus. I had no doubts that Michael would make good on his threat to make me take one, if he had any reason to think my growing child wasn't his.

* * * *

A week and two days passed for Lash and I in captivity, as we talked of various things, watched movies, and slept. But Lash never mentioned any escape plans, something that made me anxious. While I had given up on getting him to leave me behind, I didn't want to give up on the idea of getting home.

Finally, I couldn't stay silent. We were lying outside together in the sun, when I whispered to him suddenly, "Maybe you should try seducing one of the maids?"

Lash gave me an appalled look.

"Look, I can't seduce anyone," I said brusquely. "Michael watches me constantly, via the video camera. But you go outside to exercise, and swim, because they know you won't leave here without me."

"Sar, I can't."

"You need to try."

"I can't," Lash hissed angrily, "I don't know how."

"What do you mean, you don't know how?" I said back just as angrily.

"I've never seduced anyone," he said, shrugging.

"You've watched Dev do it for years. Don't tell me you can't try!"

"He has natural charm and smoothness. I don't."

"You had enough that day I was filing and you wanted to get it on!"

"That was different," Lash said quickly. "We'd already been lovers for a while, and I could scent you wanted me. Plus there was no pressure, because I expected you to say 'no'."

"This would be the same. Just try—"

"Sar, if Dev were here with you instead of me, it'd be a piece of cake, what you're asking. But you've got me instead, and I'm no good at that. I never have been. I told you that the third time we had sex."

"You always did okay with me," I persisted stubbornly.

"You're different than most women," Lash hissed with affection. "You let me do what I want, and say what I want. But most women want their own fantasy. I'm no good at being anything but myself."

"So be yourself, and see if you get any takers."

Lash gave me a dirty look. "I'll try, but part of the problem is that I don't want anyone but you, Sar."

Be patient and don't smack him. "You said you were attracted to most women."

"I like looking at them, sure. But that's as far as it goes. If you noticed, Michael doesn't hire women for looks. There are hardly any women here, anyway."

I had noticed the lack of female servants. But if you were gay and male, not having a lot of cute females around made sense. I had noticed that all the males other than the guards were all attractive, though some were brawny, and some looked much more delicate.

"Look, just—"

"Sar, give it up," Lash said wearily. "I was never good at lying to lovers. They'd know right away I wasn't into them, that I was just using them." He hugged me. "I'd do it for you, you know I would. But there's no point. I'd have more luck seducing Michael, or one of his lovers."

"Forget it then. It doesn't matter."

"I haven't been just daydreaming here all week with you, Mate. I've come up with two ideas," Lash whispered. "Be ready to move, and do what I tell you, okay?"

"Okay."

* * * *

The next day, Lash became snake, slithered out the window and around to the lower floor, and then back up to our floor. He killed the guard outside our room, opened the door where I was waiting, and took his gun. We snuck down the hall, looking right and left. No one was around.

We made it to the lower floor. Lash stepped outside, and I went to follow, and then another of those magical barriers descended, again knocking him apart from me.

Cyrus materialized a moment later. "Nice try, Lash," he murmured.

Lash shot at him before Cyrus's second word was spoken, but even though he emptied a clip into Cyrus, the bullets passed magically through him, striking the wall behind him. Chips of wall flew everywhere as the bullets exploded, and Lash slammed the door. I cringed, covering my head, though the magical shield repelled all the shards that came my way.

"Sarelle must remain here, where Michael can watch over her. Come back inside, if you wish to remain with her. Or leave now, if you do not."

Lash cursed him, but he slammed the door back open, and walked with us back to our room. He hugged me when we were alone, though neither of us said anything. We were too dejected to speak.

* * * *

A few days passed. A week after we had first tried to escape, Lash tried the second time.

He was allowed outside to exercise, and his movements were not restricted in any way, so long as he did not attempt to seek out Michael. For all that he'd done to convince everyone I meant nothing to him, Michael had found out the truth, that Lash loved me. Michael knew Lash wouldn't leave me behind, so he trusted him to come back each time.

There was a pond beneath our veranda, with steps leading down to it that Cyrus had made. It looked inviting, even to me who wasn't weresnake, and I had spent some days beside it this week in the sun with my mate. Lash hunted there at dusk, and as much as I liked to see him move and swim as a snake, I usually stayed inside then, not wanting to see what he caught and ate.

But when water began splashing madly, and a loud cry of pain sounded, I bolted outside to see him fighting hard with the longest alligator I'd ever seen. He was already bleeding on his back from a bad bite, the blood mixing into the water.

"Help!" I screamed. "Help us!"

A minute later, three tigers descended on us from the surrounding jungle, roaring loudly, one of them pure white. They attacked the alligator, and it turned on them, snapping its jaws. They lunged and withdrew, doing their best to lure it away from the house. Within a few moments, the sounds of the thrashing and roaring faded, as they led it away from us.

"Come on!" Lash hissed in my ear. I turned to find him clothed, the guard's discarded guns belted on him. He grabbed my hand, leading me past the pond, and along the side of the house.

"Aren't you hurt?"

"Fake," Lash whispered, looking around carefully. "I faked it with alligator blood. You know I heal."

We ran to some trees, and made our way down to the gatehouse. It was guarded well, but Lash distracted them by flushing some egret-like birds. One of the guards changed to tiger form, and ran after them, killing one. It settled down to eat, purring, and the others changed form, running over to get some.

Lash pulled me. "Hurry! That bird won't last long!"

We ran out past the gates into the road, and I breathed a sigh of relief. We were free!

A wall of fire went up before us. Lash whipped around, and began pulling me the other way, but fire cut us off, appearing on all sides.

"Stop," a demonic voice rumbled.

Lash grabbed me in his arms. "Hold onto me!" he hissed. "It's going to hurt!"

He was running before I had a chance to scream. We hit the flames, and I was bathed in pain. I screamed once, and then we were through, falling to the ground. Lash rolled with me, putting out my hair, which was on fire, and our clothes. He pulled me to my feet with a hissed "Come on!"

Blackness descended utterly. I could see nothing, and could smell nothing but burnt hair and singed skin. I let out a whimper, but Lash squeezed my hand, and continued to walk, as I followed him blindly.

What seemed hours later, but was more likely just minutes, the daylight came back. I looked around to see jungle, and what looked like strange crops standing in water.

"This is a rice plantation, I think," Lash hissed. "I think we are close to Egypt, but I'm not sure. In any case, they'll have a vehicle."

He kissed me quickly. "Stay here, Mate. I'm going in now. I'd rather wait for dark, but we can't risk it. I'll be back as soon as I can."

I squeezed his hand as he turned to go, then grabbed hold of him.

Michael stood there in Lash's path, Cyrus behind him. His expression was one of resignation, and more than a little irritation.

152

"Cyrus, take Sarelle back," he said in a flinty voice. "Lash needs a lesson in how to behave. Teach him, boys."

Tigers surrounded us, roaring and growling. Lash drew his gun smoothly and fired, killing two before the rest hit him, smashing him to the ground. Cyrus walled me off in another magical cage, and lifted me into the air.

"Stop it!" I screamed. "Michael, please stop it! Please!"

"No," he said sharply. "We have enough to occupy us, we need no more escape attempts. And if he's crippled, Lash may learn to be a good boy."

Blood was spattering now out of the tangle of slashing claws and darting tigers, and I saw with horror strips of skin, scaled skin in ragged curls, the sides bloody.

"You hurt him anymore, and I will kill your child and myself as well!" I screamed. "You hear me, Michael? Stop them!"

"Stop," Michael ordered. His men froze, then backed away from the ruin that was Lash. He was so covered with blood and shredded skin I worried he was dead. Then I slowly saw his flesh healing. He lay on his side limply in snake form, his tongue hanging out, his breathing ragged.

"Bring him."

One of the tigermen reached for Lash. He struck instantly and bit him, even as the tigerman shrieked and began convulsing, his eyes rolling up in their sockets.

Cyrus sighed, and spoke. Blue lighting shot from his hands and struck Lash, who let out a sound of pure agony. His jaws went slack, and he fell into the dust, jerking with electricity. The lifeless guard fell from his mouth, the man's face contorted in his death-throes.

"Leave him here," Michael ordered spitefully. "He can crawl back on his own. And if we've gone by then, it will be his loss."

"Let me out," I pleaded tearfully. "Let me out, I'll carry him. He won't hurt me. Please!"

Cyrus released me, and I walked carefully toward Lash, talking to him gently. When I was within reach of him, I let him sniff me. When he rubbed his head weakly on my hand, I picked him up. I put some of him around my neck, and the rest I carried in my arms. Very slowly, we walked back to Michael's house.

* * * *

That night we were moved via teleportation to a new mansion. It was the first of many such moves.

This place was also warm and wet, though there was no pond. Instead of there being grass beneath us, there was only a sheer cliff that fell away for at least a mile down to a river far below. I took one look and vowed not to go out on the balcony ever again.

Lash spent the night in bed. He'd eaten a lot of meat, and fallen into a deep sleep when we returned. But his body was ravaged, and I reasoned he needed a lot of protein, if he was going to heal.

Michael came in with Cyrus as I was finishing showering. I'd locked the bathroom door, but Cyrus somehow unlocked it and just walked in

"Get out!" I shouted, throwing a towel at his head.

Cyrus rolled his eyes and backed out, shutting the door behind him.

A few moments I went out to them in my robe. I had an inkling of what they wanted. And I was right. "Cyrus needs to check you for pregnancy," Michael said eagerly. "Just stand still please, Dear One."

"It's too early," I said slowly. "There is no test you can do so early, not and have it be right."

"There is an old one," Cyrus said in a tone that said I was clearly an idiot. "All it tells is if you've got a soul forming inside you."

"A fetus can't have a soul, it's only a few cells right now."

"This is not about your beliefs, Child, this is about what is and what is not. The soul begins to form as soon as the child is conceived. It is not fully formed until right before the child is born—"

"You're saying premature children have no souls? What a crock of sh-!"

"And I heard you were intelligent!" Cyrus sneered. "Souls do not have to be inside a female to form, they form with time wherever they are. The natural time is the duration of the female's pregnancy, which in human is usually nine months. Now stand still and silence your uneducated mouth."

I grated my teeth and stood still, fuming. Cyrus said a few words, and looked at me hard, but I didn't feel anything, or see anything either.

"Well?" Michael said impatiently. "Is she pregnant?"

"She is," Cyrus said, giving me a satisfied smile. "Twins, no less." He turned to Michael. "You are going to be a father."

"Finally," Michael breathed, swaying a little. Then he came over to me. "Do you wish anything?" he said gently. "Tell me what I can do to make you more comfortable."

"Get out of my sight, and don't come near me," I said then spat at him because I couldn't think of anything else to get my absolute hate of him across. "And don't ever let your men hurt my mate again!"

"You are not to give Lash any of your blood during loveplay as you have every week," Michael said sternly. "None."

The implications of his pronouncement made my very blood curdle. "But I did when I was pregnant with the twins before, and there was no harm!"

"No, Sarelle."

"Devlin and Danial took some! There was no danger!"

"You let him drink your blood just once, and I'll separate you until you've delivered the babies. I won't kill him, but he won't see you, or anything except the stone walls of a cell. Now promise!"

"I will not!" I shouted, grasping at straws. "I may ask for it under The Lust! I did before, no matter what I wanted, or promised my husband of the time! I can't promise what I have no control over!"

"I apologize, Dear One," Michael acquiesced smoothly. "You are right. I heard about what happened both times. But at no other time are you to give him your blood—"

"Don't threaten me with that," I said flatly. "I need him to sate The Lust. It will call to him just as it did before, and being bitten during sex was what I needed! Devlin took a lot, and I was fine!"

"Fine, then!" Michael shouted back, finally incensed. "But The Lust will be over at the latest by the end of the third month. After that, he is not to drink from you. Now give me your word, or I will separate you until you learn the error of your ways."

Lash doesn't have to worry about killing you, you asshole. I'm going to find a way to do it myself! "I promise."

"Good. Now please sit down and rest. You may also inform your mate when he awakens that he no longer must use protection with you."

They left, and I walked back into the bedroom. I sat down next to

Lash and touched him.

He stirred. "Mate?"

"Are you healed?"

"Mostly," he groaned. "I've been hurt worse, but not for years. Fucking cats!"

"Mate, I'm pregnant," I blurted out.

Lash looked instantly furious. *Don't comfort him, no matter how much you want to.* I knew I needed him to be furious, needed him to act as though everything were bad, even though I still hoped that the baby I was carrying wasn't a dhamphir, but a weresnake.

Lash got up from the bed, stalked out to the suite, and proceeded to break every breakable thing in the entire place: vases, glasses, pictures, chairs, tables, lamps, mirrors, you name it. The exception was the TV, and the stereo. I went out onto the veranda, sitting as far from the edge of the balcony as possible, not wanting to see him like this, and knowing there was nothing I could say to stop him. We were being watched. As much as this was hard to let him suffer, I had to do it. There would not be another chance if Michael discovered my duplicity.

Later when all was quiet, I went back in to see how Lash was. I found him passed out asleep, having drunk the entire contents of the mini-bar in the room, the wreckage in piles around him, holes in the wall from his fists and feet. The only single piece of furniture that was not broken was the bed where he was lying. I snuggled his body to mine despite that he reeked of alcohol. "I'm sorry," I said gently. "I love you."

* * * *

Lash was distant when he awoke, though he apologized for his behavior. He was badly hung over, and went back to sleep soon after. While he slept again, two maids came in, and swept up the broken glass, while two of the tigermen carted out the broken items. They had also left me a stack of catalogs on the bed without a word. I assumed that I was supposed to choose new furnishings, though I saw some of the catalogs were of woman's clothes, and food. There was even a Godiva chocolate catalog included.

I thought of Devlin then, and cried a little. Had he taken another lover by now? I knew him better than to think he had Oathed someone else, but I knew his desires, and knew he probably had been with another woman. But I didn't blame him for it. I hoped he got some comfort. He was more alone now than he had been in many years, despite that Danial was still most likely with him and he had V and Kyle. *At least he has Rene to talk to. Hopefully he has found a way for her to be with him, maybe even help him to find me. She has power, and I helped her. She will help me, if she can. I have to do what I can from my end, and find a way to let him or her know where I am.*

* * * *

A day later, Lash was sitting with me when he suddenly sniffed the air. He looked confused, and then he changed a little, and began scenting it with his tongue. "I smell another weresnake," he hissed. "A female."

He got up, and went into the interior room. I followed him, curious. We were both surprised to see Cin there, along with Michael.

"What the hell?" Lash hissed. "What is she doing here?"

"You are going to need to sate your animal side," Michael said simply. "But Sar cannot change her form, or she'll hurt my children. So I engaged the services of Cin, as I've heard she used to be your favorite. She will be on call for you, to coil with whenever you need her."

I was killing mad by then, but I didn't have a chance to say anything. Cin beat me to it.

"So it's true, you've taken up with a human," Cin said nastily. "I'm not surprised, I felt how hard you were that night at Davy's when you came back, even though you had just been with me."

Lash said nothing, he just walked over to her, and slapped her so hard she hit the floor. "Bitch," he hissed. "You're a fucking liar. And I wouldn't touch you for anything."

She lay there, and hissed at him, and then got to her feet. "I'll not lay with him," she hissed, glaring at Michael. "I want you to take me back home!"

"What you want does not matter, Cin." Michael said. "Cyrus?"

Cyrus motioned to Cin and she became snake before us, much how Lash changed for me when we would be together in animal form. She lay there hissing angrily, but when Cyrus threw some glittering powder over her she went quiet, then began undulating quietly, letting out soft eager hisses. *He's just given her some kind of aphrodisiac.*

"Get her out of here," Lash hissed in abhorrence. "I have a mate I love. I am not being with that disease-infested whore, not when I have any choice."

"I'll not risk my children," Michael said, his eyes red. "Do this, or I'll separate you."

"I have no longing for her to be snake," Lash hissed quietly. "There will be no problems."

"I don't believe that."

"It's true!" Lash insisted. "When my sisters were born, I felt no desire, not until they were older. I lost all of my desire when my mother was pregnant."

"I have never heard of this," Michael said skeptically.

"You must only know weres that were changed after childhood, then," Lash hissed sarcastically. "If you are born this way, the sex habits of animals are hardwired in. If you are changed from human to weresnake after puberty or later, human habits sometimes take precedence. But for those that are naturally animal, this is pure survival. Otherwise, we weresnakes would never have continued as a species, if we killed our children because of our need to mate. Children are the goal of mating, Vampire!"

"What?" I said finally. "I don't understand."

Lash turned to me. "My sexual desires mimic that of snakes. As snake, I want it often, and the woman must be of a certain age, and smell fertile for me even to perform. But if a woman is pregnant and I'm living with her, sleeping near her, I'll lose the urge to mate as snake, usually within a week if not less. Research that's been done say it's hormonal."

"Sar is not weresnake," Michael argued.

"But my human side is just that, a side, because I'm not human," Lash insisted. "It's almost impossible for me to have sex with a woman who is firmly past her childbearing years. It's fact I'm able to perform now with Sar, sure! But once the pregnancy is along enough, I'll lose my desire for sex with her, until after the children are of an age to not need me, or my mate again can conceive."

Michael looked at Lash skeptically.

"You can watch and see," Lash said, shrugging. "If you see any sign of me wanting that, or even changing form, bring Cin back. But until then get her out of my sight."

Michael nodded, and a few of his men carried Cin out still hissing in longing, him following. When they were gone, I turned to Lash in surprise, and more than a little wonder. "You never told me that."

"I never thought there would be a time you were pregnant again," Lash said uneasily. "If there was, I was going to say something. But I told him the truth. In fact, I didn't want to say it, but I'm afraid that when you are over four months, I probably won't be able to have any sex with you at all. So I hope by then The Lust is gone like last time, or I'll have to let you have someone else sate it—"

It was here I asked him to stop talking, as I'd had more than enough stress for one day.

* * * *

The next morning, I paged through the catalogs and ordered new furnishings. Part of me wanted to get back at Michael, so I ordered everything I wanted and then everything that was the most expensive. Then I made a list of everything I'd ever wanted in my life and never gotten, because I'd thought it too expensive, opulent, wasteful, or extravagant.

I expected Michael to get me the things we needed, like new furnishings, and probably some of the extravagant food I'd ordered, and to tell me that the rest should wait for another time. Instead, a talented sushi chef came to our room that evening, and prepared us every type of sushi we requested from an elaborate portable bar.

Lash was pleased and ate heavily, and I did, too. For a little that evening, we managed to forget that we were prisoners.

That next morning, I was summoned to my first breakfast alone with Michael. Lash let me go with the guards though he clearly didn't want to. I was walked to a well-lit hallway where Michael was sitting, reading a book. "Come, Dear One," he said in a pleased tone. "I have your Godiva cocoa here for you, along with the meat and eggs you requested. The pancakes will be out shortly. I was waiting to ask you what type of grains you wish them made from. Your list only said 'multigrain'?"

I cracked a smile. "Regular pancakes are fine. There are mixes that say multigrain, but really, I'm not sure what grains are used either."

"Then we will discover together." Michael said, smiling widely. "Please sit down and eat."

I was hungry, so I sat down and ate. When I'd finished the pancakes, Michael cleared his throat. "I am pleased you have taken an interest in your surroundings. Some of what you requested will be delivered today. The rest will come by the end of the week, as being where we are, deliveries are not easy, especially perishable ones. But I'm afraid the sports car you asked for will not be possible. I do not want you driving in your condition, and—"

"That's okay," I said quickly, embarrassed and thinking myself stupid that I'd done a childish stunt like this to get back at him. "It wasn't the end-all-be-all."

"But please choose something else," Michael said encouragingly. "I know you like animals. Would you like a dog, or three? A cat?"

Part of me hurt instantly, hearing his offer. I badly missed Ghost, and part of me wanted to ask him to bring me my dog, or one of my cats. But worse than that I missed Devlin, V, Elle, and T. I missed Serena, Titus, and even Danial, The Large Insufferable Ass. "No," I said hollowly. "No. You tell me that I'll be allowed to go home when the babies are born. That is not that long of a wait."

"It is not," Michael said happily. "I am glad you have accepted your circumstances. Please tell me if there is anything else you wish in the weeks ahead. A simple list like the one you made for me last night will suffice."

I nodded.

"I must be about my affairs," Michael said apologetically, rising to his feet. "Please return to your Mate. I admit I am glad he is with you, as I know if by some chance we should be attacked, he will get you to safety. My men are trained, but they are not on his level. Pity that so few assassins these days choose to go into service with us Rulers—"

I left him still talking, and stalked away.

Lash was waiting for me when I returned. "What did that fuck want now?"

"To give me breakfast, and say no Porsche," I said, sitting down beside him. "And to wax at length on your skill as a bodyguard."

"Fucking vampire." Lash paused. "I should ask him to get me some cigarettes and some Laphroig. That shit he had in the bar made me sick."

Michael apparently heard of Lash's request, as a carton of cigarettes was delivered with a few types of Laphroig that same night. Lash was content, but I was uneasy to know that everything we said to one another was so monitored. *Something to remember.*

Chapter Thirteen

Things with Michael improved after that, though that was mostly because I began to converse with him when we dined together. For all his other faults, he was attentive, and caring, and it was clear from the things he asked, and the many things he did for me that he did care about my happiness, strange as I found that to be with what he was doing to me.

I asked him one morning to elaborate on what he had begun to tell me that night we'd escaped Hector and Peter, regarding vampires. "How did you know we'd be attacked?"

"It was obvious, in how attacks were escalating against my kind. Devlin as you know is greatly feared, but he's also greatly hated. So I just watched and waited."

"And took your chance."

"That's correct, but please don't be so bitter about it, My Dear One—"

"Please don't call me that. I have a name, call me 'Sarelle'."

"As you wish. And if I had not, Sarelle, you might have been killed."

I didn't respond.

"The hunters didn't know how rare it was, whatever lives in your blood. They somehow think we are planning another Auschwitz—"

"What do you mean?"

"Stupid as it sounds, the hunters believe that you'll somehow lead to the breeding of vampire and human, with any vampire being able to have a dhamphir with any human. Then any vampire could create his own army, an army able to attack in daylight, within a few short years, given enough females and stamina—"

I nodded with sudden understanding. "They know how fast Theoron matured."

"Yes." He paused. "What I don't understand is why Hector doesn't know yet that that's impossible, both in practicality, and in the possibility that any of us Rulers would sit back and let it happen. But they fear what they don't understand."

I noticed he hadn't said anything about Peter, and figured Devlin had made good on his threat to drain him. At least that meant V was safe.

"What they don't want to understand," Lash hissed darkly from the doorway. "Fucking humans."

"Good morning, Lash," Michael said cordially. "I'm glad you took my invitation to join us seriously."

Lash ignored him. "Mate, come to me, when you've finished breakfast. I'll be on the veranda—"

"Why do you hate me so?" Michael said to him curiously.

Lash looked at him like he was an absolute moron. "You raped my mate," he hissed, baring his fangs. "You are forcing her to have your child."

"So did Devlin, yet you do not hate him," Michael said in an even tone.

"He loved her."

"Not when he first had her. He just desired her flesh. I did it because there was no other way to have a child of my own."

Lash was quiet for a minute, but by no means agreeable in that quietness. "She was not my mate, when he did that. But he was and is my friend, and you are nothing to me."

"You could both stay here with me, after the baby is born," Michael said quietly, interrupting him. "You know me, Lash, know I do not desire her. You know I would not make her Oath to me, though it would be safer. But if you both agreed to stay here, you would never have to share her with anyone else ever again, Lash—"

"You just want another child," Lash interrupted almost wearily. "I knew you would never let her go, even if she had a baby for you."

"On the contrary, I will," Michael said in an annoyed tone. "But my point is that you must share her with Devlin now and men of his choosing; even Danial, if he should ask for her. But with me, she would be all yours, Lash."

Lash glared at him. "Yeah, until you raped her again, you bastard."

"I am having studies done, to try to get an alternate method of impregnation," Michael said quietly. "I detest what I had to do as much as Sarelle did. They are having some success."

Lash glared harder at Michael. "I don't believe you."

"Why would I hurt a woman if there was another way? Why would I not want her to be happy, this woman who is giving me what I desire? Why would I not let her be with you, when it's obvious she loves you and you love her?"

Lash said nothing.

"Wouldn't it be worth it, to know she was yours and only yours? That there would never come a time when you wouldn't sleep beside her at night, or be barred from her affections?"

Lash said nothing, but his eyes were flat. I was guessing he'd shifted because he was really considering Michael's offer and didn't want me to know.

"To know you never had to be apart from one another ever again?"

Lash grabbed the nearest lamp and heaved it at the wall. "You're talking bullshit! You'd kill her, making baby after baby! I have what you're offering already with Devlin. He is not going to separate she and I, not ever!"

"The twins she is having are enough for me," Michael replied. "Unless they succeed in doing invitrofertilization, they will be the only and last children. It was too awful, what I had to do to her, to force myself to do it night after night, knowing that she hated me for it. I never want to feel that way again. There is something detestable in men, that some of us find pleasure in having women against their will." The repugnance in his words was thick as sludge. "Children should be made in love, not in fear, or pain. The act is called 'making love' for a reason."

We both looked at him in shock, but he wasn't finished. "And who said she must have only my children? Perhaps you might like one or some yourself?"

I remembered Lash's words to me and went still. My mate was quivering slightly as he stood there, his snake eyes flat, his jaw working.

"Would Devlin ever offer that to you, Trystan Valeras? You who call him your best friend? Has he ever said that you might try with her to have a child? Or did he tell you, as I suspect he did, that she'd have his children or none at all? That your impregnating her had better not ever happen again?"

Lash turned away and went over to the doorway. He stood there leaning against the doorway, his back to us.

"I know him, and I know he would not let you have what he couldn't. So I know that if Sar hadn't been on the pill when you first had her, he would have made sure you didn't have her at all! He is the one who told me gratefully about the brand you used, when I asked that first night! He has been careful right along to make sure she didn't get pregnant by you, hasn't he?"

Lash said nothing, but even though he was doing his damnedest not to show any emotion, it was plain to see that Michael was telling the truth, horrible as it was.

"I know she was pregnant with your child after saving you, and lost it, for some reason," Michael said. "I suspect it was because of your age, or else all the stress from her idiot husband of the time." His voice turned persuasive. "But if Devlin can have a child at four hundred, then you who are much younger can also have one, with a little help from a skilled sorcerer, which I have at my disposal."

Lash still said nothing, but hissed very softly now, and I knew without seeing his expression that he was fighting himself. Michael saw it, too, and knew he'd found a chink in Lash's armor, and moved in for the killing blow, gliding close enough to touch him. "Would you not like at least one child with her, after waiting your life to love someone, and be loved in return? To know the joy Devlin knows, that I will know shortly—"

Lash seemed to gather himself at those words, and whipped around to look Michael in the eyes. "Say I was considering what you are offering," he hissed. "You know so much, you must know that Devlin has given me his blood for years, to keep me alive and young. You know that when I begin to fail again, I'll need another potion, not once, but on a regular basis. I'll die eventually without it." Lash paused, looking at Michael. "And you must know that you are just not old enough to make the potion for me, not and have it work."

"There are other potions, and other older vampires I know," Michael said quickly. "Keeping you alive would not be an issue, if you'd only agree to stay. And it goes without saying that keeping you healthy would be part of the Oath agreement between Sarelle and myself."

"Let me think on it," Lash hissed, turning away and walking out. "I'll give you my answer after the babies are born."

"Good," Michael said with a smile. With that, he left, excusing himself.

When I returned to our suite, I went directly out on the veranda, and spent the rest of the day separate from Lash. That night when he came to bed, for the first time I turned from him and faced the wall. Also for the first time, he didn't say anything to me; he just lay beside me, not touching me.

That next week was awful. I barely spoke to Lash, and he to me. But I would catch him watching me from the corner of his eye, his expression bitter and angry.

Finally, I confronted him. He was smoking out in the sun, drinking tequila.

"Why, Tryst? Why are you considering his offer?"

"Because what he said was true," Lash said, finishing the bottle. "Devlin said all that to me and more besides. I'm not going to tell you what he said, or you'd hate him for it, probably."

"So it's better to stay here, with Michael? How can you even consider it?"

"Answer me!" Lash hissed, jumping to his feet and smashing the empty bottle. "Do you not want to stay because he hurt you? Or is it because being with only me wouldn't be enough?"

I walked angrily away from him, and he came after me. "Answer me!" he demanded, grabbing hold of me. "Am I enough for you? Do you really love me enough to be only with me?"

"Yes, you idiot!" I said angrily, even as a few tears leaked out. "I Oathed to Devlin to be with you, because I knew you couldn't leave him, and to have you, I'd have to include him!"

"I told you not to do that!"

"I loved you," I said emotionally, clutching him to me. "There wasn't another choice to make."

"But there is now," Lash said quickly. "We must consider what he's offering."

"But Devlin's your friend! You love him, you've been with him for years! You said you would never be jealous of him!"

"I'm not jealous of him being with you! Not ever! But I love you, and I know him, know he might hurt you, if something ever happened to me, the way…the way Michael would not, even given what he's done. I told myself nothing would happen, that Dev loved you, but after that night you came to me, so afraid…after that, I was worried about you, worried to leave you alone with him even for a night if I wasn't there! Before the attack, I had a job coming up in a week, and I didn't know what I was going to do! I'm supposed to protect you."

"You never said anything!"

"What could I say? We were between a rock and a hard place, both of us needing his blood, but especially me."

"We are still there! Nothing has changed!"

"We have another option now!" Lash hissed a little desperately. "We need to at least consider it."

"No!" I shouted at him. "I won't!" I tried to leave, but he grabbed me and held me close, as I tried to push him from me.

"Please don't be angry with me, because I want you to be safe, and because in my heart, I want you to just be mine," Lash said with a ragged tone. "Please, Sar. Not after that night you came to me, your teeth so sharp you couldn't talk, with so much fear in your eyes."

"I'm not angry, I'm just upset. I never thought you'd betray Devlin, Lash, not ever!"

"I'm not betraying him. I'm looking out for the woman I love! I vowed to protect you. I may have done a shitty job of it so far, but that doesn't mean I have to compound the error."

He let out a long breath. "I could never kill Devlin, Mate. But if you were to Oath to Michael with me as part of it, there would be nothing legally that Dev, or any of the Rulers could do. Then I could be with you, we could be together, just us!"

I knew that was true, just as I knew taking another vampire as my Oathed One would not stop Devlin from coming after me. He would always come for me as long as there was any life in his body, no matter if I wanted him to or not. That had been true from the first, and it was still true. If Michael had offered me this deal a year ago, to stay with him and have his child in exchange for his protection and only be lover to Theo in exchange for being free of Devlin, I'd have jumped at the chance.

But a year had passed, and just as Theo had accused me, I wasn't the same woman I'd been. I wanted a life with not just Lash, but also Devlin. I'd made a lot of excuses for my feelings for him over the years, calling it wrong, saying it was because of this or that reason, when the real reason was just that I loved him in spite of his dark tendencies, or maybe more truthfully, because of them. I loved that he was so over the top, that he was such a romantic; that he made me feel that I was the only woman he could ever love. I wanted to be back with him and my daughter, in his home that had become my home.

For I'd also become a lot less naïve this past year. As much as the deal Michael was offering sounded good, I did not trust him at all. No being was that selflessly giving without some ulterior motive. *Lash should also know this, just like he should know that Devlin would always keep coming. Maybe this is a ruse, some angle Lash is playing. If so, it's not worth arguing about further. We've already provided enough of a show.*

"Please, Mate, we don't have to decide anything until the babies are born," Lash hissed, seeing the look on my face. "I won't mention it again, I promise."

I nodded, and changed the subject. But like it or not, the unfinished argument was between us from then on, though we didn't speak of it again. Lash drank more than ever, and most nights, he passed out rather than fell asleep. He also began chain-smoking as well when he drank, spending most afternoons out on our balcony. Many nights I covered him with a blanket in his chair before I went inside to sleep by myself.

I said nothing to him about it. What was there to say? Part of me was ashamed of how he was handling everything. I was disappointed in him, both as Devlin's friend, and as my Mate. I knew some of his behavior now was because he knew that, even without me speaking the chastising words.

* * * *

Time passed slowly, but it passed. Michael had been holding us for almost three months. We'd been moved another three times since the first two, and I'd ingested enough Godiva chocolate to make me gain ten pounds that were not related to the babies. By now I was beginning to act very pregnant, again feeling all the normal signs of my body telling me something was up.

To my abject relief, this time my body had something additional to tell me. I woke up one morning in early August with a rampant desire for seafood. *I want eel, shrimp, haddock, salmon, crab, and baskets of it, maybe even some sardines, too.*

In that moment, I was finally sure of whose babies were within me. I wanted badly to tell Lash immediately, but our children depended on me being not only silent, but also very careful. So I ate the sushi delicately as I had before, even though now I wanted to shovel it into my mouth with a forklift. I was glad I'd had the foresight to request sushi every other day since the beginning. Silent and watchful, I waited for my chance.

* * * *

It didn't come until two weeks later. Michael had again moved us, this time to a less wet place. There were mature trees here, and the air was less tropical, though the vegetation was still dense and full. We were also surrounded by flowers galore. When I first saw them, I thought of how beautiful the gardens at Hayden must be now. *It's full summer now. Here I'd looked forward to seeing them all winter, and I'm missing them again.*

I cried for a while that morning, thinking of Rene, worried that maybe by now she'd left the convent and Shaker'd taken her soul. I worried about Devlin, with Lash not there to watch out for him. Then I was overcome all over anew when I realized I'd missed not only Lash's birthday, but also my own, T's, and would shortly be missing V's. *God, she might be an adult by the time I see her again!*

Cyrus appeared after a few moments, saying quietly that Michael was concerned about my emotional state, and asking if I needed anything. I told him curtly it was a pregnancy thing, and to get out, which he did almost immediately.

By the time Lash staggered in from the veranda about eleven a.m., I'd cleaned myself up, and gotten dressed. When he asked me hesitantly if I'd like to go out with him for a picnic later in a nearby meadow, I agreed.

I rode there on horseback, Lash walking ahead of me a few meters, very slowly. As Michael had said, there was nothing he denied me, though he'd said I would not be allowed to ride when I entered the third month, and I was only to walk on horseback now. But we'd had a fight a week ago, where I told him I was going to slit my wrists if he didn't let me get some exercise, and feel grass under my feet again. I'd done a ton of reading, watched movies, and latch-hooked a rug that was four foot by three foot in the last two months. In short, I couldn't take any more of being cooped up inside. So Cyrus had activated the tracking spell on me, and I'd been allowed to go for walks since that day, so long as Lash and some of the tigers followed along for safety.

After tethering the horse, and eating a meal of hearty meat sandwiches, we lay down on the blanket, not touching.

I looked around us to see the wind blowing, the trees creaking and rustling. Surely the weremen guards couldn't hear us over that? The lot of them were over near the stand of trees, dozing. Could Cyrus possibly overhear us magically with that racket in the background?

Damn it, I had to say something! Lash was degenerating into a drunk, from all that had happened and him not being able to stop me being hurt, or get me away, and from thinking I was having Michael's child, to say nothing of the ongoing fight about leaving or staying, once the children were born. I had to tell him what I suspected now, or he was going to destroy himself. As it was, he'd drunk most of the wine at lunch, and I could see it had no effect. But he drank at least a bottle of scotch if not two every night now.

I took a deep breath. "Lash, you have to stop drinking. You're drinking until you pass out every night: I don't care if it doesn't affect your fighting ability. You're going to kill yourself."

Lash hissed a little, and went red with embarrassment. I beckoned him into my arms, and he came warily, as if certain I would reject him. But we hadn't touched really for close to a month now.

"I'm sorry," he said softly. "I can't stand it, Sar. I know it can't be easy for you, but I'm going crazy, knowing you're having his children, knowing you're angry with me. I thought you hated me now, the way you've been acting."

"It's your children, I think, not his," I whispered as softly as I could in his ear. "You have to stop drinking so much! We need you. Your babies need you."

Lash pulled back and looked at me in utter shock.

"Hug me," I said softly. "We are still being watched."

Lash hugged me tightly, and whispered in my ear, "They can't be mine, you were on the pill."

"I didn't take any pills that first morning. And I was with you, and Michael had given me fertility potions in the food and water, so there may have been time."

"Sar, they're more likely his. Please, don't—"

"I have an urge to eat fish now almost for every meal, or meat," I said very quietly. "Even for breakfast! I like sushi, but that's way out of the norm for me. And there is no Lust at all, despite I'm well into the second month! Does that sound like I'm carrying a dhamphir?"

Lash hugged me tightly to him, and I realized by the wetness on my neck he was crying. "I'm sorry, Mate," he said brokenly. "I'm so sorry, I won't have another drop, I swear!"

"You need to keep drinking as you have been," I whispered strongly. "Just taper it off slowly. You're also going to have to help me fake The Lust. We are going to need to have sex a lot for the next month or so. Probably every day, at least twice."

Lash stroked my neck with his tongue, tickling me a little. "You know that's never been a problem for you and me, Mate. In fact, I wouldn't be opposed to a little romp right here—"

"I know," I said with a faint smile. "But I am going to need your help. Knowing I'm being watched by Michael's henchmen turns me off. I'm going to need to be over the top, too, to be realistic, like I was when I was having my other vampire babies. Just thinking about acting like that with an audience makes my stomach turn."

"I can help with that," he said seriously. "I can say some raunchy things, do some things to you. You just groan a lot, and pretend you're having a good time." He grinned. "Hopefully you won't have to pretend."

I let out a snort, and we both laughed, trying not to notice how brittle our laughter was. "Okay," I said, running over my mental list. "Are we forgetting anything?"

"Yes," he whispered, hugging me. "I love you, and I'm going to love our children, Mate. I let you down, and I will be stronger from now on, so I don't again."

I kissed him, cutting off his words, but he pushed me back, and made me look at him. His eyes were soft, and dark, and more than a little sad. "My mother often said that she wanted fish when she was pregnant with my sisters. I caught some for her every day."

I remembered his story of his youth, and hugged him tighter.

"We're going to make it through this," I whispered with fire in my words. "I'm going to have a life with you, and our babies."

"You're damn right!" Lash hissed stalwartly. "Don't worry, Sar. I'll take care of you like I promised to."

"And no more talk of staying here?"

Lash touched my cheek gently. "I considered it for you," he hissed carefully in my ear. "But most of what I said was because Michael needs to keep thinking he's subjugated me, so we have as much freedom as possible. He hasn't been moving us around every two weeks because he's bored."

I felt a rush of hope at his words. "You mean that Devlin's looking for us."

Lash nodded. "I knew he would, I just hoped he'd have found us by now. But that fucking Cyrus is good, almost even on Titus's level, even though he's younger. So we're going to have to escape on our own. I'd thought to wait until you had the dhamphirs and then escape, trusting Michael to be too occupied with them to follow. But we'll have to escape before that now." He kissed me. "Don't worry, Mate, I'll find a way."

"I know you will," I said tenderly, holding him. "I know you will."

Chapter Fourteen

All our careful planning was for naught; we didn't have to worry about faking The Lust. The next day, it came upon me like a steamroller the moment I opened my eyes. I turned to Lash, who was still asleep, and grabbed hold of his dick, making his eyes snap open in shock. "Fuck me, my snake!" I said throatily. "I want your hot flesh deep inside me, making me come!"

Lash thought I was acting, and so he obliged me, moving atop me and entering me, pumping hard and fast. "I am going to make you come, Sweetness," he hissed in my ear lustily. "You're so tight and wet around me, caressing me with every deep thrust. I can't wait, I'm going to come—"

"Bite me now!" I screamed, and he did, the feel of his teeth inside me pushing me to climax. I came hard with loud screams, and in his excitement, he did, too. I lay there after with him, panting hard. Lash knew by then that I hadn't been faking, and I could see he was wondering if I was really carrying his child, or Michael's.

"Again?" Lash offered, sliding his hand on my thigh.

The moment he touched me, I wanted him again. "Again," I said throatily. "Please!"

After six times, I knew something was wrong, and so did he. Then it hit me what this was. "The blood," I whispered. "I've not had any vampire blood since we got here. I'm going into withdrawal, Lash!"

"Shit." Lash's voice was pure fear. "I can't give you my blood, it won't help. And if you drink Michael's, you'll be in thrall to him." He paused. "His also likely doesn't have enough power to keep you partially turned, anyway; you need Devlin's blood. If you hadn't shared as much blood as you had with Dev and Danial that last night, it's likely you'd have needed it long before now, Sweetness."

I began crying, and we stopped talking, sure that all our plans were in ruins now.

But we were saved, as my sire had also sensed my need, and a package was delivered by one of the maids that very night to our room. It contained a sealed bottle and a note in Devlin's handwriting.

My Love, My Darling Sar,

I can't tell you in words how much I miss you. Please know Michael has promised to return you to me when you have born his child. Titus has helped me, and enclosed some of my blood for you, as I forbade Michael giving you any of his.

Take it, please, as soon as possible. I will see you soon.

Love Always, Dev

PS: Know I'm going to kill that fuck as soon as you're home with me, and safe.

I drank the blood, all of it. And The Lust faded as if it had never been, though I acted out a repeat of what had happened with Lash over and over for the next week, to make Michael think that The Lust was presenting itself.

* * * *

A week later, I was sitting there, having lunch with Michael, when I remembered something. Something that made me gasp, because it might be the key to my freedom.

"What is it, my Dear One?" he said at once, his eyes riveted on me. "Do you have pain? Are the babies kicking?"

"I have something for you, I think, that might mean a great deal to you," I said, thinking quickly. "But I'll need your help to get it."

Michael gave me a thoughtful look. "What help, Dear One?"

"Back years ago, Monica, a lover of Danial's, fell in love with him. Before I killed her, she talked about how she thought she could alter her blood, to make it like mine was. She needed some of my blood to do it, Terian told me. But she never got a chance to work on it further than theory, because I killed her."

"And you think she might have been on to something?"

I nodded. "I would like to take some men of yours, and go there to her old living quarters, maybe Cyrus, too, and look for her notes. Normal procedure for any employee of Danial's that died in his service was to store their personal effects. I know Danial kept some of her things, and that she had a lab like Terian. In fact, she was his friend; he was the one who recommended to Danial that he hire her in the first place. Terian would know where her magical notes were."

Michael looked at me. "I would need assurances from you."

"Lash can stay here," I said softly, meeting his eyes. "I will come back to you, with or without the notes, I promise you."

"Then I'll arrange it with Cyrus for later this evening," Michael said, nodding. "It is too good of a chance to pass up." He gently put his hand on my shoulder. "As you know, the success that my scientists had with alternate methods of conception was short-lived. So anything that might help to give me another way to have additional children would be a godsend."

I did not reply, and soon after, Michael strode out, already on his cell phone, making arrangements with Cyrus.

Later that evening, Cyrus teleported himself, me, and ten men to T's house, directly in front of the doorway to the werecompound's south entrance.

"It was the only unprotected place in the entire woods," he said with cordiality. "Now guide us—"

"Stay where you are," Terian growled. I turned to see him materialize in front of us, his eyes red. "I have roused the men, and—"

Cyrus motioned, and everything froze, save Terian and us. Terian looked at us in shock.

"You are merely seventy or so," Cyrus said with aloofness. "You are no match for me, half-breed, not alone. Now guide us to the one known as Monica's quarters."

"Her quarters were cleaned out long ago," Terian said flatly. "Danial did it himself. Except for a few personal mementos, he threw everything away." His voice turned darker. "And when he learned she had tried to kill Sar, he had me incinerate those, too."

I thought that was a lie, but kept quiet.

"Where are her papers, her grimoires?" Cyrus said, looking at Terian. "You would not have thrown them out. We want everything in regards to her work on making her blood resistant to the vampire virus."

"I have no idea," Terian said, shrugging. "I found nothing relating to that in her work, and little of her actual work anyway in her things. Most of it was just books, no notes—"

"All witches have notes," Cyrus interrupted scornfully. "Take me to her room."

Terian led us to Monica's old room, which was now the room of the werefox named Warren. He was in bed, asleep, and frozen in mid-breath.

"Stopping time isn't easy," Cyrus said with effort to Terian. "Were her things like this, arranged like this? I must hurry, we don't have time—"

"How should I know?" Terian answered angrily. "She was Danial's lover, not mine!"

Cyrus swore, and then swung wide his arms. "Unbind!" he grated.

Many things happened at once. The weretiger guards with us were mostly unaffected, but two went to their knees. So did Terian and I.

"My woman, Fiona, she's alive, you healed her, Cyrus—" one of the tigermen said.

"You killed her," the other kneeling guard stammered. "You killed my sister, you bastard!"

"Kill them both," Cyrus said absently to the other guards, as he rummaged in a wall safe that had appeared at his words. The other guards grabbed the two that were kneeling, trying to remove them from the room to shoot them in the head. The affected guards fought back, resulting in a brawl, several of the guards leaving the room.

"You helped Leri," Terian gasped at Cyrus. "You helped her hide her pregnancy with me; you came to her, after I was born! I saw you!"

"You came to me in a dream," I said brokenly to Terian, betrayal and rising anger filling me. "You came to me as Lash, and made love to me. You utter bastard!"

"You made me forget!" Terian screamed at Cyrus as he became full demon, his teeth springing forth, his eyes filled with flames, and the sudden heat of him like a 1000-degree oven. He threw a glowing fireball at Cyrus, who dodged, and the papers he was holding went up in a whiff of smoke. Cyrus put up a shield, cursing, but Terian hurled lightning at it before it fully formed, and shattered it. A bit of the lightning got through and hit Cyrus, and he staggered, going to one knee.

176

Time started. Warren woke up abruptly to find a fight going on in his room. He shouted "Help!" loudly and got a bullet from a tigerman in his shoulder for his trouble.

"Attack the demon!" Cyrus ordered the guards, hastily grabbing most of the contents of the safe in his arms. He grabbed me and teleported, the last two surviving tigerguards grabbing onto me desperately as I disappeared. The rest had already been killed by Terian, who had splattered them over everything, as he ripped them limb from limb, shrieking out over and over that he would kill Cyrus, that he would rend him into shreds and suck his bones.

We arrived back at Michael's in a disorderly pile. I struggled to my feet and then collapsed back down, feeling very weak.

Cyrus had them help me into the chair, and gave me some water to drink. "Are you well?" he asked gently. "I do not see any injuries to you."

"I think it's just shock. Can you check the babies, just in case?" I said worriedly. "Please?"

Cyrus laid his hand on my abdomen, and said some words. A minute later, he lifted his hand away. "They are fine."

I breathed a big sigh of relief. "Did you find what we were after?"

"Terian burned a chunk of it," Cyrus grumbled. "But I have most of her notes, and it's true, that they speak of something that might work. Will you let me have a bit of your blood?"

I gave him some, via a syringe he produced from the folds of his cloak.

I got up to go, and he stopped me. "Do you want to forget again?" he asked quietly. "I heard what you remembered about Terian's dream with you. I can make you forget what he did to you, if you wish it. It is a simple spell."

I didn't trust him at all. He might scramble my memories, or do something to affect my love for Lash. "No. I would like to think it didn't happen. But now I know it did, I can't go back to not knowing."

Cyrus nodded, and let me go.

I went back to Lash, and he hugged me before I was through the door. "Are you okay?" he hissed in my ear. "I heard the guards talking, that Terian fought with your little raiding party."

"I'm fine, and so are the babies. Cyrus checked."
"Good," Lash hissed. "Come to bed then."
He held me close, and within minutes, I was asleep.

* * * *

The next morning, Cyrus and Michael came to me to share that they had begun work, and that already, they had made more progress than in the previous two years. Even though I hated them both heatedly, I was relieved at their news, because if this worked, then the chances were good I would be freed as Michael had promised.

Lash had been working hard every day to come up with a plan of escape. He also didn't drink or smoke anymore now, having slowly tapered it off to nothing. But we were still no closer to having a plan that he felt might really work. And it didn't help that we had been moved again right after Cyrus and I returned from T's house.

Again we were in a place that was not truly tropical, and again the foliage was full and green. But I smelled water here, though it smelled like a river or lake, not the ocean. Lash hissed bitterly in my ear as he held me that night that we were only going to have one more shot at escaping, and to be patient, that he would go out the whole next week to get the lay of this new place, and formulate a plan for us to escape in seven days.

"If they're mine, they'll know soon," he hissed in worry. "I heard the guards speaking of an ultrasound machine Michael's purchased, so he can view the twins. If they are in their other forms, the truth will be out, and there will be hell to pay."

"Shh," I whispered. "We may be overheard, Mate. Sleep and know I trust you."

* * * *

Those next two days Lash was gone, roaming the countryside. He brought back game for me that some of Michael's people cooked for me to eat. Though I enjoyed tasting the unusual types of small deer and large sheep Lash provided, I also felt a feeling of despair settle into me.

Because this was reality, not an adventure story with a happy ending. Michael was simply too precise of a planner to have overlooked something that would give us both a way to escape, and also enough time to make it successful, barring a pure miracle. Lash was not going to find a miracle out in the woods under a rock, no matter how hard he looked. Even if he could make a distraction, the moment we left, Cyrus would sense it just like he had before when I'd tried to get away. Now that I was further into the pregnancy, I wasn't going to be able to leap through fire or even walk for very long.

In short, we were not going to make it. Though Lash told me not to worry, that he would figure out something, I could hear in his voice the echo of my own dejection.

I lay sleepless in Lash's arms that night, wondering what to do. Then it occurred to me that since I'd come here, I'd neglected to pray at all. *Idiot!*

I closed my eyes, and prayed for a way out. "Please, God, there has to be something!" I murmured. "You've always sent me a way before. Send me one now, please! Please!"

Just as there had been that night with Tatiana, there was no visual response to my prayer. But my faith was strong, and I told myself that when I awoke, a way to get free would present itself.

* * * *

I stirred, opened my eyes, and woke up in reddish arms that were not familiar. Turning, I looked up into Shaker's red eyes. "Hello," he rumbled, looking down at me in an easy manner. "And how are you, my human-kin? It has certainly been a while."

I felt shock for a few heartbeats, then I hugged him tightly, because I knew this was no simple dream, this was demon magic. *If Shaker is here, I am about to be rescued. Fuck that he's a demon, and he wants Rene's soul! He can have mine, if it buys my family's freedom and safety!* "I'm so glad to see you! How did you find me?" I said happily, clutching at him.

"I'm very happy to see you, too," he rumbled. "As you can no doubt feel."

Unease filled me. His erection was pressing into my thigh, from where I lay partially on top of him. "What is this?" I pulled back from him, disbelief and disappointment in my tone.

"What do you want it to be?" Shaker rumbled provocatively. "I'm open to suggestions."

I felt a surge of rage, then sweeping despair followed. "You've had this power all along to come to me! Why didn't you?"

"It is impolite to invade another's dreams, Sar. You had to invite me first. Being part demon yourself, there is no other way I could visit your dreams, save by a potion, and I don't lower myself to resort to trickery. I assume you had to be thinking of me, before you fell asleep?"

"No. I was praying for divine intervention—"

"How about some secular conception?" He grinned at me. "I could offer to—"

"Why are you here?" I interrupted bluntly, my words like razors. "I don't want you here, Shaker, and I don't want an erotic dream with you! You said you wouldn't help me if I begged you! You threatened Rene and me!"

"You got between us," he replied gently but coldly. "I have rules I have to follow, Sar. Don't be angry because I want not to be tortured, and am doing everything I can to save myself."

"I don't begrudge you saving yourself. I do judge you for trying to damn her."

"Enough," he said in my ear. "I did not come here to fight with you. I came to help you."

"You pretty much said you'd see me grovel at your feet and still not help me."

"Do you wish me to go?" he said gruffly, moving me off of his body so I sat beside him. "Tell me to go, and I will, Sar. But once I do, I'll not offer my help to you a second time. You can spend the rest of your days with Michael, and never see your daughter or your golden-eyed lover again—"

"Please, no!" I said, grabbing his arm. I took a deep breath. "Please, I accept your help."

Shaker moved closer to me, touching my hand gently. "Good. Do not be alarmed, delicate human. This is a dream we are both having, nothing more."

I didn't buy that for a moment. "Dreams have always been more than they are, at least in my experience. Most especially dreams that are shared, Shaker."

"Be that as it may, this is nothing more than a dream, my mind touching yours. You are not going to wake up with memory loss, or in any way bonded to me against your will."

"You're assuming we're having sex?"

"Not at all," he said, stepping back. "Though I wouldn't refuse, if you offered. I'm demon, after all. But I won't be other than I am for you, not to seduce you, or to make love to you. I am many things, but a trickster is not one of them."

"Then what do you want?" I said bluntly.

"A favor," he said, running his hot hand over mine. "And in return, I'll grant you one: I'll tell you how to call to your vampire lover across the ocean, so he can find you."

"Please, Shaker, please, tell Devlin where we are."

"I cannot, Sarelle."

"You won't help?" I said in disbelief. "What kind of kin are you?"

"Cyrus holds power over me," Shaker admitted, openly furious. "It was me that stopped Lash and you that second time you tried to escape. I cannot attack him, can't even work against him. But even in magic, there are always loopholes."

"What do we do?" I asked.

"Cyrus is monitoring your dreams. He does not know Theo's bond with you is broken, and he's been checking all along to make sure you cannot lead Theo to you. Every second I linger here it is more and more certain he will find me here with you! So we must pretend this is a social visit, and nothing more than your fantasy."

"What?"

Shaker tilted my head up and gave me a long kiss. It was soft, and surprisingly gentle. If I hadn't felt the heat of him roasting me, I'd have thought it was Danial. "Kiss me back," he murmured into my mouth. "This must be thought of as a fantasy of yours. And in fantasies, there is a minimum of talking."

No way! "I don't want to have—"

"Then there will be none of that," Shaker interrupted, trying to kiss me and not laugh. "Besides, though you may have been lover to vampires and weres, including Dev the Sex Machine, you have never tasted pure demon." He kissed gently down my neck. "We are potent in the extreme, Sar. We never tire. I could make love to you for days and not stop."

I shivered, remembering Rene's memories of her experiences with demon lovers, and Shaker held me close, thinking me worried. "Women have died that way," he whispered. "And while I'm sure it's a good way to go, I think you have other goals for your future, correct?"

"What do you want from me? Be clear, Shaker."

"For you to be my Mistress."

I gaped at him, and he quickly kissed me again. "Like 'Master,' Sar. I am due back in hell very soon. And I do not want to go."

"Why can't Dev bind you to himself?"

"He has Titus already, and Rip. Dev thought he could persuade Danial to take me on, but that didn't work out, as you know. His attempt to bind me as my master failed."

"There's a limit on how many demons a vampire can hire?"

"A limit to what Hell will allow." He sighed. "Demons are supposed to go out into the world for one purpose, Sar. We're supposed to cause a little mayhem while we're out here, and I don't deny the work we do is usually bloody and violent, and most of the time, I'm good with that. I like the kind of pleasures Devlin allows Titus. But I have needs too, and I need a Master or Mistress to meet them. I do not want to get on Lucifer's bad side, as Titus has. Between what happened with Rene and some other things I did this year, I'm pretty fucking close to that right now."

I felt better. I knew the relationship between Titus and Devlin was a professional one, or at least, there was no sexual aspect to it. "What do you need from me?" We'd just ignore that comment about Lucifer.

"A bit of your blood to put me in your service. A little of your life force or soul, for want of a better word, to keep me connected to you." He paused. "And for you to make sure Cyrus is killed, so that his bond with me is severed. I cannot serve two masters for longer than a month or so."

"Why did you go into his service?"

Shaker kissed me again, and murmured, "I didn't. Cyrus summoned me out of Hell five years ago, and bound me against my will. He forced me to help him break through Hayden's magical barriers to ensnare you, and also to perform several vampire murders this past Spring." He paused. "And it was him who made the spell that concealed Ulysses on Danial's land. He was paid for it, but the money was not equal to the spell, Sar." His voice was dark.

"So Samuel knew of the attack on Danial?"

"No. Cyrus has had something like a vendetta for Dev and Lash for years, at least, the years I've spent in his service. And it may even extend to Danial: as you know, Cyrus is the one who bespelled Theo, the one who gave the spell to Tasha to use." He took a deep breath. "I suspect he is the one who years ago gave Terian's brother that poison, killing him."

"Alexa confessed that it was her plan—"

"It surely was, but what she used wasn't rat poison, something that could be picked up in your local drugstore. Cyrus made it for her." Shaker sighed. "Cyrus even helped Manir, gave him some protection against Terian's lightning—"

"Why?"

"I can't say, not for sure." He shrugged. "I once suspected that Samuel had some grudge against Danial for a long time, from what Cyrus did to Theo, and later in helping Danial's enemies. But even after leaving Samuel's service, Cyrus continued to do what he could to sabotage Danial, Devlin, and Lash from behind the scenes, though he never did anything overt himself. He fights from the shadows. I do not know to what purpose."

"Theo was kept from me, Shaker! He was bespelled to keep him from me!"

"Was he? I am not sure. Why would Samuel put such effort into making sure Theo was happy elsewhere, instead of quietly killing him?"

"He knew Theo was Danial's friend—"

"And later on he hired a hitman to kill Theo, remember? It was just over a year ago."

I tried to think back. Danial had mentioned something to that effect, hadn't he?

"Samuel wanted Theo dead. Someone else wanted Theo out of the way, but not dead. There had to be a reason Cyrus did what he did."

"What reason?"

"I don't know."

Screw it, this was so long ago in the past, who cared, really? The point was, what did all of this mean for me and my loved ones? "Say Cyrus really did all this. What's his motive? Is he old enough to have been hurt by Dev, back before he was turned? Or did Lash kill someone he cared about?"

"Cyrus is about a hundred and fifty or so," Shaker said, quickly kissing me down my neck again, and stroking my back. "To my knowledge, he only knew the three men through Samuel's dealings with them. Cyrus has worked for Samuel for the last fifty years."

"Did he ever say anything about them, some insult?"

"In the five years I've known him, he never mentioned that he hated them, and he's mentioned all his other enemies multiple times. So there is no reason I can see. It's mysterious."

I moved to speak, but he interrupted. "You must kiss me," he said urgently. "I feel eyes on us, Sar."

I kissed him, trying to act as passionate as I could. I was sweating now, and I could feel his heat intensifying, the more I kissed him. "Can you tone it down?" I said, pulling back. "I'm dying of heat here. You'd have to anyway if we had sex, right?"

"Yes, or I'd hurt you." He kissed me again gently. "How is this?"

I felt the heat shrink, until it was just the rosy glow of mid-morning sunshine. I basked in his warmth. *Ahh.* "Yes, this is nice," I said, stretching happily.

"This is as low as I can go," he said, smiling down at me. "I am not half demon, Sar, and there is no pretending I'm human." His flame-colored eyes looked into mine. "Will you accept me as your demon servant?"

"Yes," I said, swallowing hard.

He kissed me hard, then he pushed his lower body close to mine. Shock ran through me, along with a little awe. *That can't be him. It can't.*

"It is me," he said, his tone amused. "But have no fear: you will not have to accept all of me, Mistress."

I punched him lightly, and he laughed.

It was now, or never. I kissed him forcefully with sudden motion, and then I bit my lip hard, tasting blood. And even though my lip was killing me, I pushed my mouth hard to his, and I felt him licking me with his tongue. In that kiss, I felt him draw a tiny part of me out with my blood, enough to elicit a quick gasp of pain. Then we separated, and he was looking at me in relief. "I'm yours to command, Mistress."

"It's my fantasy. So tell me some good things about me."

I'd thought to make Shaker laugh, but he took me seriously. He grabbed my hand, and began rubbing it on his chest. "You are cool as a river to me, dear human. It is so refreshing, your coolness. I could bathe in your still waters for days." He kissed me again, and then I felt him stroking my body lightly with his hand. "Do you wish anything besides words, Mistress?" he rumbled. "I am yours to command."

"Touch yourself."

Shaker actually gaped at me, and then gave me a look that was half grin, half wide rolling eyes. "You wish to see me unclothed?"

Why not? It would buy time. "Yes."

"As you wish." Shaker removed his loincloth type covering, and gently placed it aside. He lay back, baring his immense semi-rigid cock. As I watched, he reached down and began to stroke himself. He'd been partially erect, but as I watched he lengthened still more, his red skin filling out.

My God, he's bigger than Devlin! I was simultaneously terrified, and excited.

"Do you wish me to come, Mistress?"

"Yes."

Shaker stroked himself faster, and then with a low moan, he came, his semen jetting into the air, smoke rising from the heat of it. More terrifying, where it landed on the sheets of the dream bed, his come was hot enough it was setting them alight.

"Jesus!"

"Ow!"Shaker said, giving me a pain-filled look. "Please, no mention of that name. Your belief in it is too strong."

"Sorry," I said apologetically. "I'm just scared. Flaming semen? How could I not be wary?"

"Why?" he said, laying back and looking at me, looking more at ease than anyone who had just performed as he had should have had a right to look. "I would not burn you, if I was inside of you. I would control myself—"

Shaker went utterly still, and then he rolled over on me, still naked. I gave out a shriek, and struggled with him, trying to get him off me, but his next words stopped me cold. "We are being watched, Sar. I can feel it. Please, tell me some sexual act to perform, so this is believed to be just a dream."

Damn it! "Uh...um..."

"Mistress, please!" he whispered in my ear. "Or I will have to make this into a nightmare for you instead, so I may return to you another night! I cannot let our bond be severed, not when I'm so close to being free."

I looked at him, and knew I had no choice. "Rub yourself on me, slowly, over and over. But don't come, and don't actually go inside me, ok?" That should at least give anyone watching the appearance that we were having sex. It was the best I could do, and the most I was willing to dare.

"Yes, Mistress." Shaker pushed up my nightgown carefully, held my hips still with his hands, and very slowly, he rubbed me. I felt guilty, from the rush of pleasure I felt at his touch. But before the head of his penis was even inside a little, he withdrew it completely. Then I felt the press of him again, rubbing gently and then withdrawing. A few minutes went by that way. By now, I was slick, and he was rumbling, letting out groans every time he rubbed against me.

"Please, Mistress," he whispered. "Let all of me inside you that there is room for. You have only to tell me to withdraw, and I will. We are still being watched, and he is no voyeur, so he does not believe this to be just a dream of yours! He is waiting to see if we'll make love, to make sure this is your fantasy, and not my act of betrayal!"

"Yes," I breathed, and I felt Shaker push inside, but this time, instead of quickly withdrawing, I felt him sliding deeper, a low bass note of pleasure in his throat. He gently came up against my cervix and stopped.

"Farther?" he rumbled, eagerness and tension in the single word. "I have no wish to hurt you."

God, he was only half inside? Fuck me, this is unbelievable. "That's far enough." I drew a great shuddering breath. "Now stroke me, over and over until I come."

"Mistress, with respect, I have been having sex for the better part of a thousand years," he smiled down at me. "I am asking only so I know your tastes."

I gave him an annoyed look. "I don't know why you're—"

"In short, Devlin has nothing on me."

I opened my mouth to reply, but Shaker began to move on me leisurely, and my words became moans.

When a few moments had passed this way, Shaker suddenly stopped.

I opened my eyes and whispered, "What's wrong?"

"We are no longer being watched, Mistress." His red eyes looked into mine. "Listen carefully. Tonight, when you are with Lash, make some pretense for drinking his blood."

"We are watched constantly."

"Michael will not care, so long as it is not your blood being consumed; pretend it is part of The Lust, or something. Let him make love to you, and as he comes, drink his blood, as much as you can stomach, and think of Devlin. Concentrate on him as hard as you can—"

"What good can that possibly do?"

"Lash does not have a tracking spell on him. Magic cannot affect him, I have it on good authority—"

"Cyrus was able to hurt him with magic! He hurt him with that electrical charge!"

"But his other spells, like the magical barrier, had no effect whatsoever. Cyrus does not know this. No one knows. It is a well-guarded secret. I confirmed it, when I cast a spell of Unending Night on you both, and Lash led you through it as if I'd given him a pair of sunglasses."

"So?"

"So, that spell that blocks magic has been part of him so long, and it is so powerful, some of it is in his blood, and in his semen. Drink some of his blood, and call to Devlin with your mind. The influx of Lash's semen and blood into your body may be enough to momentarily weaken Cyrus's dampening spell on you, so you can make your whereabouts known to Devlin."

"'May be'?"

"He'll hear you, for sure," Shaker rumbled, kissing my throat gently. "You've had too much blood from him recently not to. If you were nearer to Devlin in distance, say twenty miles, he himself would likely be able to sense you, to track you down. But being so far away he can't, which is the only reason Michael let you consume his blood. But I can help with that by amplifying your mental voice, and focusing it through our mind connection. As soon as he senses you calling to him, Dev will get Titus involved. My brother can track you, once he knows what Devlin will tell him. But you'll need to do it over and over, for a few days, for him to track you successfully."

I nodded, real hope forming in my heart for the first time in months. "Okay."

"Now," Shaker said, resting on his elbows. "Do you want me to continue, or withdraw?"

"I want you to relinquish Rene's soul," I said quickly. "Please tell me you have not taken it?"

"I have not," Shaker said a little regretfully. "Rene still hides behind blessed walls of stone with those penguins."

My lips quivered, but I forced myself to stay solemn. "Will you relinquish it?"

"If you honor your duty to me as my Mistress, yes," Shaker said with a sigh.

Say it, Sarelle. Now. "Does doing this with you mean you'll own my soul, like you did hers?"

Shaker's red eyes glinted down at me, something unreadable in them. "We are kin," he said finally. "I do not act against my kin, not when I have a choice not to."

"Answer me," I said firmly, though my voice cracked a little.

"No, I won't own your soul. The trade is information for my freedom from Cyrus, and that's all."

"And for Rene's soul, Shaker. That's part of the deal."

"She must have enough faith to stand before me and ask me for it back, Mistress, as is the rule. And I will agree to this on the conditions that we already discussed this night, that all of them are met." He leaned in closer. "I am a demon, Mistress. Do not think to treat me like a human lover, or a plaything. Treat me fairly, and I will treat you the same. Do not, and you will be in Cyrus's shoes one day. Or in Rene's."

"Enough," I said, trembling. "Please, get off me Shaker."

"I apologize, Mistress," he said, both amused and a little embarrassed. "I wanted to be clear so you didn't push things, not to terrify you. Let me bring you pleasure, please. There is much I'd like to give you the experience of, and I swear that all of it will feel delectable. And we have some time yet—"

Another would-be lover. Sigh. Well at least, this one isn't professing his love, and has no desire to get me pregnant. That's something. "Withdraw, please. I must go back to Lash immediately, and try to contact Devlin, Shaker. There is no time to waste."

"May I come first, Mistress?" he rumbled, his eyes inches from mine. "One stroke of my flesh in yours, and it will be done."

I nodded, before I could think. Shaker withdrew a few inches, and then drove himself all the way in with one great thrust. I let out a shriek of pain, as he roared out his orgasm, the heat of him engulfing me.

I awoke with a scream in Lash's arms. Lash started, and looked over at me, but I kissed him passionately before he could speak. He rolled me on top of him at once. "What a way to wake up!" he hissed happily, sliding into me with a grunt. "You must have had—"

"Do you trust me?" I whispered, kissing him.

"Of course," he said, looking at me curiously. "I always—"

"Then come for me, my snake!" I said urgently. "Pump yourself into me as deep as you can! I need to hear you come!"

Lash was already hissing at my words, and he moved me on him fast and furiously. A few seconds later I felt him jerking, and as the warm font of his seed flowed into me, I bit down on his neck as hard as I could, screaming out Devlin's name in my brain.

Lash yelped, and pried me away from his neck, even as I tried to swallow his blood. I managed a few swallows, and then he was holding me down to the bed, looking at me like he didn't know me. "Sar?" he said hesitantly. "You bit me? Why'd you bite me?"

"I needed your blood," I said, pleading with him to understand without needing many words, in case Michael was again listening to us. "I wanted it…like before."

Immediately, Lash's eyes went flat, as he looked down at me, though he said nothing. He stared down at me for a long time, and then nodded. "You did before, too, that one time at Davy's," he lied. "I'd forgotten. It's okay. It must be from the dhamphir, and that The Lust is close to ending." He paused. "Take it, if you need it, Mate. I want you to have anything you need of me."

I knew he had gotten what I needed him to get, that he didn't understand why I'd bitten him, but that he trusted me anyway. I hugged him to me with tears in my eyes, loving him so much my heart broke a little.

Chapter Fifteen

The next day, I was summoned to Michael. Every time before, I had joined him in his dining rooms, or on his various balconies, or in rooms resembling living rooms, though there was never a TV. But this night, I joined him in his office.

He told me to please sit, and I did, in a large leather armchair, near a propane fire which was the only light in the room. A few moments later, he joined me, handing me a glass of wine.

"I've already had one," I said politely. "They say more than one a day—"

"You'll need it, Dear One," Michael said in a tired voice. "Put it on the table near you."

I did as he asked. I looked over at him, but his face was in shadow.

For a while Michael just sat there not speaking, looking into the flames, and I took in my surroundings. On second look, this seemed more like a library than an office. There were a good deal of books, but more of the titles I couldn't make out from my chair, and I didn't think Michael wanted me to be poking through his things, anyway.

"You hate me," he said finally. "You try to hide it now, but I still see it in your eyes. Please, Sarelle, do not hate me."

I thought of what to say, and decided not to reply.

"Do you know why I'm here?"

I turned my head to look at him, at the oddness of the question. "You live here."

"Do not be boring. I meant why I exist."

"Because you are vampire, and you keep drinking—"

"What is the purpose? What is my destiny?" Michael said with a snarl, and I realized this was the first time I'd seen him truly angry. But there was desperation in his tone, too, and hopelessness.

"What did you want, if it wasn't this?" I asked.

"You think I was a lord?" he said a little bitterly. "You think I was royalty?"

"You said you were betrothed—"

"I was. But the truth is I didn't ever even meet her."

"What happened? Did she die? Did you marry someone else you loved instead?"

"Neither," Michael said, sipping his blood. "I became a priest."

I felt my mouth working, but nothing came out.

"So surprised, and why? You know of my interest in religion."

I felt like I should apologize, but I would be damned if I apologized to him for hurting his feelings, if I even had. "I did know of that, yes."

Michael sipped his blood. "I wish to tell you a tale, if you'll listen."

I nodded.

"I grew up a child of a peasant family. We were poor. It is likely somewhat like Racklan's tale of woe, save I had no connections, even illegitimate ones." He paused. "But I liked the church, and I spent all my free time there, listening to Mass, and trying to learn Latin, that I might understand what was being said. They still said Mass only in Latin, in those times."

"When I was old enough, I began serving as an altar boy in the church. Soon enough, I was summoned to the nearest Bishop, to answer questions about my faith. They knew of my betrothal, and were willing to intercede on my behalf, if I felt called by God."

Michael's voice took on a happy note. "I told them 'yes.' In a few years, I was ordained. And the next ten years were the most fruitful of my life." He sighed. "I gave sermons, and took confessions, and forgave sins, and I felt as if every day mattered, that the work I was doing mattered. I was making the world a better place, giving people hope, and helping them to be better people. I had nothing, and owned nothing, and it didn't matter, because I had God. My superiors saw this, and praised me, that I was everything a priest should be. I was notified that soon, I would be promoted to Bishop myself. It was almost unheard of, me being only thirty. But my master, he said my zeal came from God himself—"

I sensed a "but." "What happened?"

"I'd always known I liked men better than women," Michael said darkly. "But despite the evil men of the cloth in these times, I never broke my vows with a man, or with a child."

I let him go on, not speaking.

"It was a woman. Her name was Claire," he said in a longing voice. "And from the moment I saw her, everything changed."

Michael had been a priest, and loved a woman? *A woman?* He was gay!

"I see by your face you don't believe me. But it's true, I think I loved her almost on sight. That day I followed her through the streets of France, until I managed to ask her for her name. Once I told her mine, she said she knew who I was. I had dinner with her family that night." He paused. "And later, Claire came to my room, and we became lovers."

"I will not go into details, Dear One. But I'd never experienced being close with another human, not in a physical way. I cried in her arms afterward, wanting to never leave, knowing that I couldn't marry her, knowing I'd betrayed my vows of celibacy, so unhappy I was damned, and feeling all the more damned, because I'd felt something in her arms I'd never felt in God's house."

I tried to hold onto my hate for him, but part of me was already feeling his pain. "Were you found together?"

"She said that God had put our desire in our hearts, that it wasn't wrong. She kissed my tears away, and didn't cry, when I told her that I could not be with her, that I had to be true to my vows. And we parted ways that night, vowing that we would remember what we shared with happiness, but never act on it again."

Michael laughed in a self-incriminating way. "You can guess how long that lasted. I found reason to go to France in the next month, and my feet led me straight to her door. And she welcomed me, as she had before." He sipped. "This went on for months, until a year had passed."

"Didn't her parents suspect? Did she have other suitors?"

"In those days, having a priest visit was tantamount to having the Lord visit, at least for the devout. And Claire's parents were devout. Plus there was my reputation, my zeal for Holy Father's church well-known. They encouraged her to spend time with me. Yes, she was beautiful, but she had no dowry. Women in those days needed a dowry, for a good match. Her parents were negotiating with an older richer man; in fact, they asked me to help them."

"Did you?"

"I tried to. But Claire would hear none of it. I didn't want to end what we had anymore than she did. So I delayed things as much as I could."

"But it did end?"

"I was promoted. The assignment was in Germany. I went, telling myself that this was God's will, that all along I'd been going down the wrong path. That this was the right one, and I needed to follow it. I wrote Claire, and told her that it had to end. Then I also wrote another letter, using my new title, to secure her marriage to that rich husband."

Despite everything, I was enthralled now. "What happened?"

"I heard nothing for six months. Then I finally got a letter." Michael's voice sounded old. "Claire wrote to tell me she was pregnant, and it was my issue. And she was to be married in a month's time."

"Did she tell—?"

"She said she would tell no one that it was mine. She asked me for nothing, not my love, or my support, or my influence, which by then was substantial. She said this was God's will, this child, and she was willing to go to a halfway house, to have it. And later, she would join the nunnery, and give the child up for adoption."

"Something broke in me, hearing those words. I left that same night, to go to her. I knew that it would ruin me, that I'd be cast out, but that didn't matter. All that mattered was her, and that I fulfill my duty to her, and my child."

"Her family cursed me, and struck her name from their Bible. I was thrown out of the church, and my religious titles taken along with all my wealth. We went to the small village of my birth, but even my parents had turned against me. So we left, journeying to London."

I brushed away tears, and took a sip of my wine. "Please go on."

"I spoke to a pastor there of another Christian denomination, one that allowed men of the Lord to be married. He'd heard of me, and was sympathetic. But he said that there was nothing they could do for me, that he couldn't offer me a job, as what had happened with Claire and I was too well-known."

"I was desperate. Nathanial had been born by then, and we had no food. So I asked if there was not some other country we might go to, where I was not well known, to work for God, spreading His word. The priest told me there was, that missionaries were needed to go to the Far East, to bring God to the oriental races. I agreed to go."

I nodded. I'd always wondered why a white vampire ruled Asia.

"We got married. For the next eight years, everything was wonderful. There was strife, and bad times, disease and turmoil. But there were successes, too. And Claire was a good wife to me, and a good mother to our son."

Another "but" was coming. "What happened?"

"A man came one night, seeking shelter from a monsoon. He was Asian, and richly dressed, and offered to pay for lodging, but I told him our home had only enough room for us, as I didn't like the smell of earth about him. He asked to sleep in the church. I refused, but allowed him to sleep in our shed. That next afternoon, while I was away ministering to a dying woman, Claire, pregnant with our second child, went in to get a shovel. An hour later, Nathanial went in looking for her."

I took Michael's box of tissues he offered me. "I'm sorry," I whispered.

"When I found them, they were dead, and the stranger was gone." Michael's voice was dead. "I tracked him for the next week, and finally caught up with him. For whatever reason, he didn't put up much of a fight. I shot him, stabbed him, and even burned him with fire, but he laughed, even as he healed before my eyes. My cross and rosary had no effect on him at all."

Michael swallowed. "He told me 'you can't kill me, unless you drain me of blood, Priest!' I slit his throat, but it healed! I staked him to the ground with a metal rod, holding him in place, and I drank his blood, though I gagged. I cut off his head. In the dawn's light, his body turned to dust, even the very bones. But that same sunlight when it struck me burned me, too. I wept most of that day in the closest shelter, an outhouse, knowing I was truly damned now."

Michael leaned into the light, and I saw for the first time that he was rough-featured, that his face had a friendly look, though his eyes were tortured. But the beard that had covered his face for so long was missing.

"It kept away some of the biting flies," he said in a worn voice. "I grew it when I first came to this country, though I hated it. Now like Devlin, I can't go back to being clean-shaven, save between feedings."

I didn't know what to say. I settled for nodding.

"The worst thing is that I'd have still killed that vampire if I'd known by doing it I'd become vampire myself. That is my one act I don't regret: killing him. He took everything I had left in this world."

"I'm sorry, Michael."

Michael went to his knees before me, putting his hands on the arms of my chair. "Please, Dear One, do not hate me. I don't ask that you love me, but please, please do not hate me. I only want someone to love of my own. I want back some small part of what I lost."

I sighed. Because right or wrong, evil or good, it was true, I didn't hate him now. But I didn't like him, either.

His hands touched my abdomen gently, and then he laid his head against it. "Our children will be leaders of faith, Dear One. Through them, I will find my way back to God."

Oh shit. I repressed the urge to shudder. I managed to say, "God has not abandoned you."

"True. But I have not felt Him, as I did when I was mortal. And no matter how many religions I try, or pursue, I cannot reach Him. I need to know that I am doing what He would want, or to know I am not, so I can change paths. I cannot have gone through this earthly Hell to find myself in another one when I die."

I didn't speak. I held my breath.

Michael released me, and moved back, getting to his feet. "I can see I've scared you a little, and I'm sorry. I just want my life to mean something, Sarelle. Because sooner or later it will end, and I will face Him. I would like to go to Heaven. I would like to know I made a difference, in my time here." He held out his hand. "Come."

We began walking back towards my rooms.

"Dear One, you are silent. Does talk of God unsettle you?"

"No." I had no idea what he wanted me to say. "Everyone wants to think their life meant something, to go to Heaven," I said finally. "I do."

"Do you think you are doing as God wills?" Michael said seriously.

"I've always tried to." *Except maybe a night ago, with Shaker.*

"That is all you can do then," he said quietly. "Sleep well. I will see you at breakfast."

I realized with a start we'd arrived at my rooms. The guard nodded to him. After I entered, I heard his footsteps walking away.

I went inside, and into the bathroom, and drew a bath. Lash joined me, when I was easing into the tub. "What did he want?"

"I'm not sure," I said, adding more hot water. "He told me how he got to be a vampire, and about his life. He was a priest once."

"A sad story, right?"

"Yes."

Lash eased into the tub with me, and groaned a little. "He tried to pull a Devlin on you," he said, after a moment.

I gave him a look. "What?"

"He learned of what Devlin told you, and how you forgave him. And that was the start of you loving him." Lash leaned closer. "Did he ask you to forgive him?"

"He asked me not to hate him."

"Close enough." He paused. "Do you?"

"I don't hate him. But that doesn't mean I like him."

"Be careful, Mate," Lash hissed quietly.

"I'm trying to," I said back to him, hugging him. "I'm trying to."

* * * *

I kept making love to Lash that next week, and every time, I drank his blood. I was embarrassed to say I found it not too bad. There was enough of Devlin's in it to make it taste somewhat like vampire, almost. Lash let me, even as he grimaced from the pain.

Devlin felt me, every time I called out to him. Always his reaction was instantaneous, a faint presence in my mind that was both joyous and frantic, reaching out for me in vain and failing. Finally, on the seventh night, relief struck me as Titus's calm mind appeared with Devlin's and touched mine, his presence both comforting and familiar as he tried to calculate where Lash and I were being held from the many images in my mind.

Michael was the same as he had been, respectful and considerate, but I noticed he now touched me casually, where before he'd kept his distance. I let him, as it was always when he spoke of the babies, and they were never intimate touches, only reassuring ones.

Thinking of his story in the days that followed, I wondered why he'd never introduced his lover to me. With all the hot men walking around here, he surely had one, didn't he?

I asked him about it finally the following Saturday morning when I was feeling sick and irritable. I tried to be tactful for once, and not my usual blunt self. "Michael, when I leave, you will need help raising your children. What do you intend to do?"

He gave me an odd look. "I have already contacted several nannies, Dear One. My children will be well cared for."

"Will your lover take an interest?" I asked delicately. "Or will he be jealous?"

"You are a good mother, asking that question," he said in an approving tone. "But do not worry. I have no lover right now. The one I last had was not interested in more than my power, and what I could do for him. So I broke off the relationship. And there will not be another…partner for me until my children no longer need me."

"That could be a few years."

"I hope so," Michael said, breaking into one of his rare smiles. "I want this time to last, Dear One." He cleared his throat. "Which leads me to ask you, have you given any more thought to my proposal to you and Lash?"

"No," I said honestly, and then got right to lying through my teeth. "But my mate is thinking it over. I'll do as he tells me."

"Good mother and good wife," Michael said again in that approving tone. "No wonder Devlin wants so much to regain you. He's been causing me no end of trouble."

"Might I telephone him?" I said hesitantly. "He might calm down, if he heard my voice."

"No, he won't," Michael said, his eyes tinged red. "He's told me he'll kill me, Sar, no matter what I do or don't do. So you'll neither talk to him or see him, until it's time for you to leave. Understood?"

I nodded. "Yes."

"Return to your rooms," he said in a softer tone, getting up. "I have affairs to attend to. We'll be moving operations again at dusk."

I walked back to my rooms, feeling miserable. *Why weren't Titus and the cavalry here already?* If we moved locations again, I stood a good chance of all my effort with Lash and Shaker being for nothing!

Lash was watching TV when I returned. I was surprised he wasn't out on the balcony. A glance showed me a darkening overcast sky. Rain must be coming, or else it was getting dark early. Maybe that explained the darkness; it was early September by now, right? *The days are getting shorter.*

It was going to be fall again soon. The entire summer had passed, and I'd neither planted a garden, nor even done any kind of real work. I felt another wave of despair hit me.

"Hi, Mate," Lash hissed softly. "How was your breakfast/lunch?"

"Fine. We're moving again."

"I thought we might be. The guards below have been busy all day, moving boxes into vans. They only went inside a few minutes ago. It looks like a storm is going to hit soon."

"What's wrong? Your voice is so tired. Are you sick?"

"I'm tired, Mate."

"You slept all night. What's wrong?"

Lash didn't reply. I looked back again at him. *There was something different about Lash's face. What was it?*

I moved closer to him, and then felt utter hopelessness hit me.

Lash was aging. His face was lined now, as it had been when I first met him, though his features were the ones I'd come to know, not the ones he'd been born with. There were gray hairs in Lash's goatee, and in his hair. Here was my confirmation that my blood had been helping him renew his body. He'd needed it regularly to keep him in his prime. But he hadn't had my blood for more than two weeks now. And the blood I'd taken from him during that time had speeded his decline.

No matter what happened now, it might be too late to save him, now that his body was beginning to fail again. I began to sob, and ran over to him, wrapping my arms around him. What if he died before I had his children? It was too awful to think about.

"I'm sorry. I see it too, Mate, every time I look in the mirror," he whispered sadly, as I hugged him.

"Take some from me. It might not be too late!"

"No," Lash said. "I knew all along what you were doing, letting me drink your blood so I wouldn't need that potion I used to take. So long as it was your choice, that was good with me. I hated myself for needing it, for having need of you that way, for not being a stronger man who'd refuse."

"Take it! Just a few swallows!"

"No," he said, hugging me. "I wouldn't want to risk the children. Because I'm in pain again, Sar, and it's not a little, like it was last time. This time it's happening much faster than before. Every time you drank from me, the pain intensified. If I tried to only take a little of your blood, I might take too much, because it's starting to feel like my bones are breaking inside me piece by piece. And I know if I took enough from you, I wouldn't hurt at all."

"Take it! Your life means more to me than anything—!"

"But it doesn't mean more to me than anything," he hissed gently. "You mean more. Your children mean more. Now hush."

He pulled back from me. "Come to bed with me now. I want oral sex."

I gave him a stunned look. *He has never asked that of me.* He took my hand, and brought me into bed, laying on his back, and arranging me, so I was above him, lying between his legs, my hands on his chest supporting me.

"Go down on me, Sweetness," he hissed, his voice very emotional. "I want to feel your lips on me."

I heard a metallic whisper, and saw a small homemade knife in his hand, even as he took one of my hands, and rested it on his hip. I felt a slight strange bulge beneath my palm. *Something is there, under his skin.*

What was he trying to tell me? "What do you want, Mate?" I whispered.

"I want you to swallow what I give you to swallow," he said lustily, but I looked in his eyes, and saw they were sad and resigned, opposite from the false lust in his voice.

He clicked on the stereo system, turning it to mid volume, then pulled the covers over us, hiding us from the cameras. "Listen carefully," he whispered quickly. "As soon as we're done, I'll go with you outside, and help lower you over the side to the ground. As soon as your feet touch ground, run!"

"I'm barefoot, and pregnant!"

"Run as fast as you can. There is no camera on the outside of this room, I checked. You'll hear me swearing and shouting, making it seem as if we're fighting out there on the veranda. Do not stop, or give up, no matter what. Make your way to the lower stand of trees—"

"That's a mile, if not three!"

"You'll feel your skin buzzing the whole journey, and when you get on the other side of those trees, it'll stop. Try to teleport to Hayden, as soon as you get there—"

"I can't teleport!"

"Listen and stop talking! You have to try! You may not be able to, but try over and over! If you feel your skin began to crawl, start moving again."

"Where?"

"To a place beyond that, after a meadow, and another forest. There's a cave near the lake there where you can hide. Stay there until what I'll shortly give you passes out of your system. Then you'll be able to teleport for certain. You'll be safe there for a while, beyond Cyrus's reach, and off his radar—"

I grabbed his face in my hands. "I'm not leaving you here!"

"You are, Mate," he hissed softly. "Because we can't go together, not and get away. And I'm certain now that Michael's wanted to kill me all along, that was always his plan. I went to him earlier this week, when I first felt pain and told him I was dying, and he's promised me blood for days, and keeps delaying—"

"I'm not leaving you here to die!"

"Yes, you are," he said sadly, gripping me tightly. "I wish I could've died in your arms, Mate, but it's enough to have known you, and loved you." He gently caressed my stomach. "And to know that part of us is going to go on, if I can only get you free."

"Come with me!"

"We can't share what I'm giving you," he hissed. "And you need me to stay behind here, to create a diversion. They know I wouldn't leave without you, Sar, so when they don't sense you, they'll look for me. And I'll make sure they find me, and that I stay out of their hands long enough so you can get away. And I'll kill Michael, if I can, on my way out—"

"Don't throw your life away!"

"I'm not," he said, with a faint smile. "Knowing you made it mean something, Mate. Now please, make love to me one last time."

I kissed him, tears running down my face, and then I began to kiss my way down his chest.

Suddenly, there was the sound of a key in the lock. Lash whipped the covers off us, and grabbed his shirt, shoving me off of him.

The door opened, and two tigers stalked into the room, growling. Michael strode into the room with a snarl, Cyrus and his guards at his heels. He stood and folded his arms across his chest, furious. "I had them check," he hissed, his eyes glowing red. "I never bothered, before now, as I'd been so careful to make sure there couldn't be a question of paternity. Why bother?"

Oh shit. Lash got in front of me, and slowly we backed towards the balcony.

Michael advanced, his two tigers on either side of him. "But I wanted to know if one would be a boy, so I had you tested. Cyrus had some of your blood. I so wanted one to be a boy."

"Keep moving," Lash hissed at me, not taking his eyes off Michael. "Stick to the plan."

"They're both boys," Michael grated, and then his eyes seemed to fill with blood. "But there is no vampire DNA in your bloodstream! Only were DNA! Snake DNA!"

Lash and I had backed out to the balcony by now. The morning was dark, almost like night. Thunder boomed above us.

"I gave you everything you asked for!" Michael hissed, still advancing. "Everything you asked for, both of you!"

"Except our freedom, you fuck!" Lash shouted loudly.

"You're going to die in agony, you slithering piece of shit!" Michael said. "Get him, boys!"

Lash swore and pushed me behind him. An instant later the two tigers lunged for him as one, knocking him to the ground, even as he fought them.

I turned and ran. I was almost to the balcony's edge, when I felt

Michael's cool hand close over my wrist. "You deceitful girl!" Michael snarled in my ear. "You had to know, even if he didn't! How could you let such creatures grow within you?"

"You hypocrite! You lied to us both!"

"A lie to an evil being is no sin in God's eyes," Michael replied, curling his lip. "Snakes have and always will be an animal of Satan's." He motioned to Cyrus. "Take care of this, Sorcerer. But don't harm Sarelle permanently, though you have my permission to give her some pain for her deviousness!"

"Step away, Michael," Cyrus said calmly. "Or you'll be harmed as well." He had produced a vial from his cloak and was putting powder into it.

"Please, don't!" I cried, holding onto Michael and thinking desperately. "Please, let him go! Let him go, let my children live, and I'll do whatever you want me to, Michael—"

"You're going to do that for me anyway!" Michael hissed in my ear. "I'm through being nice to you." He turned me around with a sharp twist of his hand, and I felt my wrist bones snap under the pressure of his fingers. I let out a scream, as he grated them together with a faint crunching sound. "You're as dishonest as Eve was to Adam!" he hissed at me, his fangs bared. "And my affection for you is just as deadly to my soul!"

Thunder boomed, and lightning arced from the sky, hitting one of the trees near the balcony. We all scattered as the tree splintered and split, half of it falling onto the balcony, shattering the stonework balcony edge, and cracking the floor.

Michael pushed me away, as Cyrus held a hand out to me crackling with energy. I backed away a step, the stone under my feet cracking further under my weight.

A sudden loud scream and shouting swelled up from below us, but I couldn't take my eyes off Cyrus. A lightning bolt formed in his hand, and then without a sound he was hurling it toward me, and it seemed it took on a glow, a blue glow...

"Sar!" Lash shoved me aside, blocking my body with his own, and most of the blast hit him, though some hit me, and it knocked me to the stone floor, my whole body jerking a little from the electricity running thorough it. I looked up to see Lash convulsing, screaming, as he went to his knees, hair alight at the ends, smoke curling up. There was an open raw wound oozing over his chest in a huge patch, some of his organs visible inside, partially blackened and melting. He collapsed beside me, and then everything happened at once.

"You weren't supposed to kill her!" Michael screamed, turning on Cyrus "You know we need her blood! You would have killed her with that powerful of a bolt!"

"I don't take orders from you!" Cyrus sneered, and then he hit Michael with another lightning bolt.

Michael let out a snarl, knocked to his knees, even as his talons grew in his rage. "How dare you—"

"Stay out of the way," Cyrus said to him, advancing toward me. "There has been enough trouble in the vampire upper ranks over this woman. It is better she ends here with those abominations inside her."

"I'll not let you kill her!" Michael shouted. He went for Cyrus, and Cyrus flicked his wrist, encasing Michael in another one of those invisible barriers. He tore at it in vain, shouting for Cyrus to stop.

Rain began to pelt down, soaking my dress and my hair almost instantly. It hissed where it struck Lash's prone body, sending up curls of smoke.

"Why hurt me?" I said desperately, cradling my broken wrist, as Cyrus again began to form lighting in his hands. "Why now? You saved me from the hunters!"

"You were warned not to have any children other than a vampire's," Cyrus said darkly.

"Why the fuck do you care?" I yelled. "You stopped working for Samuel!"

"I don't care," Cyrus said, and then the first smile I'd ever seen graced his features. It was horrible, like a skeleton's grin. "But your death will end the troubles between vampire and human hunters, between vampire and vampire. The balance will be restored. That is worth the cost of one woman's life."

"Please!" I said, falling to my knees. "Please, I'm begging you!"

Cyrus flung the bolt at me, and I closed my eyes, covering my head with my arms. But the blow was deflected as if by magic, the bolt slamming into the building's side. In the same instant, the windows of the entire side of the building shattered outwards, and the glass seemed to find Michael's people as if they were missiles, seeking them out almost. They were werecreatures, but with glass stuck into most organs, slicing them from tail to ear, they began dying, their bodies incapable of healing so much damage.

"Cyrus!" roared a voice from above me. Theo leapt over the top of me from the tree's trunk, shooting at Cyrus, even as he sheltered me from being hit.

Cyrus moved fast, enlarging the shield around Michael and using it now to protect them both. The bullets hit it and stopped, falling to the stone floor to clatter and roll off the edge of the balcony. Tigers erupted from inside the building, white and orange, roaring as they bounded up to us.

"Stay here!" Theo shouted to me. Before I could nod back, he was in their midst, shooting and fighting with them as human, even as they slashed at him with their claws.

Cyrus and Michael were retreating slowly within their barrier, even as more tigers surrounded them in a living shield. But lighting arced down from the sky and struck the shield, shattering it with a sound like breaking glass. Michael bolted over the balcony, but Cyrus flung up another shield, even as he began to form a ball of blue fire in his hand.

In the next instant, three separate fireballs hit his shield, disintegrating it, and I saw Terian, Titus, and Rip began to close in, forming a circle around him. They were enraged, their eyes red flames, as they hurled blue fire at him. The first fireballs from their hands Cyrus somehow stopped. But when the fourth and fifth ones hit, he succumbed. They continued to strike him over and over with magical fire and within a minute he was only smoldering ashes, a twisted melting skeleton in a puddle of black slime.

I crawled painfully to the unmoving shell of Lash, and held him. His skin was still hot to the touch, still steaming from the rain that fell on us. There was blood all over him, and he wasn't breathing. God, he had to be dead, he'd been starting to fail without my blood!

I felt evil blackness envelop me, and then a warm hand on my shoulder. "Kin-daughter, can you stand?" Titus said gently.

"Please help him!" I sobbed. "Lash is hurt, we have to—"

"Rip is preparing something," Titus said comfortingly. "We'll do what we can—"

I fainted.

Chapter Sixteen

I smelled something. Something sweet, like the scent of cherry trees in blossom, but sweeter. *Myrtlewood trees. I smelled myrtlewood trees...*

I opened my eyes and looked into worried golden eyes a few inches from mine. With a cry, I lunged for Dev desperately, knocking over the vase of roses beside me as I grabbed hold of him.

"You are safe, Love," he whispered. "Shh."

"Lash! Where is he?"

"He's sleeping," Devlin said into my hair. "The potion Rip made worked. He is alive, and mostly healed. But his features are more as they used to be..."

Devlin trailed off. I looked at him blankly, as he pulled back from me.

"He is not as handsome as he was," Devlin said quietly, his eyes on me worried again. "You remember how he looked before? And he does not appear as he did in his twenties. He looks in his late forties or so, as he did when you first met him—"

Relief flooded me. "I do. I'm just glad he's alive."

"He took that blast of lightning for you," Devlin said, and this time he brought me into his lap, hugging me tightly. "He asked about you, when he awoke briefly. Your name was the first thing he whispered. To ask if you were still pregnant with his children was the second." His words were very measured. But he didn't sound mad, as Lash had insinuated he would be.

"I think so?" I said finally. "I haven't miscarried, unless when I was out?"

"No," Devlin said, relieved. "You didn't. Titus healed your wrist also."

"Is Michael dead?"

"That miserable fuck!" Devlin snarled, his eyes bleeding to red. "He escaped in the confusion of killing Cyrus. But we killed all of his men, and burned his home, after of course taking everything of value." He paused. "Terian told us of your visit looking for Monica's notes. Rene thinks she may be able to use them, when she returns." He paused again. "I believe she wants to try to have one with me, Sar, though she has not come out and said that to me as yet."

I wasn't sure what to say to Devlin about that. But I knew one thing I had to say. "Did you tell Lash that I was never to have his child? That he was never to do anything that might result in that?"

Devlin looked uncomfortable, and nodded.

I debated asking him what else he had said that Lash had refused to tell me, and decided I didn't want to know. "Why? Were you that jealous?"

"Simply, yes," he said defensively. "But that was not the whole reason."

"Why? I'd already given you a child of your own, Dev. Why begrudge him one?"

"You don't understand," Devlin said. "You told me you didn't want any children, after what happened to Devon. I thought nothing had changed about that. We both heard him admit that night at Davy's that he had tried to get you pregnant without telling you, and I thought he might try it again. I remember also what happened with you and Danial, Sar, when you first broke things off with him. So I said if he fathered one on you, or tried anything like he did before with you, I would remove him from the Oath you took to me, and break his "mating" to you."

"You had no right to say that," I said gently. "I understand you did it because you thought that was what I wanted, but Lash knew that already, after I miscarried. He wouldn't have tried to make me pregnant against my will."

"I had the right to say that and more," Devlin grumbled, "I am your Oathed—"

"Hush," I said, holding him as tight as I could. "Just hold me, Dev. Let me feel your arms around me. I've missed you very much, and I thank you for the blood you sent. You were just in time."

"You should have more," Devlin said tenderly, cradling me to him.

"You are colder than you should be, Love."

"And you must be weak, from giving Lash so much of your blood," I said, worried "When we get home will have to be soon enough. Could you convince Danial to maybe part with some of his, so I don't weaken you more than you are?"

"He might," Devlin said thoughtfully. "He has said he would give me some, if it was needed. But things are not dire. We were able to give Lash some older vampire blood that was magically stored in Cyrus's workshop, along with mine and Titus's. As I said, it healed his injuries, which were ruinous. But it was not very old, maybe a hundred and fifty at the most. But there was a good bit of it, and it was fresh, or so Titus said—"

He let out a sigh. "Rene told me Lash would be hurt badly, that he would need my blood. She told me I was not to join the fighting, as I would need all my strength intact for that. And she was right."

"She can see the future?" I said, half in disbelief, and half in awe.

"Sometimes," Devlin said cryptically. "She said her gift of sight has returned."

"Is she at Hayden?" I asked, wondering how to tell him about Shaker, and the deal I'd made with him.

"She is not. She said we were to wait a week after returning home, and then to send you to get her at the convent."

"Devlin, I can get her now, I—"

"No," he said, shaking his head. "She has said it must be this way. I know her well enough to listen, Love, especially when I heard in her voice how much she wished to be back with us. We will wait, as she asked us to. She has a reason for all she does."

Okay…whatever. "How is V?"

"She is much the same. But she is dying to see you, and loves you as much as she ever has."

"I can't want to see her either."

"T also was glad to hear you are safe, as is Elle." He hugged me tighter. "I missed you so much, Sar."

"I love you," I said, burrowing into his throat. "I missed you too, Dev."

Dev sighed a little. "It's been agony, these four months apart from you, not seeing you smile, or hearing you laugh, watching your things gather dust, but being unable to bring myself to even touch them, sleeping in bed alone—"

Abruptly, he stopped, and gave me an uncomfortable look.

"Did you take other lovers?" I asked as gently as I could. "It's okay, if you did."

"I went to Serena," Devlin said very softly. "She consoled me, knowing how awful it was, missing my lover and my best friend, worrying constantly that you might be dead. Only her. And Hillary and Tiffany, as usual."

Oiy. There was going to be a lot of baggage there to work through when I got home. But I didn't blame him or her. "I'm grateful to her, then," I said "And if you want to be with her again while I'm pregnant, it's okay with me, Dev…" I trailed off.

He pulled back and looked at me with glowing eyes, but said nothing.

"I'm sorry," I continued quickly. "But Michael used Lash to get me to let him have me."

"Love, I know that. You don't have to say—"

"Our Oath is broken. My choker fell off, and wouldn't refasten."

"Hush and hold still," Devlin said. He hugged me close, then put the choker around my neck and fastened it. The links slid together for him easily.

"Nothing is broken," he said quietly. "Our Oath stands. Metal and magic does not always understand love or tragedy, but I do. You did nothing wrong, Sar. Don't even think about it ever again. All right?"

"Yes." *God, that was a relief.*

"Are you ready to see Lash?"

"Yes. Can you carry me to him, please?"

Devlin picked me up, and slowly took me to the middle cabin of the plane. It appeared we had been in the back. Lash was there, though it was true, he didn't look the same. He looked older than I'd ever seen him. And he was more sinister looking now. There was a cruel cast to his face that was familiar, from when I had known him before, and he was not as handsome as he had been. His features had mostly reverted to the ones he had been born with. Perhaps his fingerprints had as well. But he was my mate, and I was very, very glad he was alive.

"Let me take some of your blood, and give it to him," Devlin said quietly. "Titus took as much of mine as he could, but I could only give so much—"

It was truth that he looked haggard, though just as gorgeous as ever. But I felt too weak to donate any blood anytime soon. "Can't Titus give him something else?"

"Sarelle, I need to take it now, he won't awaken again unless he has more—"

Shit! "Argh! Take it now! Please!"

Devlin looked at me warily, as he took a syringe, and drew some of my blood. A moment later, he injected it straight into Lash's vein. He did that five times, and then said he wouldn't take anymore, in case it somehow affected the babies.

Would it be enough? I hoped so....

With more of my blood, Lash would be safer. His looks could change, revert, or do whatever, so long as he woke up. I wanted him to see his children be born, to be young enough so he was able to move with no pain. I wanted his fingerprints to be altered enough so he could stay Trystan, and not have to change his name again to hide from his past.

"We need to wait, to give the potion and blood time to work," Devlin said, interrupting my thoughts. "And there is someone else you need to see."

I turned to see Theo watching me from the front of the plane, looking at me through a gap in the curtain, his face unreadable. I swallowed hard, and went to talk to him.

"Devlin said he's going to live," Theo said flatly.

"He'll be okay," I said confidently.

"I'm glad he saved you," Theo said quietly. "I tried, but I couldn't get to you in time."

"It's okay," I assured him. "You came and saved us right in the nick of time, Michael wanted to—"

Theo reached out, and pulled me to him, hugging me, and I let him. "I tried to dream of you, to find you," Theo whispered. "But I couldn't, even though Terian made me that same potion he made for you, because he thought it was worth a try. When I couldn't, I knew something had happened. I went to Titus. He admitted breaking the bond between us. He said you had asked him to."

I was quiet in his arms, unwilling to answer.

"He told me why you asked him to do it, that you knew I was going crazy. I'm grateful you did, Sar. Titus said that Terian did it wrong that first time. It wasn't supposed to be that strong of a bond, that it subverted my werecougar urges, changing my very nature."

I stayed silent, waiting for him to finish.

Theo held me closer. "But I wish you hadn't broken it," he whispered. "I might have found you sooner, if we'd been able to talk to one another in dreams."

It was in his tone that finding me hadn't been his only reason. "Thank you for saving me," I said, giving him a real hug. "I'd be dead otherwise."

I thought of something and smiled.

"What?" Theo said, grinning a little.

"You're even now with Lash," I said quietly. "You getting to us in time, you saved Lash's life. They were going to kill him."

"And you," he growled, holding me more tightly. "That bolt of lightning was meant for you." He hugged me. "I tried, but I couldn't get to you in time."

I was starting to be uncomfortable. "It wasn't your fault."

"It seems forever since we were like this, Sar—"

Okay, that was enough. "How is Jenny, Theo?"

"Good." Theo's voice went cool immediately, and he moved away, letting go of me. "She likes living at Danial's old house. She, Cia, and Janice have become good friends."

I stifled my burning temper, and forced a smile. *This is not worth fighting about, not ever again.* "I'm glad, Theo. I'm glad you're happy."

"Are you feeling better?" Titus rumbled from behind me. I turned and hugged him, and then Rip, who was behind him.

"Thank you for coming and saving us," I said, tears in my eyes. "I hoped that calling to you would work."

"Lash was smart to think of it," Titus said with newfound respect in his tone. "I had hoped he would find a way to escape."

Don't correct him. "He didn't want to leave me," I said, wiping my eyes.

"He was right not to," Rip said, his voice angrier than I'd ever heard it. "On your own, you two wouldn't have gotten far. The asshole Cyrus had a demon working for him, helping him. When we find the bastard, he's toast."

I nodded, and said nothing, knowing the demon he meant was Shaker. But he wasn't the only one missing. "Where is Terian?" I asked Titus.

"He left, to go home."

"Why not teleport us all?"

"It's not good to teleport, when someone is unconscious." Titus rumbled. "It can be done in an emergency, but sometimes, um…bad things happen."

Well, we'd leave that alone completely. "Oh."

I walked back to Lash, and sat down beside him, taking hold of his hand. I thought of Shaker, wondering if he'd teleported back to America and would be waiting for us. Immediately there came a sound in my mind, a whisper of a low, low voice. "I am here, Mistress," Shaker rumbled in my mind. "Come to me in dreams, if you wish, or call me."

Thank you, I thought to him.

"Thank you," he whispered. "I'm free now."

Not really, I thought back to him. *You are still bound to me.*

"Yes," he rumbled, sounding happy. "Until you release me, which I hope never happens."

Will you be waiting for me, at Hayden? I thought.

"If you wish me to be there," he said in my mind.

No, I said mentally, thinking of Terian, and what he had done to me, and of Devlin and Serena's intimacy, and Lash still unconscious, and my unborn children, and Rene, Theo, and V, and Danial, too… No, I had enough to deal with. *No. Wait for a while.*

"I can come to you in an instant," Shaker said in my mind. "Wherever you are, as you are part demon, Mistress, and I can sense you. Our bond is blood, and it was made in a dream we shared, and no spell can sever it, ever. Just call out to me in your mind."

And you'll hear me?

"I'll hear you," he rumbled suggestively. "And your every wish will be my command."

Then he was gone.

The End

About the Author

Tara Fox Hall's writing credits include nonfiction, horror, suspense, action-adventure, erotica, and contemporary and historical paranormal romance. She is the author of the paranormal action-adventure *Lash* series and the vampire romantic suspense *Promise Me* series. Tara divides her free time unequally between writing novels and short stories, chainsawing firewood, caring for stray animals, sewing cat and dog beds for donation to animal shelters, and target practice.

www.tarafoxhall.com

Other works by the author with Melange Books, LLC
Return To Me
Surrender to Me
The Origin of Fear in Spellbound 2011 Anthology
Night Music in Midnight Thirsts II Anthology
Partners in Midnight Thirsts II Anthology
Kink in Wicked Christmas Wishes Anthology
The Oath in Wicked Christmas Wishes Anthology
Bedtime Shadows Anthology
Make Me Behave Anthology
Latham's Landing, An Anthology
The Oath
Her Frozen Heart, in Frozen Anthology
Night Music, a Novella

The Promise Me Series
Promise Me, Book 1
Broken Promise, Book 2
Taken in the Night, Book 3
Taken for his Own, Book 4
Promise Me Anthology, Book 4.5
Immortal Confessions, Book 5
Her Secret, Book 6
Point of No Return, Book 7
Lost Paradise, Book 8
Dark Solace, Book 9
Eye of the Storm, Book 10
Tempest of Vengeance, Book 11
Sundown-Serena, Book 12
Hope's Return, Book 13
Fate's Prison, Book 14
Coming Soon - *Web of Memory, Book 15*